Harlequin is 60 years old,
and Harlequin Blaze is celebrating!

After all, a lot can happen in 60 years,
or 60 minutes...or 60 seconds!

And a <u>lot</u> happens in Blaze's
heart-stopping new miniseries:

From 0—60!

Don't miss:

A LONG, HARD RIDE
by Alison Kent
March 2009

OUT OF CONTROL
by Julie Miller
April 2009

HOT-WIRED
by Jennifer LaBrecque
May 2009

Going from "Hello" to "How was it?"
doesn't have to take long....

Blaze

Dear Reader,

As far back as I can remember, I've been a voracious reader. But it was the summer before my ninth grade year of school that I was introduced to romance. My best friend's mother knew I liked to read, and she said she had these sacks full of well-read books that were taking up space in her attic, and would I like to have them. Free books? A summer's worth of reading? You betcha!

Those grocery sacks were filled with over a hundred Harlequin romances. Violet Winspear. Lucy Gillen. Kay Thorpe. And more. I was hooked! Who knew a hunky hero and a happy ending could make me such a contented reader?

This year Harlequin is celebrating its 60th anniversary. I'm honored to be a part of the celebration by writing this book for their Series Spotlight. I think you'll enjoy the characters and setting Lori, Alison, Jennifer and I have created for Blaze's FROM 0–60 miniseries. Fast cars. Hot heroes. A touch of danger. Steam. A quaint little town and heroines we can all relate to. In other words, the essence of good romance. The essence of Harlequin.

I want to congratulate Harlequin on their decades of making readers happy. And I want to thank them for touching my heart as a reader and inspiring me to become a writer of romance myself.

Happy birthday, Harlequin!

Julie Miller
www.juliemiller.org

Out of Control

JULIE MILLER

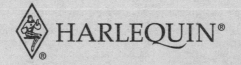

TORONTO • NEW YORK • LONDON
AMSTERDAM • PARIS • SYDNEY • HAMBURG
STOCKHOLM • ATHENS • TOKYO • MILAN • MADRID
PRAGUE • WARSAW • BUDAPEST • AUCKLAND

PLEASE RECYCLE
THIS PRODUCT IS RECYCLABLE

Recycling programs
for this product may
not exist in your area.

ISBN-13: 978-0-373-79463-8
ISBN-10:   0-373-79463-0

OUT OF CONTROL

Copyright © 2009 by Julie Miller.

www.eHarlequin.com

Printed in U.S.A.

ABOUT THE AUTHOR

While Julie Miller has never driven an actual drag racer, she has written more than thirty-five books and won several awards for her work, including the National Readers' Choice Award. In addition, she's been a *Romantic Times BOOKreviews* finalist for Best Harlequin Blaze, Best Harlequin Intrigue and Career Achievement in Series Romantic Suspense. Some of her books have appeared on the *USA TODAY* and Waldenbooks bestseller lists. Julie lives in Nebraska, where she teaches English and spoils her dog. Find out more about her at www.juliemiller.org.

Books by Julie Miller

Don't miss any of our special offers. Write to us at the following address for information on our newest releases.

Harlequin Reader Service
U.S.: 3010 Walden Ave., P.O. Box 1325, Buffalo, NY 14269
Canadian: P.O. Box 609, Fort Erie, Ont. L2A 5X3

For Lori Borrill, Alison Kent and
Jennifer LaBrecque.

FROM 0–60 has been a great collaborative
effort, and a lot of fun to boot!

Dahlia, Tennessee, really came to life for me,
working with you guys.

I feel I've been to that town and I know those
people living there.

I appreciate you sharing your knowledge
of drag racing with a novice like me.

I appreciate your humor, and
your creative energy fed my own.

And thanks to Brenda Chin for introducing us!

1

"GET OUT OF THE VEHICLE. Get *out* of the vehicle!"

Detective Jack Riley pulled his Glock 9 mm and pointed it, along with his flashlight, at the three-hundred-pound behemoth who ignored his badge and his command and started the engine. Shit.

As the drug dealer shifted his customized Chevy Suburban into gear, Jack jumped back inside the cab of his pickup and slammed it into reverse, hoping to block his target's exit from the convenience store parking lot. But Lorenzo Vaughn slipped past him, burning an acrid trail of black rubber onto the pavement as he swung out into the street.

"Screw that."

Silently apologizing to the truck's big bruiser engine, he shifted into drive and ruthlessly gunned it.

Jack flipped on the siren and warning lights of his unmarked truck, praying Vaughn would take this pursuit to the open road. With a long, straight stretch ahead of them, Jack's years of training behind the wheel would give him the advantage. But it might already be too late. There were too many hills, too many trees and houses blocking his line of sight—too many things wrong with this takedown.

The original plan he and his drug enforcement team had worked weeks on had gone way beyond south.

"Come on, baby." He urged as much speed out of the engine as he dared this time of night with so many cars still on the streets.

"Jack? You in trouble?" His partner Eric Mesner's voice crackled over the radio. "We're hung up in traffic at least five minutes away from your location."

Jack swore, yanking his steering wheel to the left to swerve around a car pulling out of a driveway. "We're already a day late and a dollar short, buddy. Vaughn didn't stick to his regular schedule. He got away from me. I'm in pursuit."

"Son of a bitch. Did you see the drugs?"

"Didn't get a chance to. But the Chevy he's driving has been modified like the others. Looks like a monster-sized race car. If it's street legal, I'm your Aunt Fanny. Whatever he's selling was either transported in there or is still hidden inside."

Rather than risk their lives or any innocent bystanders' lives by confronting Vaughn at his house—where guns, drugs, lieutenants and a reputed fighting dog stayed—they'd wanted to arrest him when he slipped out to pay a nightly visit to one of his girlfriends. "You watch your back, Jack. Don't take this guy on by yourself."

"Too late for that." Jack had been spying on Vaughn's house, tracking his routine for weeks. The closest they could figure was that Vaughn was getting his drugs stashed inside one of the new vehicles that seemed to show up at his house about once a month. The plan had been to grab the man, grab the car, and break both down until NPD had the proof necessary to bring down one of the city's biggest drug rings. But their precisely timed plan was turning into a flat-out road race. "You're coming to save my ass, right?"

"We're coming," Eric assured him. "Let's get moving. Now!" he shouted to the other team members who were closing in on Jack's lead position.

Jack switched his radio to an all-call channel and reported his location. "Officer in pursuit. I could use some backup."

Flying through intersections and leaving streetlights and startled drivers in the dust, Jack needed to think fast. He glanced at the name of a side street, pulled up a map inside his head. Hell, yes. Flexing his fingers around his truck's taut leather steering-wheel cover, Jack took a deep, steadying breath…and jerked the wheel to the right. He cut through an alley, skidded around the corner and pressed on the gas, his eyes peeled for any sign of pedestrians or civilian vehicles as he zoomed ahead of Vaughn's position on a less-populated parallel street. He couldn't safely outrace Lorenzo Vaughn, but he could damn well outsmart him.

Spotting the cross street he wanted, Jack spun left. By the time his two left wheels hit the pavement again, he had his target in sight. He floored it. "Gotcha."

Forty damn years old and Jack Riley could still play a gutsy game of chicken. Vaughn's head turned. He saw the inevitable rushing toward him and Jack grinned. He was either going to turn Vaughn toward the highway entrance ramp or T-bone him.

Only Vaughn didn't understand the rules of the game he was playing.

"Turn, you son of a bitch. Turn!"

Vaughn's SUV loomed larger and larger. He was close enough to see Vaughn's *oh, shit* expression now, close enough to count down the seconds until impact or victory, close enough to—

A blur of blue and red flashed through Jack's peripheral vision. In the same instant a bold, taunting voice blared across his radio. "I've got this one, old man! Back off!"

A black-and-white unit whipped around the corner in front of him, almost clipping Jack's right fender. Adrenaline whooshed out of his body as Jack stomped on the brakes to avoid the crash. "Shit. Billington!"

Vaughn jerked his vehicle to the left as Jack skidded through the intersection behind him. In the seconds it took Jack to regain control of his truck, Vaughn's SUV and the black-and-white unit had careened onto the highway ramp. He was blocks behind the chase already. But Paul Billington kept his speed steady, falling into close pursuit.

He'd asked for backup, hadn't he? But Jack had been looking
for his seasoned drug enforcement team to show up and save the
day—not this fast and furious wannabe who'd answered the call
from street patrol.

Cursing the young hotshot, Jack closed the distance
between them, slipping into the unfamiliar role of playing
backup on the arrest *he* was supposed to have made. "Damn
it, Billington!" Jack watched the black-and-white police car
slide into position to tap the rear of Vaughn's vehicle and slam
him into a spinout. They were going too fast. Too damn fast.
"Billington!"

The kid was cocky. Reckless.

Perfect.

In a matter of seconds, the perp's car had rolled to a stop in
the ditch and Billington was dragging a dazed Lorenzo Vaughn
from behind his deflating air bag. Jack pulled up in front of the
wreck and climbed out. "Nice driving," Jack conceded. "I appreciate the help."

"Happy to save your ass anytime, Grandpa."

Damn schmuck.

With Eric Mesner and the rest of the team finally reaching the
scene to set up traffic control around the accident, Jack lowered his
voice and reprimanded the young officer for the unnecessary risk
he'd taken upon himself. "Speeding through a residential neighbor-
hood where collateral damage is a definite possibility is not the way
to prove you've got the cajones to make the drug squad."

Billington jerked Vaughn to his feet and turned him toward
the black-and-white. "Back in the day, when you set the police
course driving record I've been trying to break since my rookie
year, you would have gotten the job done yourself instead of
calling for backup and giving me a lecture. Maybe it's time to
step aside and let some new blood into vice."

"Back in the day?" Jack winced at the mix of awe and
sympathy in Billington's tone. "I'm hardly ready to retire."

"Oh, yeah?" Billington's expression blazed with an arrogance all too reminiscent of Jack's earlier days on the force. "Who just made this arrest?"

"Good work, buddy." Eric Mesner patted his shoulder as Jack eased the tight clench of his fists. "It's good to see that bastard finally going to jail."

Nodding, Jack replayed the night's events in his head, trying to figure out where he'd lost that half-second advantage to Vaughn—and Billington—and wondering just how many other young bloods in NPD had taken to calling him *Old Man* and *Grandpa*.

Eric nodded his approval to Billington as he closed the back door of the official vehicle on Lorenzo Vaughn. "I've got the rest of the team securing the Suburban. We'll check the accessible places for any hidden drugs. Otherwise, it'll be up to the lab to break it down. In the meantime, I'm looking forward to putting him in an interrogation room and finding out how he's getting his supply into Nashville in the first place."

"You still coming over to the house for barbecue tomorrow afternoon?" Eric switched topics as smoothly as Jack eased through the gears on his truck. "I figure it'll be the last weekend we can be outside before the cooler weather sets in. The kids and the missus haven't seen you for a while. Not since you and Rosie broke up."

Hell. His ego was taking it in the shorts tonight. There was no woman at home for him anymore, waiting to listen to his troubles, willing to ease his doubts and frustrations with the lush warmth of her body. Jack's live-in lover of over a year had moved out a month ago because her job offer in St. Louis had been more tempting than a marriage proposal from him.

He liked Eric's kids, was godfather to his oldest son. Even Eric's wife welcomed him like a long-lost brother. But he didn't feel much like celebrating with the family right now. Jack turned and headed back to his truck. "I don't know."

"Don't know what?" Eric followed. "Hey. We got our guy.

We'll find where the cars and drugs are coming from. The rest will fall into place. We did good."

"No, Eric, we sucked." Jack pulled up and turned to his partner. "*I* sucked. If it wasn't for Hotshot's help back there, Vaughn would have gotten away. He could have dumped the car and the drugs and we'd have zilch. Nada. Nothing."

"So we had an off night." Eric propped his hands on his hips at the hem of his flak vest and shrugged. "How many times in the past have we had to punt and go to Plan B—or C or D— because Plan A didn't work out?"

Jack raked his fingers through his hair. "Yeah, but we were always able to make B, C and D work for ourselves. We never had to have some punk ride in to save our asses before."

Eric's dark eyes narrowed in that wise, patient way of his as he tried to assess Jack's surly mood. "We may be slowing down, but our glory days are hardly over."

Slowing down? Shit. Just the kind of pep talk he *didn't* need.

"Back in the day, my ass." Jack thumped the truck's steering wheel with his fist. It was late. He was tired. And his patience with himself had worn down to the driving need for an ice-cold beer or a long, hot lay to purge the restless frustration that gnawed at him.

But he was still on the clock, and there was no sweet, sophisticated Rosie waiting for him back home.

He couldn't keep a woman. Couldn't do the job. Eric had said it was an off day. That they'd crack the case tomorrow. Damn optimist. Probably why Eric's wife had stuck with him for almost twenty years. Probably why Jack respected his partner so much. Eric could see the promise of tomorrow. He believed in it.

Meanwhile, Jack…? Well, hell. Even with the windows down and the damp autumn air blowing in his face as he cruised along Interstate 40, he couldn't seem to cool down. Something was eating at him tonight.

And it damn well wasn't the fact that he was forty, unattached and horny as hell with some adolescent need to prove he was still the man he once was. Yeah, right.

Exiting the highway, Jack veered onto Broadway—Nashville's brightly lit, noisy magnet for tourists, partygoers and country-music star wannabes. Maybe there'd be a purse snatcher or scam artist he could haul in to headquarters. *That's it. Make an arrest. Protect and serve.*

That'd get his mojo back. Then maybe he'd believe in tomorrow again, too. Jack inhaled deeply, feeling a surge of renewed confidence.

Scanning Broadway from sidewalk to sidewalk, Jack watched for anything out of the ordinary. Neon lights blinked on and off in modern contrast to the old brick buildings they adorned, marking open-mike joints, dance clubs and honky tonks. Despite the chill in the air, every door stood open to let the music inside pour out into the street.

With a beefy bouncer standing guard at every bar, he suspected there wouldn't be anything to worry about there. Instead, Jack turned his attention to the crowds milling up and down the sidewalk. He took note of the tourists strolling toward a line of horse-drawn carriages, hoping to catch a leisurely tour of the capitol building and other historical and musical landmarks in the downtown area. He spotted a trio of derelict musicians hauling their instruments, bedrolls and backpacks in and out of doorways, looking for work and a place to sleep. Jack nodded to the two uniformed bicycle cops who'd pulled off their helmets and stopped to chat with a street-corner huckster who was probably selling overpriced tickets to something that didn't even exist. Their answering salute told him the two men had the situation well under control.

Soon, he'd run out of road—and opportunities—and hit the Cumberland River that looped through the city. Jack rolled to a stop at the next light. He drummed his fingers against the wheel, thinking his apartment and a cold shower were his best bets to save this night, when a shrill voice pierced the night air.

"You touch me again and you'll take back a stump."

A swirl of honey-gold hair drew his eye to the street-corner commotion in front of Jasmine's Saloon.

Petite yet stacked in a way that reminded him of country-music icons and teenage fantasies, a young blond woman marched down the sidewalk, bumping her way through the crowd. Her makeup had been applied with a heavy hand, and the little black dress she wore was far too short—her strappy silver stilettos way too high—for that sexy get-up to be anything other than an invitation for trouble.

Trouble followed in the form of two college-aged boys who hurried along behind her. "What if we pay you double?" the taller one shouted.

The blonde spun around on wobbly legs. Before Jack could wedge his truck into the entrance to a parking alley, Blondie drew her arm back and swung. He winced in sympathy at the slap that connected with the cheek of the gangly, red-haired young man. The young man's buddy laughed, but quickly fell silent as both Red and Blondie turned and glared at him.

There was a story behind that assault, and Jack intended to find out the details before Blondie struck again or the two men retaliated. Closing the door behind him, Jack jogged down the sidewalk for a closer look.

While Blondie tottered on her heels in a less-than-dignified retreat, the red-haired kid massaged his cheek and made some kind of suggestion to his shorter companion. With a nod of agreement, Red and Shorty hurried after their target, perhaps intent on taking what she hadn't been willing to give them.

"Easy, boys." Jack quickly caught up to the boys, stopping them with a low-pitched warning. "Nashville PD. Now turn around nice and slow."

Shorty thrust his hands into the air and whirled around, completely ignoring the *slow* part of the command. "We didn't do anything wrong."

"Shut up, Duane."

The tall one turned, as well, and Jack looked him straight in his bleary eyes.

Hell. Not one wrinkle on the kid's face. And clearly they'd already had a few. Were these two even legal? Jack pulled back the front of his leather jacket to give them a look at his badge and gun. "Let me see your IDs."

As eager to cooperate as he'd been to laugh, Duane handed over his driver's license. It looked authentic enough. Red's ID showed he was old enough to hit the bars, as well. Just barely. Jack did some quick math before returning their licenses. "Celebrating your twenty-first birthday?"

"Yes, sir."

Jack looked between their shoulders to see the young woman hugging her arms around herself for warmth as she paused outside the doorway to the next bar on the block. "What about Blondie over there? Is she part of the celebration?"

The tall one with the fading hand print on his face shrugged. "I thought she wanted to be. She hit on us inside."

Duane slurred his words and blinked sporadically, trying to send a double entendre with a wink as he tucked his license back into his wallet. "She asked Isaac if he had a phone in his pocket. I sure had one in mine when I got a load of those gazongas."

"Yeah. It was a come-on line if I ever heard one."

"I told her that money was no object—that we'd pay the going rate. But she said she wouldn't take our money—"

"I thought she meant she was gonna give me a birthday freebie."

"Maybe she doesn't do two at once, man. I don't mind waiting. It's Isaac's birthday, anyway."

"All right, boys, I've heard enough." Jack raised his hand to end the discussion. These two were clueless but apparently harmless. "Move along. Make sure you call a cab when it's time to go home. I don't want to see either one of you behind the wheel tonight. Understood?"

Both young men nodded with obvious relief. "Yes, sir."

They quickly turned and tottered back into the saloon. "I mean it, boys—" Jack called after them. "No driving tonight."

"No, sir."

Now, back to the real trouble.

Despite her lack of height, Jack easily spotted all that pale bare skin and golden hair as Blondie gave up the idea of going into the bar and, instead, joined the stream of partiers and tourists heading on down the street. Jack picked up speed as he threaded his way through the crowd in pursuit. The woman walked with a purpose. Though if she was running *to* something or running away, he couldn't tell. He supposed Isaac and Duane back there weren't up to her standards or they just hadn't been willing or able to meet her price.

The spaghetti straps on the little black dress she wore had no chance of holding up those puppies if she continued to bounce along at that furious pace. Jack tried to ignore the rush of masculine appreciation that bubbled through his veins and pooled behind his zipper. Hookers weren't his thing, but Blondie was hot, in a trashy sort of way that made him long for a fast car and a one-night stand. No commitment. Nothing complicated. Just pure, any-way-he-wanted-it sex. He wasn't the only male in the vicinity to notice the possibilities, either.

"Ah, hell."

Now she moved to the edge of the curb, stumbling backward in those spiky heels, her thumb in the air. She shouted something obscene to one car that slowed, then sped away without stopping.

Hitchhiking was just as illegal, and no safer than turning tricks. Jack needed to get to her before she got herself in a train wreck that would completely ruin what was left of this night.

"Miss?"

The instant he touched the cool skin of her arm, she started. Before he could identify himself, she jerked away, tilting her chin up, ready to do battle. "If you ask me for a blow job, too, I swear I'm gonna smack you."

He crushed the erotic image of honey-blond curls at his crotch that instantly leaped to mind, and did his damnedest to remember he was a cop. Jack pulled his badge from his belt. "Well, that would be assaulting a police officer, and we frown upon that here in Nashville."

"You're a cop?" Instead of expressing relief or laughing at the joke, she muttered a curse. "This is not happening to me."

2

WAS IT POSSIBLE for one woman to be any stupider about men than she'd been tonight?

Alexandra Morgan briefly flashed back to the crippling knowledge that she'd once proved the answer was *yes*.

Still, there was little comfort in knowing that tonight could actually be worse. She'd shunned the idea of dating for so long that she'd known it wouldn't be easy, but she thought she'd get *something* right. After that awful night in high school, and the handful of doomed attempts in the nine years since that had turned her into a closed-up, guarded, spinster tomboy, she'd finally gotten frustrated enough to try embracing the sexy, feminine side of her nature again. She was anxious to learn about all the good things she'd been denying herself. The intimacy. The trust. The orgasms. She'd wanted this.

But nothing had changed. Wanting wasn't the same as knowing. Her feminine instincts—or lack thereof—had failed her once again.

College had given her confidence in other aspects of her life. Her four years of the University of Tennessee made her rethink how she handled the small minds that had dictated the course of her life. She'd gone to work for her father, outlined new ideas to improve the family auto-repair business. She'd made a success of her life despite the concessions survival had forced her to make. But a degree in business management couldn't prepare her for nights like this one.

Tears began to chafe like grit beneath her eyelids again, and Alex blinked them away along with the painful memories from her past. She was smart enough now to grab hold of the anger that gave her the strength to bear the disappointments of her life. Like tonight.

The big bruiser with the badge here was just the icing on the cake. Her feet were blistered. She was cold, embarrassed. Accepting a blind date with the friend of a friend hadn't proved to be the fresh start she'd hoped for. "What did I do wrong?"

He clipped his badge back beneath his black leather jacket, giving her a glimpse of a gun and a rip of muscles that warned her getting away from him wouldn't be as easy as getting away from Dawson Barnes had been. "Relax, sweetheart. I'm not necessarily taking you in. But we do need to talk about what you're selling."

"Selling?" Alex planted her hands on her hips in a defiant pose. "Do you see a purse? Pockets? A suitcase? I don't have anything on me to sell." Dawson had left her with nothing but the clothes on her back. She'd thought his offer to drive all the way to Dahlia to pick her up for dinner had been a gentlemanly gesture.

But when he'd started tearing at her sweater before they'd even gotten inside the restaurant, she'd fought her way out of the car without thinking about her phone or purse or the fact he might drive off and leave her.

Oh. My. God.

The blood rushed from her head down to her painted toenails. Those two boys in the saloon who'd seemed harmless enough to approach? That jerk in the car? Mr. Tall, Dark and Serious here? "You think I'm a hooker?"

"Well, that dress doesn't exactly say all-American sweetheart now does it." His sarcasm burned through her.

Alex glanced down at the twin curses bulging over the low-cut neckline, seeing for the first time just how close she was to popping out over the top of the tight rayon knit. She quickly hugged her arms around her chest as if she could hide her assets.

But the cop's gray eyes, dark as steel and just as hard, said it all. "I look like a hooker."

She was going to be sick.

Alex rubbed her hands along her skin from her elbows to her shoulders. Her father had assured her that her late mother had always put on makeup when she'd gone out. She'd always worn a dress and heels like a "fine lady." Every fashion magazine Alex had picked up over the years talked about how a woman could never go wrong with a little black dress.

She'd managed to go wrong.

Despite the good intentions of the military father and workaholic brother who'd raised her, Alex had managed to go way wrong.

All she'd wanted was a date. One date with one decent guy who'd treat her like a lady and maybe teach her a thing or two about the intricacies of a physical relationship with a man. But Dawson hadn't wanted to teach. He'd wanted to take.

And, by damn, Alexandra Morgan was done letting men take what she'd be willing to give the right one.

At five foot three, she didn't have much to work with in the intimidation department, but she tipped her chin up, way up, to look this cop in the eye and set him straight. "Just so we're clear on this. I am *not* a hooker."

"Then I expect you're either in trouble, or you're well on your way to finding it. Either way, you need my help."

"I can take care of myself."

"Yeah, I can see that." More sarcasm? He raked his fingers over dark hair that had enough silver in it to give the short, crisp cut a smoky cast. "Come on." Making some sort of decision, he cupped a hand beneath her elbow and turned her back in the direction she'd come from. "Let's get you off the street before I have to arrest you for public indecency."

"Are you kidding me?" She jerked her arm out of his grasp. "This is a perfectly good dress." At least, it had looked fine on the girl in the catalog. Of course, that girl was probably taller, and no way did a fashion model have a pair of 38 EEs to work with. "It's not my fault I lost the sweater that goes with it. You take a look for yourself, pal. Everything I own is covered."

But even Alex could look down and see that wasn't far from a lie. Oh, God. She was blushing hard enough that even her boobs were turning pink. Quickly, she tugged the square neckline up half an inch. But then she felt a distinct breeze down between her thighs.

What she wouldn't give for one of her brother's big T-shirts— or a hole to crawl into—right about now.

Alex didn't know whether to give NPD here credit for patience or perseverence. She saw the officer's gaze go *there*, then politely move back up to her face. He nodded toward a half-ton black pickup parked in an alley at the end of the block. "I'll give you a ride to headquarters where we can sort this out."

"There's nothing to sort out. I'm going home."

"Excuse me?"

She shook her head. "Unless you *are* arresting me, I am not going anywhere with you."

His gray eyes grew even steelier. The cool leather of his jacket brushed against her cheek as he took a step closer and pointed over her shoulder at the cars passing by. "You won't accept a ride from a police officer, yet you'll get into the car of a complete stranger?"

"*You're* a stranger to me," she countered, feeling suddenly surrounded by his heat and strength, and fighting the urge to either turn tail and run or throw herself against that wall of black T-shirt and pray his offer to help was a legitimate one. "How do I know I can trust you?"

He was going for his badge again. "You see this? This means you do what I say."

"I don't have a particular fondness for cops." And though this one with the jeans and the leather and the shoulders was a sight better looking than the good ol' boy who ran her hometown, she wasn't inclined to put her faith in any man right now.

"I wasn't giving you a choice, Trouble." He grabbed her arm firmly enough make her understand he wasn't letting go. "You're coming with me."

"Hey!" The crowd parted in front of his long, determined stride as he escorted her back to his truck. Alex tapped along in double-time beside him, struggling against his grip every step of the way. "Did you just call me *Trouble?* This is police harassment. I've got a good lawyer." A big brother who'd be indignant on her behalf, at any rate. "I'll sue."

"Sue away, sweetheart."

He kept right on walking, ignoring her protests, ignoring curious stares and pointing and laughs that made part of her wilt inside. The one man who stepped forward to help quickly changed his mind and backed off when the cop thrust his badge in the guy's face.

"You're a big bully, you know that?"

"You're a pain in the ass."

"Is that any way to talk to a lady—"

The sidewalk ended. The cop turned. Alex tugged. His grip slipped. But escape was short-lived. Her heel caught in the seam of the curb, snapped and pitched her forward.

A rock-hard arm shot around her waist to catch her. "Easy."

Alex shoved it away. Why the hell should anything go right? She stumbled sideways, plucked off the traitorous shoe and tossed it. "Get away from me."

Two big hands closed over her shoulders now, saving her from falling. "Let me help."

"I don't want any help. I just want to go home." She wanted to crawl under the covers and hide her head and heart in shame.

He pulled her back. "I'm not the bad guy."

"Let…" Alex's vision had reduced to a blur of black leather and neon lights. But she had the presence of mind to put that surviving shoe to some good use tonight. She stomped down hard on his instep. "…go!"

Cussing up a blue streak, he did just that. Alex lurched forward, nearly splatting on the concrete. Her pulse roared in her ears. Her eyes burned.

"That's it." Before she could right herself, a straight-jacket came down around her shoulders. Its warmth and softness were almost a shock to her system. But there was nothing soft about the wrap-around bands of masculine strength that pinned her arms to her sides and lifted her feet clear off the pavement.

Alex shrieked. Twisted in his grasp.

"Stop it!"

Tears clouded her vision, burned down her cheeks. "No!"

"Don't fight me."

She writhed and kicked. The second shoe flew into the shadows. "Please," she sobbed. If anything, his hold on her tightened. He locked one arm beneath her breasts, the other farther down, around her hips. She was moving through the air. He was carrying her away as easily and ignominiously as a sack of potatoes. And then she was trapped, her whole body cinched up tight, unable to wiggle anything besides her bare feet, which dangled in the air beneath her.

The humiliation of her evening was complete. She was grappling in an alley with a full-grown man who was neither her brother nor her date…nor her enemy.

The fight drained out of Alex and she sagged inside the prison of the cop's arms. She was breathing hard, her chest pushing against the jacket's silky lining. The cocoon of fiery warmth surrounding her finally pierced the blind haze of fight-or-flight emotions that had turned her into a crazy woman for a few minutes. She could finally blink enough tears from her puffy eyes to see that she was facing the bed of a black pickup truck. She was pinned against the side, wrapped up in a leather jacket and sandwiched between cold steel and warm man.

As her breathing returned to a more normal rhythm, Alex became aware of a hushed, deep-pitched sound murmuring against her neck. "Shh. There's nothing to be afraid of. Just quit fightin' me. Okay?"

Alex nodded slowly, hearing the cadence of that soothing voice more than the actual words. "I'm…sorry."

She exhaled on a surrendering sigh and instinctively leaned her ear closer to the seductive sound. Smooth like whiskey, and just as intoxicating, the deep, soft tones warmed her from the inside out.

"That's it, sweetheart. Relax. I'm not going to hurt you." The rough pad of a finger was surprisingly gentle against her skin as the man who held her wiped the tears from her cheeks. "Shh. Now, come on. Don't do that. You don't want to be cryin'."

The tears of frustration and humiliation quickly dried up beneath his tender ministrations. For a few moments, there was simply fatigue—and gratitude that there was a man whose will and strength were stronger than her own—a *good* man whose will and strength hadn't been used to hurt her. But as her sensibilities returned, Alex became aware of other things. Interesting things. Things that were as male and intriguing and unsettling as that voice.

The muscled forearm wedged beneath her breasts. The rasp of beard stubble that tickled her ear and neck. The buttery softness and furnace-like warmth of the jacket he'd wrapped around her body. Alex breathed in deeply. The jacket smelled like heaven.

She felt the belt buckle pressing into her rear, and the thigh that had been forced between her legs. In their struggle, her short dress had ridden up to an embarrassing level, leaving only her cotton panties between them. But shielded from curious eyes by the truck and the man's big, muscular body, she didn't feel exposed or embarrassed.

Instead, Alex felt…female. Vulnerable.

But not afraid.

The roughness of denim rubbed against her most sensitive

skin. And a rippling response of pressure seemed to be gathering at the juncture between her thighs, building with each flex of hard muscles against her there.

"Let's try this again." He adjusted their positions, shifting her higher onto his hip. Alex closed her eyes, her thighs clenching at the friction of his leg sliding between hers. How could being trapped—helpless—like this feel so good? "I'm a detective with Nashville PD. It's too chilly for this dress and too late for a woman to be walking the streets on her own. I'm here to help you. How old are you?"

"Twenty-five."

"Before I got to you…" He paused, went still around her—as if the next question was hard for him to get out. "Have you been assaulted?"

Grabbing hands. Buttons popping. Pushing her down in the seat. "I heard you did it for all the boys in Dahlia. Let's see those tits."

"Shh. Easy."

Something in Alex had gone rigid, defensive. But his mesmerizing voice calmed her into breathing easy again.

Alex answered. "I was on a blind date. There was a little miscommunication. I thought he'd be interesting— he thought I'd put out."

"I'm sorry." He adjusted his stance, pulling the prop of his leg from between hers, relaxing the intimacy of his hold on her without releasing her entirely. "Did he force you?"

Alex squirmed in his grasp, wanting to turn around and ease away the concern—or was it fear? Anger?—that eroded the seductive timbre of his voice into a predatory growl. But she was at his mercy, and all she had to give him were words. "No. I wasn't raped if that's what you're asking. But his plans for the evening didn't match up with mine. When I got out of the car, he drove off with my purse and sweater and cell phone inside."

He cursed. Apologized. "And you've been walking ever since?"

"Yeah. It's been a long night."

"And I thought I was having a bad one. Sounds like yours might have been worse." He adjusted his arms around her, softening his hold. Though there was still little chance for Alex to escape, it felt more like an embrace rather than a takedown maneuver. "Sometimes, it's hard to get it all right."

Alex nodded. "Sometimes, it's hard to get anything right."

"Sometimes."

This man made it so easy to sink into his strength. He was still pressed against her, his cheek to her ear, his chest to her back, his… Alex's cheeks colored with warmth. There was something more than his belt buckle pressing into her bottom. But he wasn't rubbing himself against her or demanding she do something about it. His restraint, despite the hell she'd given him, created a whole new world of confusion inside her.

But oddly enough, *this* felt right.

Even though she was the one being held captive, he was letting her be the one in control of the unexpected, yet obvious, attraction simmering between them. Control was a whole new experience for Alex. And she was beginning to think she wouldn't mind if the handsome detective asked for something more than answers from her.

She tried to ignore the strange impulse and explain what had led her to this moment—pinned against a truck by what had to be the sexiest man who'd ever had a hard-on for her. "I swear I haven't committed any crime. Although, if Dawson Barnes complains that he can't father children for a couple of weeks, then I'll argue it was self-defense. And I'm sorry that I kicked you and hit you. I didn't mean to flake out like that." She squeezed her eyes shut and sent up a quick prayer. She might have really gotten herself into some trouble here. "Are you hurt?"

Laughter danced against her ear and vibrated from his body into hers. "By a little bundle of dynamite like you?"

"Is that a yes or no?"

"Relax." His lips brushed against her nape as he pushed her hair out of his face. "I'll heal."

"You're sure?"

"I'm fine." He exhaled slowly, tickling the fine hairs on the back of her neck. A riot of goose bumps rose on her skin, despite the heat from his jacket and body. "Now. If I set you down, nice and easy, will you tell me your name?"

No. No name. Alexandra Morgan was a failure when it came to men. And she was feeling something, wanting something so badly with this man that she didn't want to blow it. Maybe anonymity would give her a safety net, confidence she normally lacked. And maybe a man with no preconceived notions of who she was, a man who saw her as a desirable woman and nothing more or less, could give Alex what she wanted—a chance to be a normal, sexual, cherished woman.

Even if it was only for one night. Or one hour.

Or one kiss.

"Just like you said, Detective," she finally answered. "It's *Trouble.*"

"I believe that. Okay, so no names. Are you flirting with me, Miss Trouble?"

"Would that be a crime?"

"Depends on if you're playing me or if this is really going somewhere."

Alex breathed out the last of her doubts. She might not know exactly what she was doing, but she understood exactly what she wanted. "I don't like playing games."

"Then this is definitely going somewhere." He let go with one arm to feather his fingers into her hair and lift the curling strands to his nose. "You smell so good. Like gardenias carried on a distant breeze."

Alex's breath locked in her throat as the atmosphere around them grew heavy. This man could read a grocery list and make it sound sexy in that voice. A compliment like that was pure poetry.

"You…smell good, too," she whispered. Ugh. Not so poetic. What was she supposed to say?

But the words didn't matter. He angled his head and pressed a hot, openmouthed kiss against the nape of her neck.

Her startled gasp tensed through her body. But when she exhaled, any surprise flowed away and settled with a purr of contentment in her throat. "That was…nice. Better than nice. I didn't know there was a bundle of nerves back there."

"You like that?" he whispered, warming the same spot with his tongue.

She trembled. Nodded.

"You want me to stop?"

They were strangers. She was needy. He was willing. And he was being so…patient. Such a gentleman. And yet, this gentleman's erection was nestled in the seam of her bottom, telling her she wasn't the only one interested in exploring whatever was happening between them. It was damn crazy to want a man so badly. A stranger, no less. But when had an opportunity like this ever landed in her lap? Or rather, when had *she* ever landed in Detective Opportunity's lap?

"Don't stop."

He nibbled the sensitive spot on her neck gently, making her jerk in his arms. Then he worked his way down her spine to the collar of his jacket, discovering nerve after nerve that leaped to life beneath his warm, moist touch.

Alex squirmed between the man and truck, trying to free her hands to grab on to something to steady herself—to try to take part in the embrace. But all she managed to do was work her dress up even higher—exposing more bottom, more damp, slick heat that desperately wanted to feel the press of his leg again.

"Careful," he warned. His arm constricted around her ribcage. His fingers clenched in her hair, pulling slightly at her scalp. But the pinpricks of pain quickly blended in with the pleasure of his moan vibrating against her skin, his teeth nipping at the taut muscle where her neck and shoulder joined. His thumb inched higher, testing the weight of one breast, hooking around the taut nipple that strained against the band of her dress. He flicked the tender nub once, twice, a third time, forcing Alex's mouth open in a gasp of need and want that matched his own. "I'm not getting my signals mixed up, am I, Trouble? Tell me what you want. It's yours. Or tell me to stop."

She'd come to Nashville, expecting to learn a thing or two about this man-woman mystery that other women her age seemed to enjoy. She was looking for the *good* part of sexual experience that had been frightened out of her by a cruel act, denied her by a small town that would never let her forget her mistake. She'd thought she'd failed in her quest.

Maybe she'd just been looking for that experience with the wrong man.

"I want you to kiss me again. Really kiss me."

Her request seemed to open up a throttle, turbocharging the leisurely, languid connection between them. Without ever letting her feet hit the ground, he turned her—using the truck and the friction of her curves bunching against his harder angles to keep her suspended in the air and aligned against him in a way that was sending every red blood cell in her body charging hard into the tips of her aching breasts and down to her full, weeping center. And then he kissed her. And kissed her. His kisses consumed her.

His jacket fell away from her shoulders as her fingers crept around his neck, then raked up the back of his head, tugging his short, silky hair into her greedy grasp. His tongue reached into her mouth, caught hers in a twist and pulled it between his lips for a light nip between his teeth.

Alex returned the bold move, his groan of approval matching the restless cries in her throat. There was nothing soft about this meeting of lips, nothing reticent about the deep, ragged breaths that moved their bodies against each other. He slid one hand down to her bottom, slipped his fingers beneath the elastic band of the cotton and squeezed, branding her, skin to skin. Alex hooked her heel behind his thigh, instinctively opening her body to the hard, thrusting need of his. The truck rocked as he pushed his body closer, drove his tongue deeper.

A wolfish whistle from the entrance to the alley was the first glitch in Alex's mindless need to fulfill tonight's quest. A familiar panic button tried to break through the haze of passion. She should reconsider this impulsive encounter.

But the dectective had other ideas.

"Stay with me, sweetheart." He kissed away her doubts, turned and carried her to the cab of his truck. With an unceremonious shifting of grips and digging into pockets, he unlocked the door, opened it and dumped her inside. "Move over," he commanded. As soon as Alex scooted backward across the bench seat, he started the engine and took off. "We need some privacy."

His growly pronouncement spoke not only of his need, but reassured a bone-deep fear inside Alex that this was a good choice. That *he* was a good choice. This man would save the night—he'd save her lovelife—for her.

Alex held on tight as they jerked around corners and sped on a straightaway. Then they squealed through a parking lot and swerved into an alley where the neon lights and music and crowds of Broadway couldn't reach. About the time she'd worked her arms into the sleeves of his jacket and had pulled her dress down to a relatively modest level, he stomped on the brake, killed the engine and turned to her.

"You still game?" he asked. The glow from the dashboard shadowed the rugged lines of his face, but his eyes reflected a need, an intent, that rivaled her own.

Alex reached for him. "Yes."

As he wrapped his arm behind her back and laid her down on the seat, the truck plunged into darkness.

Perfect.

For a brief moment, his shadow loomed over her. But Alex felt excitement, not fear. She felt his palms on her thighs, his thumbs sliding up beneath the elastic of her panties. The heady weight of his body pressed her down into the upholstery as he sought out her bruised, swollen mouth for a tender kiss. "I can't believe I'm making out in my truck like some kind of randy teenager." His beard stubble abraded the underside of her chin. His kiss followed. He blazed a trail down her neck, arousing, soothing. "God, I need this, sweetheart. I need this."

And then, there really wasn't much talking.

Driven by instincts, directed by his responsive moans, sometimes guided by the instruction of his hands and mouth, Alex became more powerful, more certain of herself, more demanding.

He pushed the jacket off her shoulders. The straps of the dress followed. The strapless bra offered no resistance. When he closed his mouth over the throbbing peak of her breast, she moaned. When he blew softly across the damp tip, she twisted. And when he pulled the straining nipple into his mouth and suckled her with the rasp of his tongue she bucked beneath him.

Her fingers flexed convulsively in his hair, wanting to pull him closer, wanting to share his attentions with the other breast. As frantic as they'd been outside his truck, he seemed to be taking his own sweet time transforming her into a heavy, quivering, raw nerve of pure desire. He brushed his rough jaw over the other nipple in a caress that made her cry out, yet savor the healing touch of his tongue against her all the more.

She wasn't sure which happened first, the mindless panting or the fist of pressure building up between her thighs. She snatched at his T-shirt, tugged it from his belt as his kisses moved lower. She was desperate to touch the warm skin and the hard muscles underneath, but he moved beyond her reach. She was sitting half upright again, leaning up against the door. He shoved her dress up and kissed her belly, nuzzled her belly button, traced the sensible waistband of her panties with his chin, making muscles clench and stretch and contract. Before she could steady herself, his hand was inside her panties, cupping her bottom, lifting her to drag the underwear completely down her legs and toss them to the floorboards.

And then he was back, his kisses moving lower still. He brushed his lips through the thatch of golden curls and pressed a kiss to the swollen mound beneath. Alex dug her fingers into his shoulders and heard him laugh. The sound vibrated against her inner thigh.

"Easy, sweetheart." He stroked his thumbs along the seams where her legs joined her hips, each stroke getting longer, opening her wider and taking him closer to her slick, pulsating center. "I'm just thinking about how good you smell. All over."

Back home in Dahlia, she would have frozen up at the wanton intimacy of their position. She would have second-guessed. She never could have relaxed enough, felt safe enough, to lose her in-hibitions like this. She would have failed to know and give pleasure.

But this wasn't Dahlia, she reasoned. She wasn't Alex Morgan, pariah of gossip turned extreme tomboy. Tonight, she was this man's mystery woman. And she was all woman—all whole, sexually confident woman.

"What are you waiting for?" she gasped into the darkness. And then she tunneled her fingers into his hair and pulled his mouth against her.

Alex's head fell back and she cried out almost instantaneously as he ran his tongue between her folds and thrust inside her. Wave after wave of sensation rolled down to her core and blossomed back like shock waves through her body. He gently bit down against the hard nub, stroked his thumb along her aching crevice, kissed her and licked her and made her come again and again with just his mouth. Alex bucked and moaned and clutched him against her, her body weeping at the newfound experience of having a man bring her to orgasm.

When he was done, when she was spent, he pulled away,

crawling up over her body to reclaim her mouth in a full, deep kiss. She inhaled her own release on his skin, tasted it on her tongue. Alex Morgan had never had a night like this. "You're good."

She felt him smile against her lips. "I kind of got that idea. Thanks."

But she wasn't done. She pushed against his chest. "Your turn."

He gave her one last kiss and pulled away. "You're sure?"

"You'll have to arrest me to stop me."

He pulled off his badge and gun and set them on the dashboard. While she hurriedly redressed, he gingerly dropped one foot to the floor and stretched his other leg out behind her, opening himself up just as she'd offered herself to him. His deep voice coaxed her across the seat. "However you want."

Alex curled her legs beneath her and scooted closer. The jerk of his leg when she braced her hand against his knee told her he might be as primed for this forbidden encounter as she'd been. "Do you have protection?"

"Shit." She'd take that as a no.

But not as a *never mind.* Alex slid her hand along his thigh, crawling closer, massaging away any noble instinct to stop her wandering hands. His shoulders were broad enough, near enough, to blot out any light from her vision. But her sense of touch worked just fine. She palmed him through his jeans and she heard the creak of leather where he squeezed the seat back in his fist.

Interesting. Alex's pulse kicked up a notch in anticipation. Maybe there were other ways to feel the strength of her femininity that had nothing to do with her own release. She rubbed her palm down the length of his zipper and traced the seam of denim that ran between his legs. He groaned. "There are ways, right? Safe ones?" she asked.

His deep breath stirred the hair beside her ear. "Don't you know?"

All the innuendoes over the years didn't mean she knew what

she was doing. But she was a quick study when given the chance. She dragged her hand up, tracing the same path. "I'm learning."

His shoulders rose and fell in the shadows. "You weren't a virgin. Were you?"

Unfortunately, no. That honor had been stolen from her long ago, trampled on, laughed away as meaningless.

Tonight had meaning. Alex pressed her fingers to his lips, easing his distress as well as her own. "Shh. Enough about me. Talk me through this."

"You are one serious package of trouble, aren't you." He made it sound like a good kind of trouble. An irresistible kind of trouble. He pulled her fingers from his lips and guided her hand down to join the other one. For several moments, he simply cupped her hands over the bulge in his jeans and rocked against her. Her breathing quickened along with his. And then he gave her a command. "Unzip me. Careful. That's it."

The trembling of her fingers lessened with each hint of praise or pleasure. She unhooked his belt buckle, slid the zipper gently downward. He shifted slightly to help her ease his jeans off his hips. She smiled at the bright white cotton that poked through the opening they'd created.

Plain white cotton? A kindred spirit. The detective *was* the right man for the job tonight.

"Pull it out." She did as he asked, stroking his length through the tight tent of cotton, then reaching inside to capture the hot, pulsing hardness of him in her hand. "Oh, yeah." His hand tightened around her wrist, holding her still while he thrust inside her grip. The moisture at the tip caught in her palm and smoothed the friction between them. With a gasp that sounded like a tight breath through clenched teeth, he released her. "You do it. Just like that. Don't stop."

While Alex slid her hand from tip to base and back again, he framed her face with his hands, sifting his fingers into her hair, holding her as tenderly as he'd been firm with her a moment ago.

"I want to kiss you," he whispered at the corner of her mouth. "I can't seem to get enough of kissing you."

And then he seized her mouth with the same vigor that Alex used on him. She braced her hand against his shoulder and worked him as his tongue thrust into her mouth. The harder he kissed, the firmer her touch. He went deeper; she stroked harder. He gentled the brush of his lips across hers; she lightly teased the ridge of skin beneath him.

He was pulsing, throbbing, driving into her grip, mimicking the same rhythm with his tongue in her mouth. As she continued to caress his silken length, something deep inside Alex began to pulse in response. He moaned into her mouth, reached down and wrapped his fingers around hers, squeezing tightly as he came up off the seat and pushed himself one last, long time into her hand.

The power of his release triggered an answering satisfaction in her own body and Alex collapsed against him. For several long, timeless minutes, he wrapped his arms around her and she burrowed against his chest, marveling at the warmth, the exhaustion, the contentment she felt.

No encounter had ever been like this for her. She felt safe. Satisfied. Serenely pleased with herself and grateful to this man. Her night in Nashville had turned out to be a success, after all.

As she became aware of the soft, patternless lines he was tracing against her back, Alex noticed the time on his dashboard clock: 2:14 a.m. Her brother would be worried about her by now, her father up, pacing the living room, trying to decide whether to call the sheriff or get into his own car and drive into Nashville to search for her.

And with those concerns, the first frissons of worry marred her contentment.

"Restless?" the detective asked.

Alex pushed away from the tempting haven of his chest and slid back to her side of the seat. She pulled his jacket more tightly around her, but couldn't seem to ward off the chill of reality that had wormed its way into her thoughts. "I'm just re-membering that I'm stranded, that I don't have any way to get home or even call there."

He sat up straight, pulling up his jeans and tucking everything back into place. He reached for his gun and badge. "I'll take you."

"No." Alex shot her hand out to touch his wrist. An armed man would hardly reassure her father and brother. She pulled away just as quickly, distracted by the warmth of his skin. "I don't usually do anything like this."

"Neither do I." The gun and badge found their place on his belt. He started the engine. "I haven't had an enounter like this…for a while."

He fastened his seat belt, and while Alex did the same, he shifted into reverse and backed out of the alley.

Alex tucked her tangled hair behind her ears. "An encounter sounds like a clandestine rendezvous. Like we were supposed to meet. I'm…"

He checked for traffic and pulled onto the street. "You're what?"

"Confused."

"Join the club."

"Yeah, but you're…older."

"So I've been told." The lights from the street and other cars let her read the hard expression that deepened the lines on his face. "Doesn't mean I've got women all figured out."

Her laugh sounded more like a snort. Yeah, she was a real femme fatale. Not. At least not outside that alley. "I sure don't have men figured out."

"I'm not going to apologize for what happened."

"I don't want you to." The old Alex's doubts were quickly re-sufacing. "I know we didn't do…everything. But, you enjoyed it, didn't you?"

"Hell yeah, sweetheart. I enjoyed it a little too much."

Alex frowned. "You can enjoy it too much?"

He swore and Alex jerked in her seat. "There are rules and

regulations to life. To my job. I think I've broken about every last damn one of them with you tonight."

"I'm sorry."

He headed up a hill, picking up speed. "Don't be sorry. Be mad. Get that lawyer of yours and sue me."

"Why?"

"I was supposed to be rescuing a damsel in distress, not gettin' my rocks off with her. You can report me for that. In fact, I'll give you the form to fill out and introduce you to the officer where you can file a complaint against me."

After a moment's hesitation, she smiled. "I don't have any complaints. No one's ever called me a damsel in distress before. That's kind of girly, isn't it?"

"I suppose." She didn't understand the 180 degree shifts in his mood from hero of the hour to angry cop, but she had a feeling she was going to be okay. "So, milady—will you let me drive you to precinct headquarters before something worse than me happens to you?"

He maneuvered them smoothly through the late-night traffic and pedestrians. "Is that where we're going?"

"Yeah."

"And you're not arresting me?"

"I'm the one who screwed up tonight, not you. Here." He pulled out his cell phone and handed it across the seat to her. "The call's on me." He stopped at an intersection and watched her punch in a number. "Contacting a friend? Family? That lawyer of yours?"

Alex smiled, feeling extraordinarily relieved and comforted by the simple gift of a phone call. "All of the above. My big brother. He'll come get me."

"Tell him to meet you at the downtown precinct station."

She slid a glance across the seat to her knight in shining armor while she waited for Nick to answer. "You won't tell my brother what we did tonight, will you?"

He scoffed. "If you don't tell my deputy chief."

Nick Morgan picked up after the second ring. "Alex? You okay? I saw Buell and his buddies yukking it up at the track tonight, and I couldn't help but think… I called your cell a dozen times. You've got me scared shitless here."

"I'm okay." The truck slowed and turned into a parking garage. "My date with Drew's friend didn't go as well as I expected. And I lost my purse."

Her brother swore. She could hear her father in the background now, asking questions. "She's okay, Dad." Nick explained a few details to their father, George Morgan, then turned his attention back to the phone. "You're not hurt?"

She'd been embarrassed, angry, frustrated and a little afraid before this smoky-haired detective had literally picked her up off the street. But she hadn't been hurt. "I'm okay, Nick. I met…" Detective Galahad was watching her, hanging on to every word. "Nashville PD has been very helpful." In ways that made her blush and turn away. "Just come get me, okay? I'm at the downtown precinct station."

"I'll be there in forty minutes. I love you, Shrimp."

"I love you too, Nick."

They were parked beneath the precinct offices by the time she handed the phone back to the detective.

"Thank you." She offered him a hesitant smile. "Big brother will save the day."

He nodded. "So now I know this infamous lawyer-slash-wonder-brother of yours is Nick. You ever gonna tell me your name?"

"Look, Detective…" She unfastened her seat belt and reached for the exit handle. "Don't get me wrong, I enjoyed tonight, but…"

She laughed. It was a sad sound, really—a sound that revealed just how much this *encounter* had been an aberration for her, for both of them, perhaps.

"This isn't reality. Let's forget the names so we can skip the embarrassment of you mentioning tonight to anybody who happens to know anybody I happen to know. Okay?"

"Okay. Your call. Tonight never happened."

So why did it hurt that he'd agreed so easily to her request?

3

"MMM. YEAH. RIGHT THERE."

Alexandra Morgan caught her tongue between parched lips as her thoughts drifted away from the fan belt she stretched between her hands and took note of how the fender of the '94 Buick she was repairing pressed against the juncture of her thighs. A pocket of pressure was gathering where hard steel met soft woman, fueled by an errant fantasy that seemed to keep cropping up at the most inopportune times.

Normally, she relegated her secret fantasies to the privacy of her bedroom or one of her late-night bubble baths where she washed away the grime of a day spent in the family garage where she worked as a mechanic. But this was a routine fix on a slow day, just maintenance stuff for a local customer. The real excitement of her job wouldn't start until tomorrow or Thursday, when the drag racers who frequented the Dahlia Speedway across the parking lot started showing up for replacement parts and tune-ups in preparation for the regular weekend races.

In other words, Alex was bored. And when she was bored, her mind wandered. Wandering into something as pleasant as her fabricated forbidden affair with the big-city cop with the wide shoulders and hushed, seductive words was a welcome respite from the grief and anger over her brother Nick's recent death that normally filled her head these days.

Outside the open doors of Morgan & Son's Garage, the afternoon air was heavy with the promise of a spring rain. Maybe the green scents of budding trees and flower blossoms hanging in the mist and dappling her bare arms with moisture had reminded her subconscious mind of those bubble baths where a cop with stormy gray eyes had had his way with her time and again in an assortment of imaginary story lines.

Her imagination took her to places far removed from tense, worrisome reality.

"You like that, milady?" her knight in shining armor drawled, sliding his hand between her legs and cupping her warmth.

"Yes," she moaned, closing her eyes against the pleasure of his strong hand reaching into the water and rubbing against her clit. "Please don't stop."

"Ah, my damsel is in distress, is she?" Broad shoulders filled her vision as he bent over her to gentle her soft cries with a kiss. "You don't have to beg with me."

Her diaphanous bathing gown floated in the water, its sheer material hiding nothing from his eyes. The smoky gray orbs lazily looked their fill, each visual caress like the stroke of his hand on her body.

He was unlike the other men in her kingdom. This one came from a far-off country. He served her willingly, while the treacherous knights of her own kingdom were not allowed to touch her. Her mystery knight, the Silver Fox, spoke in hushed, seductive tones. He ruled his own lands with an iron fist but always treated her as nothing less than a lady.

"Will you join me, good sir?"

"You only had to ask." His tunic and breeches became a taut black T-shirt and jeans as he peeled off his clothes and slipped into the tub with her. Water sloshed over the sides and she laughed as his big frame displaced all the bubbles. Alex's thighs clenched

*together when he wrapped his viselike arm around her waist and
pulled her onto his lap. A well-honed warrior, he'd fought many
battles. But each evening he returned to her chamber to take her
in any number of ways. Tonight's seduction was to be slow and
sensuous. And merciless, she thought with a gasp of pleasure, as
the bulging evidence of his arousal poked against her bottom.
"Milady should never have to beg for pleasure."*

*He kissed the back of her neck as he palmed her breasts. His
big hands lifted them and kneaded them with a gently urgent rev-
erence—like the patient, mature man he was, not some grabby,
greedy teen who could earn ten bucks on a bet if he touched them.*

Teen? Eeuw. Reality tried to nudge its way in and mess with
her fantasy.

Alex squeezed the humiliating memory from her mind and
tried to *feel* the hardness of the grown man pressed against her.

"You don't think I'm common, do you?"

*"You talk too much, milady. Let me show you my apprecia-
tion."* No. She smiled wickedly. This time she'd show him. *She
spread her thighs slightly, boldly catching his arousal and
squeezing it. "Alexandra…"*

*How did he know her name? That was one of the rules
between them. No names. Ever. She squeezed him again, gently
punishing him for forgetting.*

*Alex squirmed in his lap, guiding him closer and closer to
where she wanted him to be. Inside her.*

"Alexandra…" No names. *She adjusted herself over him. He
moved beneath her. This time they'd come together. He wanted
it, too. She was a lady.* His *lady. The kingdom need never doubt
her fine qualities again.*

*The pressure was building. The water on their skin—lapping
between them, surrounding them—simmered with heat. Their heat.*

"Alexandra…"

Someone was shouting her name.

But not in passion.

"Alexandra Morgan!"

Alex jerked at the drill-sergeant shout, bumping her head on the open hood of the Buick. "Ow. Damn." She slid off her perch on the fender and tugged her tool belt back into place, embarrassed to think that an errant monkey wrench and a tan sedan had triggered one of her stupid fantasies.

"Daddy?" Alex rubbed at the sore spot beneath the yellow bandanna wrapped on top of her head, clearing her brain of naughty thoughts and ignoring the male laughter coming from underneath the car in the next bay. She quickly scanned the length of the garage, from the lube pit to the office hallway door, trying to account for each of the employees who hadn't gone on lunch break yet. No one had seen her squirming on top of the car, had they?

But she had bigger problems.

"Alexandra!" Her father's deep, booming voice—as crisp and quick as his military stride—announced she was in trouble. Again.

The door to his office slammed, jolting through Alex's body with dread. "Oh, no. He found it."

"Found what?" Winston "Tater" Rawls, a longtime employee of the garage and the closest thing to a big brother she had now that Nick was gone, rolled out from under a Ford hybrid in the next bay. "What'd you do this time, Alex?"

She grabbed a rag off her tool chest and wiped her hands, mentally shaking her head at the lanky blond goofball's question. "I was thinking for myself again."

He made a tsk-tsk sound behind his teeth. "That'll teach you. I think I'll just listen to the fireworks from here, if you don't mind."

"Thanks for having my back, Tater." Sarcasm dripped from her voice.

"Anytime." He rolled back beneath the Ford, his laugh echoing from under the chassis. "Anytime."

Alex dashed toward the exit leading to the business offices. She made it all the way around the sedan before the stale smells of body odor and cigarette smoke stopped her in her tracks. *Not now.*

She tipped her chin to the black-haired mechanic who blocked her path. Artie Buell was nothing if not persistent. Of course, she wished he'd also learn how to wash his stained coveralls, use a little less gel in his hair, and take no for an answer.

Using his tongue, he rolled a toothpick from one side of his mouth to the other with a suggestive swipe. "I'll watch your back, Alex," he drawled. "You need me to smooth over anything between you and your daddy, I'm your man."

Right. Ever since their sophomore year of high school, when dating his older brother hadn't worked out so well for her, he'd tried to be *her man*. She'd grown up, moved away and learned to dream of bigger things than small-town stereotypes. She'd come home again because her father and brother had needed someone to manage their home and feed them. She couldn't cook as well as she could fix a car. She couldn't sew or garden as well as she could grow a business. But she loved the men who'd been her only family from the time she was a toddler, and for right now—especially now that Nick was gone—she'd be whatever her father needed her to be.

Artie Buell, however, hadn't changed a bit in nine years. If he wasn't such a good mechanic—and the sheriff's son—she'd have raised a stink about him working here. But she had her own reasons for wanting to stay on the Buell family's good side now. The truth might depend upon their cooperation. And for that reason alone, she summoned a smile. "I can handle my dad just fine. Thanks."

"I think I impressed him when I won the Moonshine Run last month." Damn. The polite chit-chat wasn't over. Alex froze her smile into place and endured. "You know, I didn't see you at that race. I kind of thought you might want to root a friend on, especially seeing as how I rebuilt most of that car right here in your daddy's garage. Remember I ran some of those last-minute calibrations by you?"

"Sure. I'm glad they helped. Gotta go."

When she would have scooted around him, Artie's hand snaked out to grab her arm and halt her beside him. "You should have at least helped me celebrate at the party afterwards."

Working with Artie was one thing. Anything more personal would be like reliving a nightmare. *Keep it nice.* "I told you I was busy that weekend. Congratulations again, though." She tugged against his grip. "Dad's waiting."

Instead of releasing her, he pulled her close enough that she got a whiff of the cigarettes on his breath when he leaned down to whisper. "You haven't even been down to the pit to see my trophy. It's a bigun."

Right. Like she'd ever venture down into that sunken room that reminded her of a burial chamber unless she had a damn good—work-related—reason to do so. The fact that it was Artie's main work space at the garage probably added to the eerie claustrophobia she got whenever she went down there. "A bigun? That's a pretty lame line, even for you."

"C'mon, Alex. I'm not the bad guy in the family. Remember?"

"Artie." Tater was out from underneath the Ford again. This time, he wasn't laughing. "I thought I asked you to get the specs for this car off the computer for me."

Artie winked one dark eye at Alex but spoke to Tater. "I got 'em."

"Then move it."

"I'm movin'."

When he pulled the printouts from his pocket and released her to deliver them, Alex glanced down at her forearm. She didn't know which bothered her more, his grimy fingers on her skin, or the memory of another Buell's touch. Both turned her stomach.

"Alexandra!"

The steel door connecting the garage to the office corridor swung open. Alex jumped as her father's barrel-chested physique filled the doorway.

For a moment, his stern green eyes looked beyond her into the garage. "Get to work, Artie. I need you back down in the lube pit to change the oil on Jeb Worth's car before he stops by at one to pick it up. I don't pay you to stand around and flirt with my daughter."

"Yes, sir."

As Artie handed off the papers to Tater and both men returned to the cars they were working on, Alex hurried on over and greeted her father's ruddy expression with a wry smile. "Thanks for the rescue, Daddy."

But Staff Sergeant George Montgomery Morgan, USMC, Ret., didn't smile back. Instead, he waved a bill at her face. "What is this? What new scheme are you cooking up now? You know I don't like surprises. I told you I wanted to be cautious about expenditures now that the Fisks are selling the track to Whip Davis."

Alex's relief came out as an embarrassing snort. Thank heaven. He hadn't found the papers she'd taken from Nick's things, after all. She stuffed the shop rag into the back pocket of her baggy denim overalls, using the moment to compose her thoughts before she gave away what she'd been working so hard to hide. "I thought something serious had happened."

"This *is* serious," he groused.

"Right. The money. Of course, it is." She should have known her father wouldn't go snooping through her personal things. But if he'd found the stash of notes she'd been sorting through regarding her brother's death, he'd be in a whole new world of hurt. She'd worried and confounded him enough over the years. Not enough of a lady. No husband. No man. She knew he didn't blame her for their trouble with the Buells, but still, it had to be disappointing for him to know how Artie's older brother had forever changed her view of men and relationships. Causing her father more pain was the last thing she wanted. In fact, she was doing her best to help her father climb out of the emotional pit he was already trapped in by investigating the truth behind Nick Morgan's car crash.

Artie's father had declared it a tragic accident—said Nick had probably fallen asleep at the wheel and careened off the country highway into the bottom of a ravine. Maybe she was grasping at straws, but Alex had seen two sets of tread marks on the muddy shoulder before winter rains had washed the evidence away that night. *"Somebody probably stopped there to see if they could help him,"* the sheriff had suggested. So how did he explain away the twin sets of skid marks on the road near the crash site? Sleeping drivers didn't slam on their brakes. And what was the likelihood of a second driver laying tread in the same exact location?

Sheriff Buell had come up with many plausible scenarios to explain away Nick's death, but Alex wasn't buying them. The rain hadn't started until after the crash that January night. The family business was taking care of cars, for God's sake, and Nick's had been in top-notch condition. Nick had raced at the speedway before heading to law school. He knew how to handle a car. Knew how to handle any road condition. The crash made no sense. His death made even less.

Though George Morgan seemed to accept walking through life with his son in the ground and his heart buried there beside him, Alex wasn't ready to let this town deal her another cruel blow. Especially not when, in Nick's last phone call before his accident, he'd told her that he'd be missing their traditional New Year's Eve game night because he was working on something for the state attorney general's office—and that that *something* could have serious consequences if the wrong people found out what he was up to.

"Wrong people?" she asked. *"Here in Dahlia? Who?"*

Nick laughed at her curiosity and ignored her concern. "Don't worry, Shrimp. It's just some paperwork I need to finish up. Boring stuff. I'm afraid you'll have to find someone else to play that marathon game of RISK with this time. But I'll be looking for a rematch next year. Okay?"

"Okay. I'll give Dad the message. Happy New Year, Nick. I love you."

"Love you, too, Shrimp."

The next time she saw her brother was at the county morgue. That night Alex had wept with her father and vowed to uncover how *boring paperwork* could get a good man killed.

But right now she had to deal with whatever current crisis she'd brought into her father's world. "Is there a problem?"

"A five-hundred-dollar problem." He smacked the paper with his hand. "I appreciate you stepping up to help with the business side of things now that—" Alex's heart twisted at the hesitation "—now that Nick isn't here. But the racing season has only been going for a couple of months. I don't want to be spending money we may need to see us through the rest of the year."

Alex reached out and wrapped her fingers around her father's fist where he clenched it at his side, holding on until the tension in him began to relax. When he turned his hand and squeezed hers in return, Alex knew he was going to be all right. For now. Her secret was safe. Suspicious bills she could argue—suspicions about Nick's death she could not. Not until she had something more to back them up with, at any rate.

"This doesn't have anything to do with the Fisks or Mr. Worth or changes at the speedway. You're afraid I'm going to screw something else up. But I've really thought this through, Dad." Alex pointed out the letterhead on the paper. "The Nelson Racing Team is making a name for themselves on the circuit. Skyler Nelson won the Missouri Flats in 4.89, running with an LSX 427 iron block motor. Exactly what we specialize in building. If he puts our name on his car, just think of the advertising. Our business could grow exponentially. We might have to open a second garage."

"I suppose you'd want to manage it?"

Why not? Nick had been the lawyer. *She* was the one with the business sense. "During my internship my senior year at Tennessee, I worked in that auto parts store in Knoxville. In six months' time, my business plan saved a struggling business and helped put them in the black."

Her father scratched his fingers over the top of his silvering crewcut, gradually transforming from the grizzly bear who'd stormed into the garage into the gruff teddy bear who might love her, but who rarely understood her. "I'm not interested in opening another garage or going nationwide. We have a thriving business right now, right here in Dahlia, growing as attendance at the track grows. I hope we'll continue to turn a profit once the speedway changes hands, but during this transition time, I can't guarantee what kind of cash flow I'm going to have. I want to see how things pan out with Davis managing things before I start dipping into our cash reserves."

Alex used his perfunctory explanation as an opportunity to steer the conversation away from anything remotely personal. "What about sponsoring a local driver, then?"

"This is five-hundred dollars out of our budget already. And you want to spend more?"

"We have to spend money to make money, Dad. We need to sponsor a car, not just service the cars whenever the driver needs something. If we hook up with a big name and he or she is successful, then we'll be successful." Oops. Open mouth, insert foot. Retreat to the brig. "I mean, we'll *continue* to be successful and you won't have to worry about our future, no matter who's running the speedway."

But his eyes shuttered and the debate was over. Her father drew back his shoulders, silently reminding her that it was his experience and own two hands that had started this business twenty-two years ago. Nick and Alex's mother had died and George Morgan—former chief mechanic at the Camp LeJeune motor pool—had left the marines to settle in one spot and raise them. The garage had been built from a small military pension and big dreams. "My decision stands. I can absorb this bill. Just don't surprise me with any more new ideas." He reached out and tapped the point of her chin in a gesture he'd used as far back as she could remember. "Okay?"

But Alex wasn't Daddy's little girl anymore. When he opened

the door to the office corridor, she followed right behind him. "Drew Fisk and his father and grandfather have poured a lot of money into the speedway to bring it up to code, modernize the track and add the amenities that racers and fans want nowadays." Her father's sigh told her she wasn't making any headway, but he held the door to his office open for her and let her keep talking. "Those upgrades brought in the Farron Fuels Racing Series, and Dahlia is turning into a booming little town again. We can do the same—increase our promotional budget, sponsor a team and take advantage of the influx of business and money."

He swiveled his leather chair forward, pointing to the door as he sat behind his big walnut desk. "I want to be careful about who we sponsor and where our logo shows up, honey. Remember, it's my name on this company."

Alex's hands fisted at her hips when she glanced back at the red-and-white logo painted on the safety glass. Morgan & *Son*'s Garage. It was a sad reminder of dashed hopes—for her father, and for herself. That sadness painted her voice when she turned back to face him. "It's *my* name, too."

"Ah, honey, I didn't mean…" A powerful engine gunned outside the front of the garage, loud enough to be heard in the interior offices. But George Morgan ignored the potential customer and reached for his daughter's hand, pulling her closer as he sat on the corner of his desk. "I didn't mean you aren't an important part of this family. Or this business. Or that it hasn't meant the world to me to have you close by these past few months. It's just…"

"Dad—"

"Let me say this." He grasped both her hands now, and Alex willingly held tight to his strong grip, wishing she knew the right words or actions to ease the pain that deepened the grooves beside his eyes and mouth. She couldn't be hurting any more than he was. "I had it in my head all these years that Nick would be taking over the garage and running it with me one day. Even when he became a lawyer, he always found a way to stay involved." He brushed his knuckles beneath her chin, and Alex did her best to summon a smile for him. "You've always been my little tomboy. But I hoped you'd grow up to be a fine lady like your mama was. I guess I'm still hoping to see you in a dress, with a good man at your side and little ones running around your feet."

Work boots, overalls and dirty hands hardly lived up to that legacy. "I'm sorry, Daddy. I've tried. I just don't seem to have much success when it comes to being that lady you want." Besides the fact she'd been raised by a marine, and hadn't had much feminine influence growing up, most of the eligible men of Dahlia—like Artie Buell—didn't see her as much of a lady. One man had created the lies about her being a teenage tramp, but it took the well-oiled gears of small-town gossip to perpetuate them. "But I do know my way around cars and business. I'm good at this. Please give my ideas a little thought, okay?"

He leaned in and pressed a kiss to her forehead. "I'll think about it, honey. I promise. In the meantime, just run it by me first before you spend five-hundred dollars on anything besides car parts. Okay?"

Not exactly a victory. But Alex wrapped her arms around his neck and hugged him tight, anyway. "Okay."

A sharp knock on the door ended the father-daughter moment. George stood as Alex pulled away.

"You two open for business?"

"Well, look who's here. Drew Fisk." George reached out with a smile. "Where have you been keeping yourself, son? You weren't at the track during last weekend's races."

Alex tilted her head to welcome the blond-haired man in the tailored blue suit and white dress shirt. As usual, the tie was long gone. "Hey, Drew."

"Alex." He winked by way of acknowledgment and reached

in front of her to shake her father's hand. "George. How're y'all doing? I've been in and out of town, taking care of business."

"For your father and grandfather? How are they?"

"Fine. Dad's in India, trying to work out an agreement to build an aluminum fabrication plant there like the one we have here. Grandfather is as cantankerous and crusty as ever."

"I can't imagine him slowing down, even now that he's retired."

"He seems to keep his nose in everybody's business, for sure." Drew turned his attention to Alex, his bright blue gaze traveling up and down her body, appreciating her curves in the same way he had from the day he'd realized his best friend's younger sister had sprouted breasts, and was no longer just a tagalong for his adventures with Nick. "Alex. You're looking as pretty as that spring day outside."

"And you're full of it," she scoffed, burying her dirty hands deep in her pockets. Though he used that same smooth BS on every female, it was nonetheless good to see an old family friend again. She smiled, knowing he liked talking about his cars almost as much as she liked working on them. "I thought I heard a seven liter V8 engine driving up. Did you get that new sports car you were bragging about?"

"I did." He arched a golden brow in a devilish smile. "As I recall, somebody here wanted to know how the engine runs on one of those. Care to find out for yourself? It's clouding up outside, but we can take it for a spin before the storm hits."

Alex shrugged, appreciating the invitation, but knowing she had too much on her plate right now to have time to fritter away. "I've got Mrs. Stillwell's Buick out in the shop that I need to finish."

She felt her father's hand in the middle of her back, nudging her toward Drew. "I'll put Artie or Tater on it. I think I can spare you for a half hour or so."

"But Dad, I—"

"Go. With his grandfather selling the track, Drew might not be around quite so often. Better seize the moment, as they say."

His hopeless matchmaking wasn't obvious, was it? She had responsibilities here. "Oh, by the way, honey." He reached back across his desk and picked up a pink slip of paper. "I took a phone message for you. From a Daniel Rutledge?"

Dan Rutledge? As in Nick's friend from the state attorney general's office Dan Rutledge? The man whom Nick had been going to see that awful night? Alex snatched the memo from her father's hand, her fingers trembling. "Thanks."

"He a friend of yours?" her father asked, no doubt hoping for news of a decent man in her life.

"I've never met him." Technically, that wasn't a lie. She only knew Daniel Rutledge through Nick's notes and a series of phone messages and e-mail inquiries she'd asked him to return. Alex stuffed the note into her pocket. "I guess I'll have to call him to see who he is and find out what he wants."

She couldn't reassure her father with a better answer than that? Especially with a mixture of excitement and fear that was no doubt stamped all over her face. Did Rutledge have suspicions about Nick's death, too? Answers for her? Alex lowered her head, feeling her cheeks steam with her lousy cover-up.

Fortunately, her father was perplexed enough by the mystery to miss her reaction. "The name's familiar. Wasn't he a friend of Nick's back in school? Did you ever know him, Drew?"

Drew shook his head. "Must be from law school. Nick and I lost touch for a couple of years when Grandfather sent me off to Princeton to finish my education."

"I hope he wasn't looking for Nick." George sank back onto the corner of the desk. "Maybe he doesn't know about the accident, and he was trying to reach him. Oh, hell. Somebody else I didn't tell."

"Daddy?" Alex reached out, but he was already drifting away from her, shrinking back into the distant shadow of the man he'd been before grief had ravaged him. "I'll take care of it. Don't worry."

George Morgan barely nodded. Tears burned behind Alex's

eyelids. Some son of a bitch was going to pay for what they'd done to this man. "Daddy?"

A long arm wrapped around her waist and pulled her into the hallway. "Let's give him his privacy." Drew closed the door softly behind them and turned her against his chest for a hug, pressing her nose into the scent of designer cologne at the open collar of his shirt. "He'll be all right, Alex. Give him some space."

When she felt his lips brushing against her temple, she pushed away. "No. I want to fix this."

"You can't."

"Watch me."

"Alex." His familiar, indulgent smile stopped her from retreating across the hall into her own office. "I miss Nick, too. I thought he and I would be a team forever. You can't make your father's hurt go away for him. You have to let him grieve."

"In my head, I know you're right. But:..." Drew Fisk was no fantasy knight in shining armor. But he was a friend, and he drove a fast car. And right now, Alex needed some speed to drown out the frustrations roiling inside her. She mustered up an answering smile. "Maybe I could use a little fresh air, after all. Give me a few minutes to find Tater to tell him I'm leaving. Start your engine, Drew. I'll be right there."

4

JACK RILEY LEANED BACK against the wall at the Headlights Ice House, a bustling food and drink establishment where picnic tables and stacked crates formed eating areas that were anything but private. The lights were bright, the noise was loud, but with thunder rumbling in the night sky outside, it offered a warm, dry place where a man could fill his belly and get a crash course in who was who in Dahlia, Tennessee.

Stretching his long legs out across the bench seat of his table, he took a long swig from his second bottle of beer.

He'd come here to catch a criminal. Or two. Or six. Or however many sons of bitches it took to stop the flow of drugs and money that he'd traced from Nashville back to this deceptively innocent spot on the map.

Located about thirty miles east of Nashville, Dahlia had once been home to plantations, horse breeding and tobacco. According to his current investigation, Dahlia had nearly died during the Great Depression. But one of its founding families, the Fisks, had built the Dahlia Speedway in the 1960s, and the town was reborn. Now, instead of racing thoroughbreds, they raced cars.

The Chevy Camaro he'd been working on since he was a teenager—a lifetime ago, it seemed—was Jack's ticket into town. Secured in the trailer he was hauling behind his pickup, the modified street car would qualify him as an entrant in the track's Outlaw 10.5 Division Drag Racing Series.

He needed to become a part of the track.

He needed to become a part of this town.

Because someone here had murdered his partner.

When Lorenzo Vaughn had agreed to reveal his source for the drugs he'd sold in Nashville, in exchange for a reduced sentence, a fatal chain of events had been set into motion.

Vaughn had sent Jack and Eric to a chop shop. The business of tearing down racing cars from across the country and selling parts on the black market had also been a front for the even more dangerous business of smuggling heroin and other drugs inside some of the vehicles. But by the time the task force moved in to make an arrest, the business had closed up and moved its location. To ferret out the new distribution center and the men behind the drug import scheme, Eric had gone in undercover as a buyer looking to make a purchase. He'd stayed with the job, perfected the role of a new dealer in town, worked his way up through the hierarchy of thugs and lieutenants to the men in charge of the operation—who made him as a cop and had him gunned down in the street. Whoever was running the Dahlia-Nashville smuggling connection was going to pay.

The cop bleeding out on the pavement three months ago could have been Jack. Should have been Jack. He had no wife to grieve over him, no children in shock, no family left in ruins.

Eric had started this investigation.

Now Jack was going to finish the job.

He was going to find the drugs. Find the smugglers.

He was going to find Eric's killer.

Despite plenty of hotshots on the force who could drive their cars fast, Jack had volunteered for this undercover assignment himself. He could drive. Billington was still gunning for his record on the police academy driving course, but Jack had the experience. He knew the S.O.P. (Standard Operating Procedures) of the drug game—when to step on somebody, when to make nice, when to duck for cover. A young stud like Billington wouldn't have the patience for the nuances of undercover work. Besides, this assignment was personal. For almost twenty years, his partner's family had been *his* family. Nobody hurt one of his own without there being hell to pay.

According to an Internet search, the name Jack Riley was almost as common as John Smith. With thousands of Jacks to blend in with, no personal link to Dahlia, and the driving experience to back up the role he had to play, he'd decided to simply become a civilian version of himself—Black Jack Riley, an over-the-hill racer staging a comeback.

He was here to find out who was shipping the drugs and how it was being done without the local cops and track officials putting a stop to it. They were either unaware of the problem or they were unwilling to deal with it.

But Jack would.

And if he found the Glock 9 mm that had taken his partner's life, as well, in this hamlet, then the owner would be taking a trip with him back to Nashville.

He intended to get *this* job done. And done right.

Son of a bitch. Jack squeezed his fist around the neck of his beer bottle and weathered the punch of grief and anger that hit him in the gut as he remembered his partner's children weeping, and the weight of Eric's casket on his shoulder as he helped carry him to his grave. *Double-ass son of a bitch!*

Jack tipped the bottle and let the tang of the icy liquid slide down his throat, forgetting for a moment how important it was to bury his emotions and keep his wits about him. It was the key to any undercover operation. Especially one as personal as this. Eyes open. Be tough.

He eased his death grip on the bottle and set it back on the table. He wouldn't fail Eric Mesner because he couldn't keep his emotions in check.

"You ready for another one, big boy?"

Jack turned his gaze to the waitress who'd shown up at his table. She smacked her gum a little too loud, wore her blue-jean skirt a little too tight, but her friendly smile was just right.

Jack smiled back. He remembered her introduction when she'd first taken his order. "Sandy, is it?"

"You bet." *Smack.* Smile. She propped a hand on her hip and nodded toward his drink. "How many can a big fella like you hold?"

Draining the bottle must have been the cue she'd been looking for to come back to his table. Though she didn't appear to be much over thirty, Sandy walked and talked as if she'd been a fixture at this place for years. She was probably a good source of information about the town and its residents. At the very least, she was a friendly face. The service had been as good as the food. He'd remember to leave her a big tip. "One more, at least."

"Comin' right up."

As she cleared the bottle and headed for the kitchen, Jack heard a slurred voice from next table over. "Hey, Sandy—ain't you gonna ask me how much I can hold?"

Hoots and laughter from the drunk's table applauded his clever come-on.

Jack glanced over to see a man palm the waitress's butt. She swatted away the offending hand with a laugh. "The problem with you, Hank, is that you *can't* hold your liquor."

The stained cuticles on Hank's fingers marked him as a man who worked with his hands. "Maybe I wasn't talkin' drinks."

"Honey, you are nothin' *but* talk." The laughter turned to oohs and verbal jabs and more laughter, deriding Hank's failure to score points with the lady. "Why don't you run along home before you get yourself into trouble, Hank. You've had enough."

"Now Sandy, you aren't shooing us all out, are you?" A short man with a shaved head, wearing a jacket that matched the silver Fisk Racing jacket that handsy Hank wore, draped his arm around the awestruck brunette sitting beside. "As far as I'm concerned, this party's just getting started."

Most likely a "drag hag," a woman fan of drag racing who followed the circuit to get close to her favorite driver or top mechanic, the brunette curled her body into Baldy's. "I'll go home with you anytime you're ready, Jimbo." She trailed her finger over the dome of Jimbo's head. "You just say the word and I'm yours."

Jack's beer soured in his mouth at the shameless invitation. Give him sass and fire over that coy crap anytime. Like the blond mystery woman who'd turned him inside out that night in Nashville—and had haunted his most erotic dreams ever since.

Don't go there. With a ruthless denial of any distracting emotions, Jack forced his thoughts to the job at hand. He'd do a damn sight better by his partner if he concentrated on figuring out all the players at the track in Dahlia. Starting with Hank and Jimbo and the crew at the next table.

Jack looked back in time to see Jimbo break off a liplock with the brunette. Then he pointed across the table to Hank. "Now that's how you get a woman in line."

"Shut up," Hank drawled. He tucked his fingers into the waitress's pocket and tugged her back to his side. "Come on, Sandy. You and me. We've been dancing this dance for years now. When are you gonna give in?"

"When are you gonna grow up?"

"Burn." The youngest man at the table, a ringer for Hank with his black hair and downhome drawl, had his cell phone out. But he wasn't so busy texting that he couldn't trade a high five with Jimbo. "She nailed you, big brother."

Hank didn't miss a beat. "No. *Nailed* is what she wants me to do to her. Ain't that right, Sandy?"

The table erupted with laughter. Even the fourth team member sitting with them, a silent giant with a full beard, joined in. The quiet redhead cozied up next to him giggled. Another fan from the track, no doubt.

Jack sat up a little straighter, appalled, but not surprised, by the crude innuendoes. Those boys and their babes had probably won big at the races, and were drinking their way through the celebration. Something had given them plenty of profit to allow them to set a stack of bills on the table, bold as brass. They were showing off their momentary wealth to the other patrons and making sure everyone in the restaurant noticed that they were the big men in town.

Jack noticed. It might just be pay day for the locals. But he'd seen the same kind of behavior working undercover in the drug world. Show the world that you were top dog, and nobody messed with you. Hank and Jimbo, Text Boy and the big guy were all going on Jack's list of possible suspects.

As the laughter waned, Sandy deftly slipped away as though she'd had plenty of practice avoiding that table already. "Down, boys. I'll bring you all a cup of hot coffee."

"Don't tease me, woman. I don't want coffee." Hank nearly fell off his bench seat, shouting after her. "Unless you're gonna put a little of that sugar in it."

Jack admired the waitress for ignoring the taunt. He relaxed back against the brick wall, feeling confident that she had enough experience to take care of herself. Besides, the noisy table with the Fisk Racing team wasn't the only group he needed to assess.

As his eyes swept the room from his corner table, he knew he'd made a good choice in stopping here for drinks and dinner. The perfectly grilled burger and the generous slice of home-baked apple pie he'd eaten were only partly responsible for the mental pat on the back he gave himself. Even for a Tuesday night, the joint was hopping. If he wanted a quick introduction to the town, he'd come to the right place. The clientele here at Headlights provided a clear cross-section of the people who lived in and moved through Dahlia.

Besides the crew from the track, there were yuppies at another picnic table. Still wearing their suits despite ditching their ties and high heels, they sipped margaritas and discussed art galleries and business investments.

But most of the place was filled by locals dressed in jeans and other casual work clothes. With one obnoxiously tipsy exception, they were more subdued—probably feeling at home, relaxed, and therefore they had nothing to prove. He saw everything from Southern belle housewives with proper, pretty dresses and proper, pretty children, to farmers and factory men. There was a table of silver-haired retirees, probably all descendants of Dahlia's founding fathers.

Then he took note of a final table, with two men wearing tan shirts and brown slacks. He didn't need to see the badges on their shirt fronts or the wide-brimmed felt hats with the plastic rain covers hanging off the corners of the table to know that they were the law in this town. He pegged the fiftysomething man with the slicked-back hair and evidence of a growing pudge as the one in charge. The younger man would be his deputy.

Jack imagined the balance of customers would shift come the weekend, when the drag races were in full swing at the track, and the number of visitors to the town tripled or quadrupled. Then he'd see more drivers sporting their sponsor's ball caps and jackets. More women, following their favorite drivers.

The faded black ball cap on the table beside him winked at Jack. Nashville Paint & Glass wasn't a racing sponsor so much as a secret tribute to Eric. Jack and Eric had coached Eric's son and his middle-school baseball team to a city championship a few years back. Now the cap was more than a prop in his quest to find the drug runners in Dahlia. Like an ever present conscience sitting on his shoulder, that cap represented Eric, and the justice Jack was determined to find here.

SMACK. JACK GRINNED as he heard the waitress's approach. "Here you go. Enjoy." She served his beer and carried her tray to the next table. "And here's your coffee."

For a few seconds, Jack toyed with his drink, running his fingers up and down the cold glass, catching the icy condensation with his fingertips. He preferred the feeling of soft, warm skin beneath his hands, but ever since Rosie had left him—with the exception of one amazing, unexpected encounter in a Nashville back alley—he'd been without a woman.

It wasn't the eight months of celibacy he minded so much. After all, when the right woman came along, he'd be primed and ready and it'd be worth the wait for both of them. His nostrils flared as he inhaled to soothe the tightness that suddenly constricted his chest. There'd been too many times these past weeks when he'd been crazy with anger and grief, and had longed to bury himself deep inside the heat and solace of some sweet, willing woman, and escape into a night of passion.

He'd even cruised the late-night streets of downtown Nashville, wondering if he should pick up a woman at one of the honky tonks, or even pay one for a night of nameless, mindless sex. In the end, he'd gone home alone and eased his frustrations in other ways. Maybe it was the cop in him, hating the idea of victimizing a woman or breaking the law for his own pleasure. Or maybe it was just the fact that no one had piqued more than a passing interest.

Not one woman had awakened his senses or jump-started his hormones the way one had that crazy night when he'd run into a tiny blonde with too much makeup, too few clothes and a mouth that wouldn't quit.

That night he'd been twenty again. He'd felt strong. Whole. Hell, the way she'd responded to him had made Jack feel like some kind of Don Juan superhero. But with no name, a protective big brother with a law degree and a truckload of guilt over how he'd bent the rules with her, Jack knew the passion of that hour they'd spent together wouldn't be repeated.

No more real to him than a pinup girl or celebrity, green-eyed Trouble should have been filed away with the embarrassing mistakes of his past that he knew better than to repeat. Because, all these months later, even the memory of her scent and those curves and that mouth could still make his blood simmer with want when he shouldn't be thinking about anything except his investigation.

"Hank." A smack—not gum, but hand against hand—startled Jack from his thoughts and drew his attention back to his surroundings.

"Five'll get you ten that you're gonna strike out again, big brother."

"Shut up."

"Artie, don't egg him on." The waitress was having trouble at the next table. "I said to keep your hands to yourself, or I'll have Eddie come out from the kitchen and put you in your place."

"Come on, Sandy. Eddie's busy cookin' right now." Hank was nothing if not persistent. Jack dropped his feet to the floor and sat up straight, trying to determine if the waitress's expression reflected annoyance or fear. "It's Tuesday night. What are we gonna do for fun if you don't help us out?"

"Drink your coffee." When she turned to walk away, Hank's hand latched on to the hem of her skirt and pulled her back to the table. She swatted at his grip. "Damn it, Hank. Let go. Your father's sittin' right over there."

Hank laughed. "He knows that boys will be boys."

Jack glanced across the room to see if the sheriff would intervene, what passed for law enforcement in this town seemed more interested in carving up the chicken-fried steak on his plate.

Jack fought the urge to flash his badge and haul the drunk to jail. But he couldn't do that without blowing his cover. Now, Hank's entourage was daring him to make good on his attempted conquest. Hank obliged by pulling the waitress onto his lap. She shoved his lips away from her cheek and pushed to her feet.

The sheriff still wasn't moving. Jack squirmed inside his skin. But only for a moment. Experience had taught him to think before he acted. He wanted to make a place for himself in this town? Show them who wasn't to be messed with? Here was an opportunity. He'd ordered the third beer, knowing he wasn't going to drink it. It was all for show, to establish his reputation in Dahlia. A hard-drinking man didn't stop with two beers. And a hard-livin' man didn't walk away from a fight.

He rose from his seat, setting his beer bottle down with a thud as he stood. "The lady said, 'hands off.'"

"Lady?" Hank smirked as he turned to see who'd spoken. "All I see is Sandy Larabie standin' here."

"I don't know if you're too stupid or too drunk to understand." Jack moved out from behind his table. He twisted Hank's wrist, hitting a pressure point with his thumb and forcing the other man's grip to pop open. "Get your hands off her."

Jimbo pulled his arm from the brunette's shoulders, and slid a warning glance to the big guy. Artie snapped his phone shut. "Mister, what are you doin'?"

Hank's watery eyes blinked as though trying to bring Jack's face into focus. "Who the hell are you, stickin' your nose into my business?"

Jack released him and the drunk rubbed at what were most likely numb fingers. "Give them their check, Sandy. These boys are ready to go home."

Hank shot to his feet, rattling the mugs before he got his legs free of the picnic table. "I'll leave when I'm damn well good and ready to leave."

The waitress tugged at Jack's sleeve. "Mister, you don't have to stick up for me. I've dealt with him before."

"Well, apparently, he didn't get the message."

"You lousy son of a—"

It happened fast. A woman shrieked. There was a stream of curses. A plate shattered. Hank cocked his arm back and took a swing. The man was big and stocky enough that he could have done some damage, but Jack was sober. He ducked beneath the unsteady blow and came back up, clamping his fingers like a horseshoe around Hank's neck and driving him back against the wall.

"Mister—!" Sandy warned.

He knew Hank's buddies were back there, ready to pounce on him from behind. Jack was years past coming out on top in a four-on-one fight. Still, a cover was a cover—

"Now, now, boys. What's goin' on here?" a deep, slightly nasal voice drawled behind him.

"Hank's drunk and won't keep his hands to himself, Henry." Sandy was quick to position herself between Jack and the sheriff. "This gentleman stepped in to defend my honor."

With Hank thrashing harmlessly at arm's length like a fish on a hook, Jack looked back over his shoulder to meet the sheriff's dark eyes. With his napkin still tucked in at his neck, he didn't look like much of a threat. But the deputy standing behind him had his hand resting on his gun, ready to provide some serious backup if this little introduction to the fine folks of Dahlia got out of control.

Time to cement his role as the new bad boy in town and snag the attention of whomever the real bad boys might be. He gave Hank one more shake for good measure. "I was just clarifying a few things for Mr. Grabass, Sheriff. Since no one else here seemed to want to stop him."

The sheriff hooked his thumbs into his gun belt and assumed a smarter-than-you-think good ol' boy pose. "You let him go now, son." Son? Suspecting he was closer to the sheriff's age than to Hank's, Jack was amused enough to comply.

Hank dropped to his feet, rubbing his collarbone and nursing his pride. "Ain't you gonna arrest him for assaulting me?" He turned to his friends for help. "You saw. He started it."

The sheriff pulled his napkin from his shirt and dabbed at his lips. "Hank, you pay your bill and scoot along home with your buddies. Artie, you drive. I don't want no accidents."

"But Dad—"

Dad?

"Now, Hank. I'm not in the mood to argue with either one of you boys."

The young men grinched and grumbled, but with a pair of

"yes, sirs," they snatched up their money from the table and left. When Jack moved to do the same, the sheriff stepped into his path. "I don't know you, friend. You passing through?"

Yep, he was earning himself a reputation, all right.

"I'm here to race at the track," Jack answered. "I'm not looking for trouble. It just seems to find me sometimes."

"I see." The sheriff turned to the waitress and smiled. "You get on back to work now, Sandy. You okay?"

"Sure, Henry." She smiled up at Jack. "Thanks."

"No problem."

As Jack went back to his table to retrieve his cap, the sheriff turned to the curious onlookers who'd come out from the kitchen or were staring from tables across the restaurant and announced, "There's nothing to see here, folks. Eddie, you go on back to your grill. The rest of you enjoy your drinks and dinner."

Sandy was right behind Jack when he turned around. "Mister, uh—?"

"Riley. Black Jack Riley."

She reached out to shake his hand. "Well, Black Jack Riley. You always have a friend here." She gave Sheriff Pudge a less friendly look before smiling at Jack again. "Good luck at the races."

As he set about cleaning up the mess at Hank and Artie's table, Jack placed money on his table and turned to leave. But the sheriff blocked his path. "Mr. Riley? I'm Henry Buell, sheriff here in Dahlia." He gestured toward the front door. "Since you're going to be around for a while, we need to have a talk."

He headed back to his table where he dropped off his napkin and picked up his hat and a yellow rain slicker, expecting Jack to follow.

So Sheriff Buell wouldn't lift a finger to stop the sexual harassment of one of his citizens—or discipline his own sons—but he was ready to lay down the law to a complete stranger. That might explain a lot about the illegal drug trafficking going in and out of his county. Jack scratched nitwit off his list. Henry Buell's dark eyes were too sharp to miss much. That meant he was either a coward who turned the other way, or he was on the take.

Neither of those options gave Jack much comfort.

Jack wove his way through the tables and followed the sheriff out the door. The spring storm had ebbed into a steady rain that dripped from the brim of his cap and quickly soaked through the cotton of the black T-shirt he wore.

Though he was working his investigation in cooperation with the state police, they, along with NPD, had left it to his discretion as to when and how much information he would share with local authorities. Thus far, he wasn't inclined to talk about his suspicions with Buell, so the need to maintain his badass persona was more important than respecting the uniform at the moment.

In a subtle show of defiance, Jack ducked his head and jogged across the parking lot to his truck. After unlocking the cab, he pulled out his black leather jacket and shrugged into it. When Jack was good and ready, he shoved his hands into his pockets and faced off against the older man. "Like Sandy said, Sheriff, I was defending her honor. I wasn't looking to cause any trouble."

"It's not the first time my Hank couldn't hold his liquor. I imagine he'll go home and sleep it off." He strolled along the length of Jack's truck and charcoal-gray trailer. "I haven't seen you on the circuit. Where have you been racing?"

"I haven't for a while." Jack let Buell check out his license plate numbers before giving his well-rehearsed story. "I ran into some trouble a few years back and had to get out. Turned forty this year—decided I wanted to make one last run for a title before I give up the dream. I heard Dahlia was a good place to get my wheels back under me until I can hit the big-money races again."

The sheriff paused a few feet away, giving Jack the same careful once-over he'd given his rig. "Dahlia's starting to get some big money. The way we used to. Drew Fisk took over running the track from his daddy, and has really been turning the place around."

"Fisk? As in Fisk Racing?"

"Yep. The Fisks are selling it now. But to good people who know their stuff. You heard of Whip Davis? He used to be crew chief for Corley Motors."

"I've heard of Corley Motors." The track was changing hands? Transition and new ownership tended to make people with something to hide nervous. Maybe he'd better order a complete listing of track employees and investors, and see who was scrambling to save money or a job.

"Davis is settling down in Dahlia now. Hooked up with Cardin Worth, daughter of the folks who own this fine establishment." The sheriff thumbed over his shoulder at the restaurant behind him. "You mark my word. The speedway's making a comeback. I don't know what kind of trouble you're talking about, but as long as you keep your nose clean, you can make a comeback here, too."

"Thanks, Sheriff." Jack shifted his boots on the gravelly asphalt, giving the false impression that he was relaxing his guard now that Buell had given him permission to stay. "Say, you know a place where I can store my Chevy while I'm working on it? I can sleep in my truck, but I want my baby to stay someplace safe and dry."

Buell grinned and pointed down the highway. "Morgan's Garage. Out by the track. For a fair price, he rents out space where racers can work on their cars while they're in town. He's got a spare room out there you can sleep in for a few dollars more. They'll be up working late tonight."

"Sounds perfect. Thanks." Ready for the conversation to be over, Jack climbed in behind the wheel and started his truck.

When Buell tapped on Jack's door, he rolled down his window to hear what the older man had to say. "Mr. Riley? One more thing."

"Yeah?"

"I like to keep things peaceful in my town. I don't put up with troublemakers. You watch yourself. Because I'll be watching you." Buell tipped his hat, dripping water down the sleeve of his raincoat. "Evening, now."

Jack turned on his lights and the windshield wipers, clearing away the rain and his less-than-friendly first impression of Dahlia, Tennessee. He was definitely running this op without Henry Buell's help.

Jack pulled out of the Headlights parking lot and turned toward the speedway.

He pulled his cell phone from his belt and punched in a number, keeping his eye on the dark road out of town as the call picked up. "Daniel? I'm in. The local sheriff has already promised to keep an eye on me, so I think my cover is set. If there's any action in this town, the players will come looking for me to see what I'm about. I've even got a lead on a bunk right next to the speedway, so I'll be able to get in there and check it out after hours."

"Sounds good, Jack." Daniel Rutledge, his temporary boss at the state attorney general's office was younger than Jack, but the ambitious attorney seemed to have a good grasp of the details of the case, and had no problem keeping the joint operation between NPD and his organized crime investigation team running smoothly. He was probably gunning for a big promotion, or even a state office, once they solved this case and could make the news public. Rutledge could take the credit for it, as far as Jack was concerned—as long as this drug pipeline was shut down and Eric's killer was behind bars. "I'll report your progress to the task force at tomorrow's briefing."

"We're going to get these bastards. I promise."

"I believe you. Just keep your head down and don't blow your cover."

"I will."

"When you need backup, call. I know you think I'm nothing more than a paper pusher, but I know how to rally the troops. Keep me posted."

"I'll call in tomorrow at the regular time."

He heard an uncharacteristic hesitation in Rutledge's voice. "Jack? I know this is personal for you."

"Yeah?"

"Don't let anger over your partner's death keep you from thinking straight. I've already lost a good man trying to bring this crew down. I don't want to lose another."

"I'll get the job done."

A few minutes after disconnecting the call, Jack pulled into the parking lot at the track. Though the dashboard clock said it was half past nine, there was enough illumination from the security lights for him to see the three-story tall white skyboxes and viewing stands rising above the cracked brick walls that formed an entrance arch into the track. Driving past the main gate, Jack familiarized himself with the layout. Tomorrow, he'd get inside and start snooping around the offices, pits and control tower.

He pulled up to a steel-gray building adjoining the track. "Morgan and Son's Garage." He read the sign over what looked like an office entrance out loud. That part of the business was dark. But with eight garage doors—one standing open with light and the loud strains of Toby Keith pouring out—he knew he'd reached his destination. "Look out, Dahlia."

Big Black Jack Riley had come to town.

5

"DAMN IT, PICK UP," Alex whispered into her cell phone, her free ear plugged with a finger to drown out the music from the garage.

Give me a break, already. She got up and closed her office door, pacing as she waited through a third and fourth ring.

Drew Fisk, Tater, Artie and a couple other friends from the racing crew Drew sponsored had the radio cranked up for their impromptu party to celebrate Drew's latest acquisition. Not only had Drew spent his paycheck to buy the new Corvette, but he'd plunked down a huge chunk of change on a Mustang that had been fitted with a nitrous comp engine and rigged to race at the Outlaw series time trials this weekend.

Drew's "quick ride" had lasted until Alex was obliged to let him drive through one of the local fast-food joints to buy her a burger and fries for dinner. Tater had covered her at work, finishing up Mrs. Stillwell's car, and her father had seemed pleased rather than irritated to hear she'd spent the afternoon with Drew—as though his rebelliously single daughter had gone on some kind of date.

Dream on, Daddy.

Even with the drone of the Corvette's powerful motor humming through her body, Alex had grown impatient as the minutes ticked on. Shirking her workload was the last thing she needed to do if she wanted to prove to her father that she could be a viable partner in the family business. And it had taken far too long to find the privacy she needed to return Daniel Rutledge's call.

"…leave your message at the sound of the beep."

"Great. Just great." Alex stopped in front of the desk, her eyes fixing on a family picture of her and her father with Nick at his law school graduation. She shouldn't really have expected any kind of breakthrough with her amateur investigation into Nick's death, should she? Still, she'd hoped. *Beep.* "Mr. Rutledge. It's Alex Morgan, Nick's sister, again. We seem to be playing phone tag." She left her number and a request he return her call. "I really hope you can help me find some answers. I just want to know why Nick went to see you that night. Thanks."

Alex snapped her cell phone shut. She squeezed it in her fist and tapped it to her lips, as if she could maintain some kind of connection to her brother if she just held on hard enough. She stared at the photograph until the image blurred behind a veil of tears. Nick had been a six-foot tall, golden-haired, handsome son of a gun. Valedictorian. Cum laude graduate. He'd had a successful practice in Dahlia, aspirations to work for the State in Nashville. Women wanted to be with him. Men wanted to *be* him.

And he'd been her big brother. Nick had been there through the fiascos in high school. The gossip. The shame. He'd defended her honor and boosted her morale. He'd made staying in Dahlia not only possible, but bearable. She'd lived in the shadow of his charmed life and felt blessed to do so because she'd loved him. She missed him.

It didn't get any simpler—or more painful—than that.

A stinging swat on her rump jerked her from her grief.

Alex whirled around to attack the offending hand. "Damn it, Drew!" Recognizing her friend didn't ease her irritation. She hadn't heard the door open, hadn't heard him sneak up behind her. And she sure as hell didn't want to hear whatever excuse he had for startling her like that. She shoved him out of her personal space and tucked her phone into the top pocket of her overalls. "Don't you know what a closed door means?"

"Come on, Shrimp. What are you doing in here, hiding away

from the party? I'm beginning to think you like my cars better than you like me." Right now, she did. "You all right? Hell. Did that phone call upset you? Are you missing Nick?"

"I always miss Nick." She swiped the tears from her eyes and sashayed past him, burying the hurt and frustration deep inside and assuming the perky, one-of-the-guys role the good folks of Dahlia allowed her to play. "Come on. Show me this guaranteed-to-win car of yours."

"Hey, now." Drew reached for her hand, his tone contrite. "If you need some time—"

"I want to look at the damn car." Pulling her hand from his grip, Alex marched down the hall.

The spurt of temper that had added kick to her stride sputtered out when she stepped into the garage and saw the circle of men with beers and flasks gathered around Drew's cherry-red Mustang. Unexpectedly, she flashed back to being a teenager again. Back to that awful night when she first discovered what kind of hero her brother had been.

But the cold chill of remembered humiliation lasted for only a moment. Alex breathed in deeply, taking in the smells of pit grease and new car and testosterone. These were grown men, not boys. Members of Drew's racing team—all friends of hers from the track. While it was never a thrill to run into Artie Buell after hours, she was relieved to see that his older brother knew better than to show his face around here. Seeing a couple of women she didn't recognize, Alex figured this was a party that had moved from someplace else. The only things these guys were interested in tonight were getting laid by one of those sexy women in their tight jeans, and revving up the Mustang's engine.

Pulling her hands from her baggy overall pockets, Alex headed straight for the middle of the pack. "You know you can't fire up that motor inside the garage, right? Dad frowns upon collecting fumes and starting fires."

Her teasing reprimand garnered a round of laughter and a

taunt from Tater Rawls. "We all know *you're* the one who really wants to see how fast this car can go."

"You better watch yourselves, ladies," she said to the brunette hanging on to Jim DiMarco's arm, and the redhead sitting on a workbench next to the tall guy she knew only as Crank. "All these bozos think about is *go* and *go fast*. I think like an architect. I want to see how this thing is put together." Alex gave as good as she got, absorbing the chest-thumping and ribbing and job-related chatter she usually enjoyed with the men who worked around the track. She nodded to Tater. "Come on, let's open it up and see what kind of horsepower this thing's packin'."

She detached the pins locking the fiberglass hood down on her side, while Tater opened his side. Together, they lifted the hood and handed it down the line to the other men who set it aside and quickly returned to gawk at the shiny new setup that included every bell and whistle that money could buy.

Lacking the height of her fellow car nuts, Alex boosted herself up onto the fender and leaned over the motor for a closer inspection. Not for the first time, she wondered just how much money the heir to a real-estate and bauxite mining fortune had in his bank account. Andrew Fisk III had spared no expense to make this Outlaw racer state-of-the-art. The insides were still shiny and sludge free—as perfectly preserved as a museum piece. Maybe even a tad boring because, while the potential power of the motor was obvious, there was nothing for Alex to tinker with.

She was almost afraid to touch anything for fear of mussing it with a fingerprint. Still, she knew that Drew had gathered them all together for some oohing and ahhing over his newest toy. "That carburetor looks hand-built."

Jimbo and the brunette moved aside so that Drew could lean over the car beside her. "It has an LS7 carbureted intake—guaranteed to give me 460 horsepower, minimum. Can't do that with a fuel-injected engine. Artie ordered it in from Nashville for me."

"Is Artie heading up your pit crew this weekend?"

"Unless I can sweet-talk someone else into doing it." Drew butted his hip against hers in a nudge-nudge offer that indicated the job was hers if she wanted it. "Interested?"

"Hey!" Artie protested. "I did all the work putting this baby together, I should get the glory of taking care of her."

Alex twisted her mouth in disappointment. Artie was welcome to it. There wouldn't be much to do on this motor except dust it.

"You gonna be driving it, Drew, now that you won't be managing the track anymore?" Tater asked. "Or is Jimbo still your man?"

Drew slid away, straightening to address the query head-on. "I'm still managing the track until the sale's complete and Whip Davis takes over full-time. I've got everything prepped for this weekend's races—the PR's out, the vendors are lined up, the prize money is ready for each class. I've been a busy man this week."

"So who's driving?" Tater was less interested in Drew's workload than in the details on the 'Stang.

He wasn't alone.

A flurry of arguments and bribes to get behind the wheel stopped abruptly when a dark, familiar voice interrupted them from the open garage door.

"Is this a party? Or are you boys still open for business?"

OH. MY. GOD. Every muscle inside Alex froze from her fingertips to her toes.

That voice wasn't just familiar. It was *his*.

Her knight in shining armor. Fantasy Man.

Tater introduced himself. Answered questions about storage facilities and a room to rent. Alex didn't hear many of the actual words, but she felt the timbre of that voice rolling across her skin. Deeply. Slightly husky. All sexy.

She'd been living with *"Milady"* and *"How may I seduce you this evening?"* for months now. He probably wouldn't even recognize her in her metamorphosis from hooker to tomboy. But

Alex would never forget Detective Opportunity from that night in Nashville.

She slid off the fender, nearly landing on her butt until she could will her legs to support her.

"Will it be available for a couple of weeks?" The sexy detective could read a muffler warranty with that voice and turn her knees to putty. "Sounds like a fair price. I'll take it. And call me Jack."

"Hey, I know you." Artie invited himself into the conversation. "You're that big guy from Headlights."

"That's right. You get your brother home all right?"

"No thanks to you."

"You work here?" the detective asked.

"I'm crew chief for this car."

Moving beyond the steadying grasp of Drew's hand, Alex pushed her way to the front of the crowd and stepped up beside Tater.

That voice was no figment of her imagination.

The smoky cast of his short, crisp hair was hidden beneath a black ball cap. But the eyes were the same—steel-gray, revealing only what he wanted. The curtain of rain falling outside the open garage door behind him had plastered his jacket to his shoulders and his black T-shirt to his chest. He stood with his hands at his hips, his jacket pulled back. She quickly looked for the badge and gun she remembered so vividly.

Though she didn't immediately see them, the rest was the same. The taut, muscled body she'd rubbed herself shamelessly against. The stern, handsome lips that she'd demanded kisses from.

Alex squeezed her hands into fists. She was shaking.

His eyes skimmed over her and past her in a guarded, all-seeing scan of each man and woman in the room. Then, boom. His gaze swung back to her. Locked on. Narrowed. So much for not remembering. "Trouble?"

She crooked her mouth into a wry frown. "What are you doing here?"

"What are *you* doing here?"

"I run this garage with my dad."

"Morgan and *Son?*"

"Um…"

Drew came up behind her. "You know this guy, Alex?"

She nodded.

"Is he a friend of your dad's?"

Detective Opportunity was drifting closer. She tried to read the hard look in his eyes, tried to communicate her own silent message. *Do* not *tell them about Nashville.* Mistaken for a hooker. First orgasm. Willing hand job. Any one of those would wreck her determined effort to blend in as one of the guys in Dahlia.

Maybe silent communication wasn't the best way to do this. Maybe turning him around and sending him back to the big city was the only way to keep the past buried.

Alex moved out to meet him halfway. "What can I do for you, D—"

"Shut up."

"What?" A knight in shining armor would never… "Look, just because you carry a—"

"Not another word." Advancing. Closing in.

Alex tilted her chin. "I beg your—"

"For old times' sake."

"What old time—?" He palmed the back of her head, leaned over her and stopped up her mouth with a kiss.

With her fists wedged between them, he looped an arm behind her back and dragged her against his chest. He straightened, lifting her feet off the floor without breaking the kiss.

Alex protested in her throat, pushed against him, twisted her hips—tried to reclaim some measure of dignity and control. But the big brute wouldn't budge.

The rain had warmed against his skin, intensifying the scents of leather and musk that clung to him—that clung to her now as her own clothes soaked up the dampness of his. Their noses butted as he shifted into a different position, driving his lips against hers, filling her mouth with the faint tang of alcohol and lust. Something inside Alex shifted, as well. Surrendering to the assault on her senses, she opened her fists to dig her fingertips into soft, damp leather and held on for the ride.

This was not some polite, pleased-to-see-you, namby-pamby kiss. It was a full-blown, tongue in her mouth, take-no-prisoners, stake-his-claim kind of kiss that shocked Alex to her core, then revived her with a liquid-hot desire that surged through her veins and throbbed in the crush of her breasts and at the juncture of her thighs. Every female cell inside her screamed for something more.

Drew's buddies were whistling behind her, laughing. Tater scratched his chin. Drew stood beside him, staring at the passionate greeting with a blend of curiosity and disdain shading his expression.

And Alex?

She wound her arms around his neck and kissed him back.

JACK HUSTLED TROUBLE DOWN the hallway, away from the hoots and questions and protective posturing of the men in the garage behind them.

That was the best plan he could come up with to keep his cover intact? Kiss the woman into silence before she blabbed his real identity and blew his investigation? The ploy had worked. But now he had a whole new truckload of problems to deal with.

He knew his grip on her arm was a little too tight, his stride a little too long for her short legs to comfortably keep up with him. But he was frustrated, damn it. Frustrated that one wrong word from this pint-sized stick of dynamite could destroy his investigation and let Eric Mesner's killer go free. Frustrated that when he knew he should be chewing her out about refusing to take a hint or obey a command, he instead wanted to ask her why she'd melted in his arms and turned that kiss into a wildly frenetic public display of affection. Why hadn't she slapped his face instead of firing his libido into overdrive?

And what was the deal with the Huck Finn look? In Nashville, she'd gone for too much makeup and too little dress. Now, she'd clamped down those honey-gold curls beneath a yellow do-rag, killed the makeup, and put on a pair of tank tops and men's overalls that were big enough to make her curvaceous figure look like a sack of potatoes. The woman definitely needed some fashion advice. Plus a good dose of common sense.

And, she needed to stop throwing herself, full throttle, into a kiss like that. Made a man think that he had nothing more important to do than to make love to a willing woman all night long.

Jack pushed open the door where she'd led him and released her inside the spare, functional office. He nudged her toward the desk and closed the door behind him, muttering a curse when he discovered that the lock on it was broken. Fine. He'd just keep his voice to a whisper and pray that she could do the same.

"So…" He spun around to face her. "Now that we're thoroughly acquainted—for the second time—are you going to tell me your name?"

Her cheeks were still adorably flushed, but with her fists propped on her hips and emerald darts shooting from her eyes, he didn't think he needed to worry about kissing her again. "The next time you want to stick your tongue down my throat, maybe you'd better give me a little heads-up first."

"A name, Trouble."

"Alex Morgan. Alexandra."

Jack whipped his cap off his head and raked his fingers through his damp hair. "Hell. That screws everything up."

"Gee, thanks, it's good to see you, too. Now that I've been found out, are you going to tell me your name?"

"Jack Riley. Look, it's nothing personal, but I'm working an investigation. Undercover." He paced off the room in three strides. Then paced back. "You cannot tell any of those people— anyone in Dahlia—that I'm a cop."

She knocked aside the finger he pointed at her. "I won't if you don't tell them Nashville thinks I'm a hooker."

"I'm serious."

"So am I."

"I'm talking about my job."

"I'm talking about my life. I'm trying to gain some respect here. I'd never live that down in a small town."

"I'm trying to live, period."

Damn it. He was leaning over her again, moving in closer with every degree that she tilted that defiant chin. Moving in close enough to realize she smelled a hell of a lot prettier than he'd ever imagined Huck Finn had. No amount of grease or working under a hood or hanging out with the local party boys back in the garage could completely mask that subtle fragrance of gardenias and woman.

Or lessen his instinctive male reaction to it.

But he needed to douse the sparks that flared between them and have a cool, reasonable conversation with Alexandra Morgan.

Releasing a deep breath, Jack tugged his cap back on top of his head and quickly surveyed the room. Even if that door locked, the privacy of this office wasn't good enough for him.

He nodded to the Tennessee Titans windbreaker hanging from the coatrack beside the door. "Is that yours?"

"Yes."

Jack plucked it off the rack, shook it open and held the jacket up for her to slip into. "Come on."

She stared at the jacket, then glanced up at him as though she didn't understand what he wanted.

"Put it on. It's raining outside." He flicked the jacket like a matador's cape, waiting impatiently. Finally, she turned and slid her arms into the sleeves. Jack pulled it up over her shoulders, then grabbed her hand and reached for the doorknob. "You and I need to go for a ride."

He shouldn't have been surprised to feel her plant her feet and tug against him. "I don't need to do anything but damage control.

There are already at least two men out there calling my father and ruining his night with questions about the stranger who just assaulted his daughter."

"Assaulted?" He pushed the door shut again. "I didn't want you to say *detective*. Or *badge* or *cop*, Miss Chattermouth. Besides, I wasn't the only one liplocked back there."

"I…" The tugging stopped. Her gaze dropped to the middle of his chest and her cheeks flamed with color. Ha! *So much for taking the high road, sweetheart.*

He took advantage of her embarrassed silence and opened the door, checking for company before leading her out into the hall. "Not one word to those men until you and I have a private chat. You're not supposed to be a part of this. But now that you are, there are things you should know about the plan and rules you have to follow. I will not let you blow this for me."

Adjusting his grip to lace their fingers together, rather than looking like a caveman dragging his woman back to his lair, Jack pushed open the door to the garage and nudged her out ahead of him. A flurry of conversations stopped abruptly.

The tall blond guy in the suit signed off on a phone call and snapped his cell shut, stuffing it into his pocket as his eyes darted from Jack to Alex to the clasp of their hands and back to Jack. He must have made one of those warning phone calls to Alex's father.

"Everything okay, Alex?" The shaggy-haired mechanic who'd introduced himself as Tater Rawls stepped forward to block their exit. He ducked his head to make eye contact with the woman at Jack's side. "I mean, you do know this guy, right?"

She nodded. "I met him in Nashville." She turned her head to Jack's chest and muttered out the side of her mouth. "I can tell him that much, right? It's what your cap says."

Jack tugged on her hand. "We need to go."

"He's a little old for you, isn't he?"

Alex jerked her head to the left. "Drew!"

Suit boy was on his feet now, his hands in the air in a pose of surrender—as if he hadn't intended the dig in his words. "I'm just saying—you're not trying to replace Nick, are you? Looking for someone older, wiser in your life?"

"Don't say that." She surged forward, her cheeks flushed, her teeth practically bared. "This has nothing to do with Nick. No one could replace him. I'm with…Jack…because…"

Jack pulled her back to his side. She'd said plenty enough already. He did not need her defending him. Once that mouth got going, there was no telling what might slip out.

"I don't believe we've met." He held out his hand. "Black Jack Riley."

"Drew Fisk. Andrew Fisk the Third." Fisk's mouth curved into a friendly enough grin as he shook Jack's hand, but the name and title were meant to remind Jack of his place. "I didn't mean any offense by the age crack. Alex's late brother and I were friends from way back. I'm just looking out for her."

"Well, Andrew Fisk the Third, let's just say I'm old enough to know a good thing when I see it." He looped his arm around Alex's shoulders. "And this little lady is old enough to know her own mind." He turned to make sure everyone in the garage understood they were a couple. "Excuse us for a while, ladies and gentlemen. I'll be back another time to get to know the rest of you. But Alex and I have some catching up to do and we thought this reunion might go a little more smoothly without an audience."

Her body stiffened against him. The angle of her chin dropped a good forty-five degrees.

A smattering of nervous laughter from around the garage was quickly stifled by an arch look from Drew Fisk. What the hell? First she went off at the mention of her brother and now she was burrowing into his side?

Tater nodded. "I can understand that." He moved aside, tucking his hands into the pockets of his coveralls. "I'll probably head over to Headlights to check in on Sandy before they close. But you've got my number if you need anything, Alex." He glanced out at the low-hanging clouds that were still dumping rain on the asphalt surface of the parking lot. "Don't stay out too late in this mess, or your dad will really worry."

When Alex didn't immediately respond, Jack pulled her forward, keeping her on her feet when she stumbled. "She won't."

It was just as well that she'd finally run out of words. Until he could brief her on his investigation and drive home how vital it was that she play along, he wanted to keep her away from any potential suspects who'd be keeping a close eye on him, already.

Faking a relationship with Alex would probably get him into the inner circle at the track sooner, but using Alex as a cover would be a definite risk. Jack had eighteen years of experience and a dead partner to prepare him for the dangers of infiltrating a drug-smuggling operation. He didn't need a civilian novice endangering herself—and him—by letting the wrong word slip to the wrong person at the wrong time.

"Let's move it, Trouble." The parking lot lights were dim moons in the night sky above them as Jack urged Alex into a jog and dashed toward his truck and trailer.

When Jack stopped to unlock the passenger-side door, she pulled her hood up over her head and hugged her arms around her middle. "What's he doing here?"

Following her gaze, Jack noticed the beat-up black truck parked just outside the closed garage door at the end of the building.

Son of a bitch. Hank—the sheriff's son who got away with shit Jack would have tossed him into jail for—was sitting inside the truck. Talking on his cell phone. Sipping from a silver flask. Staring at them.

"You know him?" Jack asked.

"Hank Buell." Compared to her usual fire, her voice sounded dead. "He's part of Drew's crew, too. I imagine he's here to check out the new car. Why is he just sitting there?"

Jack would like to say Hank was waiting for the weather to let up. But after putting him in his place at the restaurant earlier,

Jack imagined there was something more sinister than the elements keeping him in his pickup, watching them, in the dark.

He opened the door and reached for Alex's hand. "Get in the truck."

But she scooted away from his helpful grasp to check out his trailer. "No. I'm not going to let him intimidate me."

"He intimidates—?"

"Hank and I have history."

"Well, Buell and I now have history. We had a run-in at dinner. I guess it's your friend Tater's girlfriend that Buell was hitting on. Hank couldn't control his hands, so I helped him."

"You rescued Sandy Larabie?"

He'd done what any man should have done.

"I stood up to a bully. If Hank's looking for a rematch, I don't want you caught in the middle of it."

But the seconds he took to check on Buell were the seconds she needed to unlatch the back of his trailer. "What are you driving?"

"Crazy woman." Jack looped his arm around her waist and pulled her out of the way as the metal doors swung open.

Just as quickly as he'd moved her to a safe distance, she was pushing his arm away, wiping the rain from her face and climbing up inside. She slipped between the wall and the car, caressing the Camaro's smooth lines and fading paint as she inspected it from tail-light to grill. "I'd love to see this baby in the daylight. And look under the hood. Is it vintage?"

Ouch. Any pride at her interest in the car was short-lived. Jack climbed into the trailer and dragged her back outside with him. "It was my high school car."

"Oops. Sorry."

He appreciated her deference to his age about as much as he appreciated the slap of cold rain on his face. Keeping one hand on her arm, Jack closed the doors and latched them shut. "It's not as bad as it seems," he mocked. "I've been replacing parts and keeping her in shape over the years. She may be showing signs of wear on the outside, but she's in primo condition under the hood where it counts."

The double entendre wasn't lost on her. "I said I was sorry."

"Just do what I ask and get in the truck." The slamming of a vehicle door diverted his attention back to the garage. "Buell's on the move."

A tiny orange glow briefly illuminated Buell's watching eyes as he sucked the last drag of his cigarette and flicked it out into the parking lot, plunging his expression into darkness before he turned toward the party going on inside the garage. Right. Nothing suspicious about that.

"I wouldn't worry too much about Hank. I mean, it's cool that you rode in to Sandy's rescue and all." This time, Alex let Jack guide her to the open truck door. "Creep though he might be, he won't try anything on his own. He has to have his crew behind him before he'll sprout any balls."

Beyond the frank language, Jack was impressed by what he'd bet was an accurate assessment of Buell's character. But he was more impressed by the potential danger of their situation. He'd been outnumbered by Hank and his posse at the restaurant—he'd be more than outnumbered here if all those men in the garage turned out to be friends, as well.

"You mean *crew* as in a bunch of his buddies inside your garage drinking beer and 'looking out for you'?"

"You think they would…? Oh." Her face blanched beneath the orange-ish glare from the parking lot lights. The potential danger must have finally sunk in. "Maybe we should leave."

"Wish I'd thought of that." Jack reached around her to brush away the moisture hitting the bench seat of his truck. "What's going on with you? It happened back in the garage, too. Somebody says the wrong thing and you go quiet instead of mouthing off— which I'm guessing is your usual modus operandi."

"Modus operandi?" The sass was back. "First you tell me to keep my mouth shut, and when I do, you think something's wrong."

It wasn't hard to figure out that the tough talk and boyish exterior was a defensive armor for Alex. But what she was hiding, he had no clue. If she wasn't going to talk about it, he'd have to let the mystery slide. For now. Not knowing all the facts could come back to bite him in the ass if there was a problem, but right now his first priority was ensuring that his cover was safe and that she didn't blow this case for him. "I'm here to race. That's the plan. Black Jack Riley is making his comeback at the Dahlia Speedway. All you have to do is play along."

"Have you ever raced before?"

He wrapped his hand around her elbow to help her inside. "Don't worry, Trouble. I know how to drive."

"Is that a yes or a no?"

"Will you just get in?"

She spun around in the triangle formed by the seat, the door and his body, and tipped her face up to the rain. "Who are you investigating? Is it Hank? Someone else?"

To hell with this. Jack cinched his fingers at her waist, ignored her startled gasp, and lifted her onto the seat. "Do you argue every damn thing a man says to you?"

He looked straight into eyes that were deep green and dart free. She'd propped a hand at the center of his chest to balance herself. She curled up a palmful of leather before answering. "Only when I don't understand or trust what he's saying. Or I don't think he's listening."

Jack's fingers splayed out over her hips, finding the womanly curves he remembered masked beneath the butch outfit. His gaze locked on the delicate pout of lips that begged to be kissed. Not in haste. Not in a rough burst of passion. Not because of some damn charade. But gently. With reassurance. He wanted to kiss Alexandra Morgan. Taste the rare moment of vulnerability that softened the lush pink bow of her mouth. He wanted to press his lips against hers and take his own sweet time exploring this softer, more feminine side to the woman.

He bent his head, drifting closer.

The second he felt the whisper of her breath caress his cheek, Jack pulled back. What the hell was he doing? He was supposed to be laying down the rules here, driving home the danger of the situation, not succumbing to the need to drive himself deep inside her.

Removing his hands from the lure of her body, he pried her fingers from his jacket and stepped back to close the door. He circled around the front of the truck and climbed behind the wheel, starting the engine and pulling away from the curious onlookers inside the garage before speaking. "I've heard everything you've said. It's what you're *not* saying that has me worried. I may not be wearing it, but I still have a badge. You don't trust me?"

Alex pulled off the windbreaker's hood and wiped the dampness from those distracting lips. "I don't know you well enough to answer that yet. I never even thought I'd see you again."

"Likewise."

"That's a bad thing, isn't it. Seeing me again?"

"It sure as hell complicates things. I'd planned this as a solo operation." He glanced across the seat at her, wondering at the methodical way she rubbed her hands together in her lap. Damn, this woman was a puzzle. After ensuring the lane was clear, he pulled out onto the highway. "There's not a boyfriend or fiancé I need to worry about, is there?"

She snorted. Charming. "Are you kidding?"

"Why would I kid about that?"

"At any time during our brief acquaintance, have I struck you as a woman who gets a lot of action in this town?"

A remembered encounter, with her hand on his dick in this very same truck, leaped to mind.

"There are ways, right? Safe ones?"

"Don't you know?"

"I'm learning."

She hadn't known about hand jobs or oral sex. Her natural instincts had been right on the money, but even that night, he could tell she hadn't had much experience.

But with that figure of hers? The full-body kisses? Jack swallowed hard, shifting gears and picking up enough speed to divert his attention away from his crotch. Of course, she did have that whole Huck Finn thing going on—hiding her hair, hiding her curves, hiding any hint of weakness behind that mouth of hers. And there'd been obvious innuendoes about something bothering her.

Her world was obviously complicated. "Let's just drive. When I'm sure no one can overhear us, I'll fill you in on those rules."

"All right." She opened her jacket and pulled a cell phone from the top pocket of her overalls. "But I should call my dad—tell him I'm fine and that he doesn't need to wait up for me."

"Tell him you're taking a couple of hours to catch up with an old boyfriend."

"How about I tell him something he'll actually believe? Much to his chagrin, I don't date anyone here in Dahlia."

"Perfect. Tell him *I'm* the reason you haven't been seeing anyone here."

Honey-gold curls bobbed against her neck as she shook her head. "Look at me, Jack. I'm willing to help you, and keep your secret. But I'd rather we tell people that we're just friends."

He scoffed at that idea. "There are eight witnesses back in that garage who'd never believe that you and I are just friends."

"You don't know this town, Jack Riley. You don't know me."

"Trust me, Trouble. That's all about to change."

6

JACK STARED THROUGH the windshield at the still, utter darkness of the Tennessee countryside, so unlike the noise and neon of the nights in Nashville. The clouds overhead blotted out the moon and starlight, while the thickly forested hills and rain shut out everything else.

It was a perfect setting for illegal activity, especially if Sheriff Buell didn't keep a better eye on things out here than he did in town. A sizable group of men and an entire fleet of trucks loaded with East Coast drugs could cross state and county lines without ever being seen, unload and break down the shipments, smuggle them into cars or parts being shipped out of Dahlia to Nashville— and no one would be the wiser. Jack wouldn't have to work hard to figure out *how* the drugs were being shipped. Finding the men behind the smuggling network would be the real trick.

Only, Jack wasn't thinking about smugglers and drug busts right now. Not parked on a gravel road, with Alexandra "Trouble" Morgan sitting across the seat from him, filling up the cab of his truck with her unique scent. Too subtle to be perfume, the rich, evocative scent of fragrant flowers seemed to emanate from her very skin. His brain translated her scent as the essence of femininity. And every cell in his body remembered that scent, and responded to it with the same hunger they'd shared seven months ago in Nashville.

Kneading the steering wheel with both hands to keep from reaching for her, Jack glanced across the truck to find her sitting with her arms folded protectively across her chest, staring out into the same black nothingness he had. Though she wasn't a classic beauty, there was a porcelain-skinned freshness to her face without all that makeup she'd worn in Nashville. And that body…Jack breathed deeply to counteract the interest stirring south of his belt buckle. Petite and packed, and responsive to every touch of his hand and mouth, that body was a treasure, as hidden now beneath the man-sized overalls as it had been on display for him in her little black hooker dress.

He shifted in his seat to ease a bit more room into his jeans.

"So…Alex. How have you been?"

"You didn't drive me all the way out to Hickory Road to ask about my health."

Ah, yes. The mouth. He hadn't forgotten the sass hidden behind those full pink lips, either.

Something had changed from that night to this one, though. Was this guarded, older, almost disguised woman the real Alex? Was that curious, brave, bold woman in Nashville the real deal? Or was there another role he'd yet to discover that was closer to the truth? "Were there any…ill effects or repercussions after our close encounter in Nashville?"

"I'm fine." Not convincing, but he'd take it. "You?"

Seven months of misery every night, wishing he could reclaim the connection they'd shared, complete what they'd started. After Eric had died, the need to recapture the strength he'd felt that night, and the healing gifts of trust and surrender she'd given him had only intensified. But he could lie, too. "I'm fine."

She turned to face him. The lights from the dashboard offered enough illumination for him to see the turbulent emotions in her eyes before she looked down. When she looked back up at him, her eyes glistened with tears.

Hell. The instinct to hold her, to heal her, made the muscles of his stomach clench. He reached out to her. "Alex?"

But she swiped the tears aside and his hand fell to the seat between them. "My brother died in January. I think he was murdered. Is that what you're investigating?"

Double hell. Things *had* changed. But he was powerless to help her. "Sweetheart, I'm sorry. I'm so sorry. But I can't discuss my case, other than sharing a few basics you need to know so you don't blow my cover. It's safer that way—for both of us. If you don't know, then—"

"Nobody can get that information out of me. Logically, I understand that. But in here..." She pressed her hand to her heart. "I am damn tired of being out of the loop. Of officials not returning my calls, of Sheriff Buell patting me on the head and telling me that I'm trying to justify losing Nick."

"That was a cruel thing to say to you."

She inched closer, rising up on her knees. "I know Nick was in the middle of something that he couldn't talk about, either. He told me if the wrong people found out what he was up to that there'd be consequences. And there were. Damn serious ones. My brother's dead. Run off the road on his way to Nashville. His body burned..." Her voice caught on a tearless sob and Jack pulled her hand into his, holding on tight, silently offering his comfort and support. "If you know something about Nick's death, tell me. Please."

The plea in her eyes was hard to resist. So hard that Jack had to lower his gaze to the grip of her fingers around his. An attorney with a sharp eye, handling the right case, could conceivably have stumbled onto the same people Jack was looking for. Like Jack's partner, Alex's brother might be another casualty in the drug war Jack and Dan Rutledge and the Nashville task force were fighting. He'd be curious to know just what Nick Morgan had been working on. So yes, the drug smuggling and Nick Morgan's death could be related, and he intended to look into it.

But he couldn't tell Alex any of that. Instead, he lifted her hand to his mouth and kissed the back of her knuckles, apologizing for not being able to say what she wanted to hear. But he could honestly answer, "I'm not investigating your brother's murder."

She snatched her hand away. "Then, what?"

He needed to tell her something, or she'd keep asking questions he wasn't supposed to answer. And a man wasn't meant to look into eyes that held that much disappointment and accusation. Jack turned his gaze back to the night. "I'm investigating some activities at the Dahlia Speedway."

The energy flowing back into her expression was a tangible thing. He didn't even have to look to know he'd just given her hope. "Nick did work at the speedway. For Mr. Fisk. The blond guy you met—Drew. That's his grandfather. He owns the track. Well, he's selling it. He had Nick going through documents for him before he put it on the market. I've seen some of Nick's papers."

"Whoa, whoa, whoa." Jack faced her with a stern look. "You've been snooping through legal documents?"

"Not exactly. After Nick's death, I found some files in his things—tucked inside a box of books—paperwork from the Fisk offices. A lot of it is financial stuff that I recognize. But then, he's jotted notes, circled some things he questioned. I don't know if it's illegal, but it's certainly poor accounting." She had potential evidence? That'd go over real well with the thugs he was after. "I was going to give them to Drew. He manages the track. Well, he has for the past three years, and he's acting as interim manager until Whip Davis takes over. But then I thought there might be something in them to give me a clue about Nick."

Jack closed his fingers around her upper arm. "You still have these papers? Have you told anyone else about them?"

She shook her head. "They're in my desk at work. The rest of Nick's papers either burned in the car with him, were returned to his clients or were seized by the sheriff."

Seized by the sheriff? "I thought you said Buell ruled your brother's death an accident."

"He did. Even though there were two sets of skid marks on

the road that night. But only Nick's car was found in the gully. And Nick…he raced at the track. He wouldn't—"

"Uh-uh, sweetheart." He tightened his grip, giving her a little shake. She wasn't grasping the danger she'd be in if the wrong people suspected she was sitting on potentially incriminating information. And that jackass of a sheriff had just moved to the top of his suspect list. "There's no point in seizing legal evidence if Nick's death was an accident."

"That's what I thought. That it was some kind of cover-up. But I have history with Sheriff Buell. That's why I've kept the papers hidden and I'm trying to find answers on my own."

Jack pulled away, his eyes narrowing at her offhand comment. "You and the sheriff have history?"

Even in the shadows, he could see her face go pale. He didn't believe her when she tried to laugh it off. "I haven't been turning tricks in Dahlia if that's what you're worried about." He wasn't. The false smile disappeared. "It's personal."

"Something to do with Hank Buell?"

But he wasn't getting an answer. Instead, she tucked a loose golden curl back inside the controlling cap of her bandanna. Hiding herself again. Hiding the fact she was a pretty, vibrant woman. Hiding her emotions along with the truth.

Jack hated watching the transformation. He wanted to see the passion in her eyes again—for the truth, for success, for him. He wanted to see the confidence in the tilt of her chin.

Sliding over from behind the steering wheel, he draped his arm around her shoulders and tucked her to his side. She didn't mold herself to his body the way she had back at the garage, but she didn't push away, either.

"Hey." He tried to cajole a smile out of her.

"Hey, what?" *Wiseass.* A glimmer of spirit tried to show itself.

"If it means anything, I think it sounds as though you're on the right track."

"About what?"

"About your brother's death not being an accident."

She looked up at him. "You believe me? That Nick was murdered?"

He traced his forefinger around her jaw to the point of her chin. "I can't say for sure until I see those papers of yours. But I do know that the men I'm investigating are willing to kill to keep their secrets. If your brother stumbled on to something…"

"You really listened to me, didn't you."

"Why wouldn't I?"

She turned her whole body toward him, hooking one knee over his. The contact gave him a taste of what it would feel like to have her entire body sinking onto his lap. Suddenly, he wanted her there—on him, around him, crying out for him the way she had that night in Nashville. Her heady scent, eager touches and wanton responses had filled him with a renewed strength and virility.

But even though her fingertips lightly traced the zipper of his jacket from chest to stomach, Jack shifted the desire in his veins down to idle. A taut line had formed between her golden eyebrows. He dropped his hand to the small of her back, massaging gentle circles there. She was feeling the pain of her brother's death, but something was different.

"I'm still listening, Trouble," he coaxed. "Talk to me."

With a slight tug at the front of his jacket, she nodded, then raised her dark green eyes to his. "Just how dangerous is this investigation of yours? Would they kill you, too?"

There was no way to sugarcoat the truth. "They've already killed one cop. I'm dead if they find out I'm working with the state's DEA task force."

Her pretty eyes blurred out of focus as an all-too-familiar pain sank its claws into him. Eric had bled to death in his arms because they'd found out he was a cop.

"Jack?" Warm fingers brushed across his face, dragging him from the raging spiral of his thoughts. "Jack." He had both arms around Alex now, and he was squeezing her hard. Too hard. "They killed a cop? Who was he?"

He released her to run his palms up and down her arms in apology, willing his touch to be as gentle as he was ruthless about shoving the image and pain of Eric's death from his mind. But he didn't answer. He had secrets to keep, too.

Time to get down to the reason he'd brought her out here in the first place. He wasn't going to fail at this investigation. And nobody else was going to get hurt. Not on his watch. "This is a dangerous mess I've gotten you involved in, make no mistake. I'm sorry about that. I'll keep you out of the worst of it as best I can, but you're going to have to do your part."

"I want to help."

Jack stroked along the sleeve of her jacket one last time and then dropped his hand with a possessive weight over her knee, as if that small reassurance would make all of this craziness understandable. "There are three rules I need you to follow. If you want answers—if we want answers—this is what has to happen."

She nodded.

"Rule number one. You can't tell anyone I'm a cop—not your father, not anybody. As far as Dahlia knows, I'm Black Jack Riley and I'm here to race."

"That's easy. What else?"

He released a long breath into the quietness inside the truck. "I have a feeling this will be harder for you. Rule number two. Follow my orders. If I shush you, I don't want to hear another word. If I tell you to run, you book it." He squeezed her knee. "And if something goes south, you do exactly what I say. No heroics."

"But if I can help—"

"It's not open for discussion. You won't do your brother or me any good if you get hurt."

"What if you get hurt?"

Admirable to be concerned, but the rule didn't change. "Follow. My. Orders."

The green eyes flashed. Oh yeah, that one was grating on a nerve. "Fine. What else?"

Rule number three would be the tricky one. For him. Separating his emotions from the demands of the job had never been harder. He ran his hand up to Alex's hip and back down along the soft worn denim of her overalls, recalling how her skin was softer, warmer, underneath. He had to know she could play the undercover game. And he had to remember, despite the need sizzling from each and every pore of his body, that whatever he felt for this enigmatic woman had to take second place to accomplishing his mission.

"Number three? From this moment on, you and I are officially a couple. We've planted the idea, but we can't give anyone reason to doubt us or the wrong people will question my being here and I won't be able to do my job."

"I imagine people are gossiping about us already."

"If I could have come up with a different way to shut your mouth on such short notice, this scenario might have played out differently." He tucked his finger beneath her chin and tipped her face up to his. "But I need you to be convincing. We both know the seeds of attraction are there already." Her tongue darted out to lick her lips and parts of Jack clenched in response. Yeah. Attraction was definitely there. "But you closed up like a book a few minutes ago. You wouldn't let me touch you. You wouldn't talk to me."

"I was upset about my brother." She tried to withdraw even now, but he wouldn't have it.

"Be upset. Be pissed off. But don't avoid me." Jack reached for her right knee and turned her, pulling her right across his lap so that she straddled him. She pushed against his chest and tried to wiggle off him. Jack held on, forcing the kind of intimacy it would take to make them a convincing couple. "You can't be afraid to touch me or yell at me or interact with me, or no one will believe that we're an *us*. They'll start looking for other explanations that can get me—and now you—into trouble. Don't give them a reason to ask questions."

With a warm huff that caressed his face, she finally relaxed onto his lap. "I warn you, I'm not…" Her fingers curled beneath his leather collar. Only inches separated her flushed cheeks from his, but the uncertainty in her expression put her in some distant place. "I'm not very good at being with a man. I've never been anyone's girlfriend or gal pal or whatever you're going to call us. I don't know how convincing I'll be."

"Gal pal?" Jack frowned. "Sweetheart, you were golden that night in Nashville." He shrugged, trying to make Alex smile, trying to get her comfortable with the role he needed her to play. "I wouldn't recommend the hooker dress again, unless it's a private party just for me. But as far as I'm concerned, you had all the right moves. We can make this work."

"Right moves? Like what?"

Crap. Was she kidding him with this? No, the earnest, almost studious squint of her eyes told him she was looking for a serious answer.

"I'll admit we got off to a rocky start." He moved his hands to her back, sliding them beneath her jacket. When he found the nip of her waist beneath the layers of clothing she wore, he stopped, savoring the warmth of her body, treasuring the hesitant trust that kept her straddled across his lap, waiting for an answer. "Memories of the way you responded to every touch have kept me awake a lot of nights and sent me to a cold shower more often than I care to admit."

She arched an eyebrow. "You had to take a cold shower because of *me?*"

Jack pulled her closer, spread his thighs wider to let her feel the hardening evidence of her effect on him. Her soft gasp whispered across his ears like an erotic invitation. "You do this to me, Trouble. Nobody can argue that."

She trailed one hand down his chest toward the promised

land, following the bold curiosity of her eyes as she took in the unmistakable bulge filling the space between them. His skin remembered the last time she'd taken him in her hand and his muscles bunched and nudged with anticipation.

But her fingers stopped at his belt, and her eyes returned to his. "So, even though I look like one of the guys, it's convincing if I do this?"

Alex flattened both palms at the center of his chest, sliding them under his jacket to catch his flat nipples beneath the heels of her hands. The sensitive flesh instantly popped to attention through the damp cotton of his shirt, demanding more of her sensuous research.

"Works for me." Jack whispered his approval when she obliged, catching the nipples between her thumbs and hands and rolling them until he groaned at each zing of pleasure that shot from her touch to his swelling dick. He leaned forward, resting his forehead against hers, looking straight down into emerald-green eyes that darkened with her own blossoming desire. "You are so not one of the guys."

"I've never had the chance to explore a man's body before." He jerked when she pinched him. When she snatched her hand away, her mouth rounded with an apology, Jack pressed a quick kiss to her lips and guided her fingers back to continue their experimental touches.

"That was a very good move." His words were little more than a hoarse growl in his throat. After unhooking the straps of her overalls and letting the front fall away, Jack's own hands skimmed over the round weight of her breasts and squeezed, mimicking her exploration of his body, enjoying the answering gasps and moans he could solicit from her. "You touch me however you want. Wherever you want. I'm okay with that."

"Just okay?" This woman might look all tomboy on the outside, but her inner temptress had taken over. She was smiling now. Alex dipped her head, replacing her hand with her tongue, laving the hard bud through his shirt. "Is that any better?"

"Damn, sweetheart." His muscles quivered in response to each stroke. Groaning, needy, feverish with want, he moved his hands down to the firm curve of her butt and pulled her tighter into his lap, holding the apex of her open thighs against the helpless rotation of his body. Had he ever wanted anything as badly as he wanted to be free and thrusting up inside her right now?

Patience. Jack eased his grip, closed his eyes and tried counting to a hundred. *One. Two.* He had to get her comfortable with this, with him. He had to reassure her that she could play the part of his bedmate. He had no doubts about her abilities. But a partner who hesitated was a partner who made mistakes. And with two men already dead, mistakes were not an option.

Three. Ah, hell. He couldn't even make it to ten.

Somewhere between danger and isolation, this tutoring session had become a full-on seduction.

While her mouth wet him down to the skin, she tugged at the hem of his shirt. Her knuckles brushed across his stomach and Jack sucked in a sharp breath. His hands battled with hers to get his jacket off and his shirt untucked and get her hands on his feverish skin.

Every cell leaped beneath the brand of her touch. But the wicked vixen had something more in mind, and Jack's will was powerless to stop her. She pushed his shirt up beneath his armpits and closed her mouth, hot and wet, over his rock-hard nipple. She stroked the nub with her tongue, sucking the tingling skin. Jack's arms tightened convulsively around her back. He dipped his nose to the crown of her head and groaned.

"Good move." He stretched his jeans to an almost unbearable tightness as he imagined that wet, sassy tongue directly on his skin there.

She turned her attention to the other side of his chest. "So I'm doing it right?"

He was damn well going to burst into flame if this wasn't leading to the release he so desperately craved. Could she really not know the effect she had on him? He snatched the bandanna from atop her head and buried his nose in the fragrant curls of her hair. "You're a ringer, Alex. A sexy, irresistible natural talent." He slipped his hands beneath all the layers of clothing she wore to find warm, vibrant skin to hold on to. "Don't play with me. I don't feel like standing outside in the rain to make this go away. But I'll have to if you don't stop."

Her tongue left him as she straightened in his lap. "You want me to stop?"

"No." Feeling bereft of her touch, he brought his hands up to frame her face, to make her read the seriousness of his expression. "I never expected to find you again. But I never stopped wanting you. I've been dreaming about this since…" *Don't go there.* Jack squeezed his eyes shut. He couldn't think about Eric's death now. The guilt and anger and loneliness would destroy the mood. Get him to thinking. Turn this into something more than blind lust for a woman he needed to get out of his system. He opened his eyes and kissed her hard. Kissed away his own doubts when she eagerly responded. "I don't want you to stop."

She curled her fingers around his wrists. Her eyes were dark and drowsy with passion, her cheeks flamed with a rosy blush. "I've had a few fantasies about you, too, since Nashville."

Fantasies? Jack couldn't quite seem to catch his breath. His erection throbbed with anticipation. Just what kind of things had this woman been thinking about doing to a forty-year-old man who felt a decade younger just hearing her say that?

He made one last, valiant effort to remember that getting with Alex Morgan was supposed to be about the job. "So we can do this, right? You won't be afraid to touch me or flirt with me—"

"I don't know how to flirt."

Jack tunneled his fingers into her hair, stopping her from shaking her head, stirring up her scent, making himself crazy with the need to be inside her. "Telling a man you fantasize about him qualifies as a definite flirt."

She rose up on her knees and settled herself more purpose-fully on his lap. Every accidental brush of a hand or thigh coiled his body into an ever-tightening knot. He wanted her. Here. Now. As she talked she wound her arms lightly around his neck, sliding closer. The tips of her breasts were hard little spears that poked against his chest and reassured him that the desire simmering between them was mutual. "These are strange rules of yours, Jack Riley. You really think we can convince the people of this town that you want me?"

Jack pulled her in for a kiss. "Who's acting?"

And then there was little need for talking or coaching as Alex purred into his mouth and completed the kiss.

Snaps unsnapped. Hands explored. Mouths got greedy. There was a silent instruction to sit back on his knees while his jeans and shorts came down. Her overalls wound up around her ankles as neither of them remembered her boots. He pushed up the layered tops she wore, then pulled at the cotton and elastic of her bra. He suckled a proud breast as it spilled out, palmed the inside of her smooth, creamy thigh and traced the seam of her womanhood with his thumb until panties were soaked and she whimpered with need. She skidded her palms along the stubble on his jaw and tugged at the short strands of his hair. There was a twisting of bodies and bumping of hands when he pulled a condom from the glove compartment. There were no clever words, little finesse. This was about kissing and grabbing and sliding deep inside the warm folds of Alex's body. Again. And again.

This was about burying his nose in the perfumed valley between her generous breasts and holding on tight as he came up off the seat and exploded inside her. Every muscle in Jack's butt and thighs contracted as he pushed himself in as deep as she'd take him. She arched her back, tipped her head back and cried out as the tiny muscles inside her squeezed him and milked him and cascaded down all around him.

When she was spent, when he was empty, Alex collapsed

against his chest. Her breathing against his neck was as ragged and shallow as his own. Jack waited until their lungs had resumed a more normal rhythm and she was turning away to tuck her breasts back into her bra and shift her panties back into place before he lifted her onto the seat beside him and rolled down his window to dispose of the goods. The blast of cool air and cold rain provided the wake-up call he'd needed about thirty minutes ago.

Smooth move, Detective. He'd just broken one of his own rules.

He'd had sex with Alex. Hot, fast, mind-blowing sex. No matter how he tried to rationalize the loss of control—that it was part of Alex's basic training to get her used to the idea of playing the role of lover in his investigation, that she'd seemed to want it as badly as he had—he knew he'd just made a colossal strategic error. His judgment on this investigation was already impaired by losing one partner. Now he'd gone and involved himself with his new, unofficial, partner. *Involved* wasn't a good thing for a detective on a mission to find drug smugglers and killers.

Jack knew damn well that that had been more than sex. That had been something building up inside him for the past seven months. A need to connect. A want unlike anything he'd experienced with any other woman. But emotions were distracting. Need was distracting. Worrying about Alex on any level beyond strict professionalism was damned distracting.

Watching her sidle over to the opposite side of the truck to redress herself while he zipped and buckled everything back into place definitely worried him. Why was the mouth suddenly so quiet? Maybe she was just picking up on his moody second thoughts. *Jackass. Mr. Sensitivity.* "You okay, Trouble?"

She nodded without facing him. "That wasn't exactly how I'd pictured it would be." She wiped away the condensation from the inside of the window. Was she checking the sideview mirror?

Jack pulled down the visor in front of her and opened the lighted mirror. "How you pictured what?"

"Being with you. It's been…a while for me." Thank God she

hadn't said this had been her first time. No way was this sex kitten in disguise a virgin. But she did keep harping on her lack of experience with men. "I did okay, hmm?"

"Sweetheart, if that was your idea of *okay*, then I may not have the strength to survive you on a good day. You were…irresistible." He reached over to brush a honey-gold tendril off her cheek and tuck it behind her ear. Though she didn't exactly jerk from his touch, she did seem awfully busy tying her bandanna over the top of her head just so, checking in the mirror and then checking again. On the third take, he glanced behind them to see if she had spotted something moving outside. But the night was dark and muffled by the rain. "Did I hurt you?"

"No." She shot him a smile that was about as reassuring as the hasty way she turned off the lighted mirror. "You're good for my sex life. Hell, you *are* my sex life. That's the second time I've had an orgasm with you." She slapped her hand over her mouth. "Oh my God. Did I say that out loud?"

Jack swallowed the impulse to chuckle with relief. "Sweetheart, I know the setting and the circumstances aren't ideal, but that's just about the best compliment you can give a man."

He got a glimpse of eyes that were wide and dark and unreadable before she turned away to attack the buckles that fastened her overalls into place. "So what's our next step? I'm assuming you'll want me to take you to the track. Most of the regulars come into the garage at one time or another during the week, too. The next time we have—" she swallowed hard "—an audience, I assume you'll want me to kiss you? Or hold hands or whatever?"

"Just follow my rules, Trouble." He vowed to do the same. Jack started the engine, ending the discussion. "And don't worry. You're better at your part than you give yourself credit for. I guarantee you, within twenty-four hours, no one in Dahlia will have any doubts that you're my woman."

The only person who seemed to still need convincing was huddled in the far corner of his truck.

7

IT WAS WELL PAST MIDNIGHT when Alex sank into the fragrant hot water of her bath to ease the soreness from her muscles. She wasn't used to having sex like that—a frenzied mating that left her feeling powerful, sated, spent. She wasn't used to having sex, period.

Because she'd sworn off the men of Dahlia, sex had become an enigma to her. Orgasms from anything besides her own hand were an absolute mystery. It had been her very first time when she'd been taught that sex could be used as a weapon against her, when she'd learned that her needs and fragile hopes didn't matter.

But Jack Riley had made that awful night seem like little more than a bad dream. Despite the adult-like curves of her adolescent body, she'd been more child than woman then. Completely inexperienced. Tonight, Jack had made her feel like she was all woman. Like she mattered. Like the other women of Dahlia had nothing on her when it came to driving a man crazy with want.

Alex pulled a washcloth from the shelf beside the claw-footed tub. After soaking it in the water and oils she'd used, she rubbed the soft cloth over her skin, stretching out her legs and arms one at a time to leisurely cleanse and massage every inch of her skin—finding and remembering each place Jack had touched. Remembering how much she'd enjoyed it. She'd loved the power of it, the freedom from self-doubt as much as the rapidly building arousal and intense release it had given her.

Alexandra Morgan had had sex.

And the world hadn't ended.

It might not have been women's magazine style with tips and tricks and secret moves to increase his or her pleasure, and there'd been no courtly *milady* or background music. No gown. No gentle seduction like with the knight of her fantasies. Tonight in Jack's truck had been more like a souped-up motor revving on all cylinders and charging straight to the finish line.

She'd liked it. A lot. He hadn't joked at her inexperience or been impatient with her curiosity. He'd talked in plain terms and had used his hands and mouth to explain the rest. She could do this. She could get past her self-preserving inhibitions and fear of repercussions and make believers out of the men of Dahlia.

Alex breathed out a heavy sigh and relaxed against the pillow at the end of the tub. With a little more practice, she might even make a believer out of herself.

But how was she supposed to trust her feminine instincts when they'd failed her so miserably in the past? Blinking her eyes open, Alex retuned to the reality of her cooling bath water. Proving she could have sex once—albeit shake-her-world-down-to-the-core sex—didn't mean she was on the way to getting her love life in order.

She had to remember there were rules to this game. That this *was* a game. Any tenderness, any passion, was all part of the act. Part of the cover. Part of the job. Jack might fire her up like a combustion engine, but her dreams of a real relationship didn't figure into the equation.

Alex was still sitting there—wishing she had a mother to seek advice from, wishing she had some girlfriends she trusted to confide in, wishing she had Jack Riley here with her now— when her cell phone rang.

The soft whir of sound vibrating across her bathroom shelf startled her from her thoughts. It buzzed a third time, a fourth, before she could dry her hands and pick up the phone. *ID Restricted. 1:13 a.m.*

"ID Restricted? What does that mean?" Maybe it was Jack on some kind of untraceable line. Maybe there was a fourth rule he'd forgotten to dictate to her. Reluctantly, Alex answered the call. "Hello?"

Silence.

Her heart skipped a beat, then shifted into a higher gear. "Is someone there?"

"I saw you with him."

The voice was deep, muffled, unfamiliar.

"Excuse me?"

"You slut. You need to stop what you're doing. The outsider doesn't belong here."

Instinctively, Alex drew her legs up to her chest, hiding herself from unseen eyes. "Who is this?"

Click.

The disconnect jolted through her entire body.

Not again.

As soon as she could remember to breathe, Alex shut the phone and shoved it back onto the shelf. She pushed herself up out of the water on trembling legs.

"You son of a bitch."

This wasn't happening again. She wasn't going to let some dickless bully terrorize her the way the boys of this town had nearly a decade ago. She'd lived down that shameful night—sacrificed practically every feminine, sexual impulse inside her to do it—but she'd lived it down. She was a grown woman now. She had a college degree. A job. A cause for her brother that was far more important than any drunk, adolescent ego. She might hide her body from the lewd jokes and stinging gossips of this town, but she refused to be afraid.

With a few tendrils of righteous indignation giving her the courage to move, Alex stepped out onto the mat. Dripping across the cold tiles, she pulled her father's long flannel robe off the hook on the door. She tied it tight around her waist, overlapping the deep shawl collar at her neck, and opened the bathroom door. Nick and his buddy Drew had gotten her out of that high school nightmare.

Tonight, she was on her own.

After pausing at the foot of the stairs to listen for her father's reassuring snore, she tiptoed to the front door. Even in a small town, her dad was a fanatic about security, so the door was locked. But Alex checked it, anyway, opening and then refastening the dead bolt, making sure the knob didn't turn in her hand.

She parted the curtains that hung at the front window and peeked out. The storm had abated to a gentle, misty rain, but with the moon still hidden above the clouds, it was too dark to see much beyond the circles of light cast by the lamp posts at either end of the block. No one was moving along the sidewalks. Cars were parked on each side of the street. Houses were dark. Whoever had called wasn't watching her now.

Alex's racing heart finally calmed enough to hear above the frantic pulse that beat in her ears. The night wasn't so still as she'd first thought.

She leaned her cheek closer to the front window and heard the dapple of rain on the leaves in the trees outside. And another sound—this one lower, rumbling, mechanical.

Her trained ear recognized the sound. A powerful engine, idling in Park. The rhythmic spit of the motor told her it had been driven hard, and needed its oil and filters changed.

She peered into the darkness again, grateful for the shadows inside the house that would hide her from prying eyes. She scanned each car along the street and in her neighbors' driveways, looking for something to explain away that sound.

There. Alex squinted, thinking her eyes had played a trick on her. She pressed her forehead to the cool glass, stared harder. Across the street, beyond the glow of the street lamp, a chimera appeared. A ghost of movement among the rain and shadows.

But Alex didn't believe in ghosts. An idling car expelled exhaust from its tailpipe, exhaust that would be virtually invisible at night. But a tailpipe also gave off heat. That flux of movement was hot exhaust rising through the cool, damp air. That car was running.

"What are you doing out there?" she breathed against the glass. She skimmed her gaze along the car from tailpipe to headlight. Its body was like a giant black cat crouching in the darkness, its windows blank. The silhouettes of the seats inside blended into the shadows. "Who would leave their car—?"

A fiery speck of orange light suddenly burned inside the car's interior.

Alex jumped back from the window, quickly stilling the swaying curtains that might reveal her presence.

A man was sitting inside that rumbling car, smoking a cigarette.

Like Hank had smoked his cigarette and watched her leave the garage with Jack tonight.

Sitting and smoking and watching.

Watching *her.*

Dashing through the house as quickly as her heart was now pounding, Alex checked each window on the main floor, as well as the doors leading to the garage and backyard. Once she was certain she was locked in tight, she paused and took a deep, steadying breath. She was safe. She could relax.

But when she returned to the bathroom to clean up her mess, her phone was going off again.

She picked up the phone. *ID Restricted.*

"Stop it, you bastard. Just stop." When the phone went silent, Alex nearly dropped it.

Okay. So she was a little bit scared. She was definitely confused. She had no big brother this time who could make everything right, and she didn't want to burden her father with her paranoia over a couple of crank calls.

But there was another man she could turn to.

JACK EXHALED SLOWLY INTO the rain so that the fog of his warm breath wouldn't give away his position.

After steaming things up with Alex in his truck, the wet grass felt particularly cold as he lay on his belly in the shadows of Dahlia Speedway's infield. He'd give anything to be naked and snugged up to the warmth of her body, taking that get-acquainted session into round two. But when the track's outer gate had creaked open and a black pickup hauling a toter trailer had rolled in with its lights off, thoughts of tutoring Alex in the art of sex vanished and survival mode kicked in. Jack dove for the ground behind the infield's barrier wall, which was the only cover between the flat racing strip and the viewing stands where his visitors were headed.

He was lucky they hadn't shown up a minute sooner, when he was coming out of the track offices in the three-story tower that dominated the race grounds, relocking the door he'd picked open behind him. He was even luckier they hadn't arrived a minute later when he would have been snooping around the guest services and equipment storage area behind the metal viewing stands where they were pulling up and parking now.

His late-night search of the deserted race track hadn't turned up anything he didn't already know. Drew Fisk's office had been pretty well stripped of paperwork, in preparation for the pending sale, no doubt, or possibly because Sheriff Buell was trying to cover his tracks over something Nick Morgan had found. And the officials' offices held information on stats, records and regulations rather than the local connection he was investigating.

But his night at the track wasn't going to be a total bust. Ignoring the mud soaking his knees and elbows, he crawled to the opening between the concrete barriers that ran the length of the strip to protect onlookers from crashes, fires and other dangers that sometimes occurred. He squinted into the rain and spied on the after-hours rendezvous taking place beneath the stands some thirty yards away. Nothing like someone sneaking into a locked up facility after hours to make a cop suspicious.

From this distance, though, it was difficult to make out many details through the darkness. Once they killed the engine and turned off the wipers, a curtain of rain sluiced down the windshield, further blurring any chance at a positive ID. Without sound equipment, he could only imagine what the two men sitting inside the truck might be discussing. But whatever it was, the man in the passenger seat was giving the orders.

Jack trained his eyes on the driver's-side door as it opened, but the guy had his back to him as he headed around to the rear of the trailer. The best description he could come up with was medium build, dark hair. A few seconds later, the other man emerged, his face obscured by the cell phone at his ear before he, too, turned and walked to the back of the trailer.

Both men wore shapeless generic gray coveralls and dark ball caps. But he was guessing light-colored hair for the man on the phone, or maybe he had a shaved head like the guy he'd seen at Headlights and Morgan's Garage?

What activity there was to observe from his skewed vantage point didn't last long. The dark-haired man made most of the trips, unloading large boxes from the trailer and carrying them into the concrete-block building where track equipment was stored. Meanwhile, the guy on the phone pulled a pack of cigarettes from the glove compartment and lit one as he paced beneath the stands. Periodically, he'd look up, either cussing the rain or whoever was on the other end of the call.

Though he trained his ears to the man's voice, Jack could only make out a few phrases like "…product" and "…change everything" and finally a "You know damn well that money…" that sent the boss man off on a long stalking pace behind the storage building.

By the time he returned to Jack's line of sight, the call was done, the cigarette was out and his buddy was locking up the building.

"Damn." Jack mouthed his own curse, wiping the moisture

from his eyelashes, wishing the rain would stop and a full moon would light up the suspects so he could see their faces. But as the men climbed into the truck and pulled away, the best he could do was get a partial Tennessee plate.

He rolled over and sat up with his back against the concrete barrier wall. He was soaked to the skin from his knees to his chest, but the discomfort was nothing compared to the frustration of coming away with nothing more than half a license plate and truck make that he silently texted to Dan Rutledge's office in Nashville to run through the DMV system for him.

He gave the perps a solid two minutes after closing the gate behind them before he left his hiding place. *They* had used a key to get in to both the track and the storage building. That meant they had a legitimate reason to be here, along with the illegal reason that he suspected had brought them out tonight. Jack jogged across the asphalt track and made a quick search of the concrete beneath the stands until he picked up the lone cigarette butt that the man on the phone must have discarded. Now to find out just what was in those boxes they'd unloaded. Clamping his small flashlight between his teeth to light his work, he picked open the padlock on the storage building and stepped inside.

The place was jam-packed with rows of gray metal shelves forming aisles, while spare tires and anything else too big to fit on the shelves leaned up against the wall. Every flat place had something stacked on it, with everything from concession stand supplies to boxes of nuts and bolts. But Jack would bet his next paycheck that those boys hadn't been carrying in spare hardware.

"And we have a winner." Jack grinned as his search led him to the boxes he was looking for. Partially hidden behind a row of soda pop canisters. The only boxes that had been marked by the rain.

After a quick look out the door to make sure he had no more unexpected company, Jack pulled out his pocketknife and carefully sliced beneath the packing tape on the first box. Though it was labeled Fisk Aluminum & Fabrication on the outside, inside he found a steel air filter pan for a carburetor engine.

"No way." He couldn't be this lucky. His partner, Eric, had brought in something similar during his undercover investigation—various car parts with existing or built-in compartments where drugs could be stored and shipped. Jack quickly unscrewed the wing nut on top and opened the pan. "Damn."

It was shiny and new and empty.

No evidence tonight. Although…

Jack ran his fingers between the double interior walls of the filter pan. It could be a design modification to guide more cooling air in or out of a racing engine. Or… "Someone's built in a place to stash dime bags."

Nothing major, but if enough cut bags of dope were smuggled in enough cars and parts, he could still be looking at the pipeline that supplied dealers like Lorenzo Vaughn and the thugs fighting to replace him in Nashville. It was a start. Matching a name to the license plate and truck he'd seen or finding the actual drugs would be even better. Then he might start to feel some kind of vindication for Eric's murder. "I won't let you down, buddy," he vowed, just as he had the day Eric had died in his arms. Just as he had the day of Eric's funeral. And the day after that. "I won't let you down."

Moving swiftly and silently, Jack resealed the box and reached for the next one in the stack. He was in the middle of putting away a second modified filter pan when his cell phone vibrated in his pocket.

Rutledge couldn't have a plate match for him already, could he? He doubted the young attorney was even awake to get his message yet. It had to be one-thirty in the morning. Instantly on alert, Jack shoved the box back into place and pulled his phone from his belt. Only a handful of people had this number, and none of them would be calling at this hour for any good reason.

He pulled out his phone and checked the number. Hell. He couldn't get it answered fast enough. "Trouble?"

"Jack?" Alex's voice was soft, unsure.

"What's wrong?" Jack headed toward the open door, making sure no one was lurking about who might overhear his conversation. Or sense the protective fear that tensed every muscle of his body. "Did something happen after I took you home?"

He didn't like the sound of that pause.

"I think we already have someone's attention."

Jack pulled the door closed and secured the padlock. "What do you mean?"

"I just got a phone call."

At this time of night? "From?"

"I don't know. The voice was disguised. He said—well, I'm pretty sure it was a he—he said I should stop what I was doing. And I don't think he meant taking a bath."

She was naked? Jack braced his hand against the door, trying to catch a deep breath at the image of her lush, naked body rising up from the water, smooth and wet and... *Focus.* Curling his hand into a fist, Jack turned away and jogged toward the emergency exit gate where he'd snuck in two hours earlier. "Tell me exactly what the caller said."

"Not much. He said the outsider didn't belong here, and that I should stop what I was doing. I don't know if that means investigating Nick's murder, or making out in your truck or what. And I think someone's outside the house. I mean, Dad's upstairs and the doors are locked. But there's a car, and..." Bits of gravel crunched beneath his boots as he skidded to a stop, catching a quick, bracing breath right along with her. "In high school there was a prank, and this guy...well, these boys..."

"These boys what?" What was she trying to say? What the hell was wrong? Why hadn't that bastard threatened him instead of her? "Alex?"

She'd turned her mouth from the phone, cussing like a sailor. When she came back to speak, the vulnerability he'd heard in her voice a moment ago was gone. "I'm sorry. I'm babbling like a panicking idiot, and I've outgrown that. It's just another stupid prank. I'm sorry I woke you."

"You didn't. I—"

"I'll let you get back to sleep. Good night."

"No. You tell me exactly—" The disconnect echoed like a gunshot through his brain. "Trouble? Alexandra?"

Son of a bitch. Like he was getting any sleep tonight with a cryptic call like that. She'd sounded so afraid. He located her incoming number and rang her right back. Voice mail. Damn. She'd turned off her phone.

"I swear, woman, you're going to give me a heart attack one way or the other." Jack ran for the kudzu-covered brick wall framing the main gate. Not wasting the time it would take him to pick the emergency gate lock, he hoisted himself up over the wall and dropped down on the other side. Cursing the sticky friction of his wet jeans and jacket, he stretched his long legs into a run straight across the parking lot to Morgan's Garage where he'd parked his truck.

Eric Mesner would have had his hide if Jack's obsession with solving his murder had endangered an innocent civilian.

If he'd inadvertently done something to jeopardize Alex's safety, when he'd just been trying to cover his own ass with this fake affair… Jack climbed inside his truck, started the engine and squealed away over the wet pavement.

8

WITHIN TEN MINUTES of her call, Jack was picking the lock to the Morgans' back door and sneaking into a darkened house. Dark save for the light shining through a doorway at the end of the first-floor hall. The house was quiet except for some cham-pionship snoring coming from up the polished hickory staircase. Alex had indicated her father was asleep, that she was rattled and that calling him had been a mistake.

By damn, he was going to get some answers to something in this town. Moving toward the light without making a sound, Jack familiarized himself with the layout of Alex's house, and found himself standing in the doorway to her bedroom.

"It was nothing," my ass. Alex was pacing at the foot of an old-fashioned, white wrought-iron bed, wrapped up to her chin in a man's robe, her lips moving in some kind of *sotto voce* mantra or curse he couldn't understand.

Although he had no desire to frighten her further, it was even more important not to wake her father or alert the neighbors with a startled scream, so Jack crept up behind her and reached around to cover her mouth with his hand.

Her reaction was instantaneous. A shriek into his palm, an elbow to his gut, bare feet knocking against his shins. Damn, that woman packed a punch. He cinched his arm around her waist, pulling her off her feet and into his body, flashing back to that night in Nashville.

He pressed his lips against her ear, gentling her with a voice that was as reassuring as he knew how to make it. "Easy, sweetheart. It's me. Shh. Don't cry out."

The fight ended as quickly as it had begun. When she gave an acknowledging nod, he eased his hold and lowered her to the floor.

"Jack?" As soon as he released her, she spun around. In the course of their struggle, the robe had gaped open, revealing one of the two most beautiful breasts he'd ever seen. But before he could note more than how the rosy circle of color at the tip stood out against her milky skin, she quickly covered herself, clutching the robe together at her neck and waist. "How did you get in here?"

He frowned. "I've been a cop for a lot of years. I've learned a few things. Now we need to have a conversation. Tell me about that call. And who's watching? You can't—"

"I'm just glad you're here."

She walked straight into his chest and the lecture died on his lips. As she wrapped her arms around his waist and nestled her cheek against him, the temper and fear that had carried Jack from the track to her bedroom dissipated. Her breasts pillowed against his stomach, the scent of flowery bath oils teased his nose. For one noble moment he tried to push her away. "Sweetheart, I'm a mess."

She didn't seem to care. "I've never had a man dash to my rescue before." Her lips moved against the cotton of his cold, damp T-shirt like a warm caress against his skin. "Except for my brother. And that hardly counts, does it."

With a dumbfounded sigh, Jack lowered his lips to the crown of her hair and folded her up in a snug, protective embrace. "I sure don't feel like your brother."

But this wasn't about riding in like some kind of hero. This wasn't about discovering tender, aching places inside him that had nothing to do with the need this woman stirred in him.

This was about understanding the rules. His rules.

"You and I have to get one thing straight, Trouble." Jack tugged the elastic band from the nape of her neck, hating the tight, sexless bun more than the bandanna that normally masked her hair. He sifted his fingers into the heavy golden curls, stirring up that sweet gardenia scent that was uniquely hers. "You *never* hang up on me in the middle of a conversation. Understand? Communication is everything in an undercover op. If you hang up on me, I don't know if you're in trouble or pissed off at me. And I guarantee you, if you hang up without explaining what's wrong, I will be on my way to finish that conversation in person and see with my own eyes that you're all right."

"Really?" She moved her arms beneath his jacket and snuggled close enough that he could feel every curve and muscle as if they were standing skin to skin. "That's so sweet."

Sweet wasn't what he was going for. Jack spread his legs slightly, adjusting his taller stance so that his thighs could more fully cradle the curve of her hips, lengthening the body-to-body contact that seemed to be calming her, soothing him, warming them both. If she didn't mind soaking up the mud and moisture from his clothes, he wasn't going to push her away. "That's team play, Alex, and we're a team now. We have to know what's going on with each other. Got it?"

"Yes. No more hanging up."

"Good." Reluctantly removing his hands from her hip and hair, Jack leaned back against her arms and tilted her face up to his. No signs of crying, but definitely paler than he'd like to see. He smoothed her hair from her face. "Now, tell me about this phone call. Why did it spook you?"

Her chin went down and her gaze landed at the center of his chest. "It's embarrassing."

He unhooked her arms from their death-grip around his waist. And though he could have enjoyed the view all night long, Jack folded the baggy plaid flannel over the deep vee of cleavage at the front of her robe and turned her toward the bed. "You were scared. You can't bluff your way through this one."

He pulled back the quilts and sheet and waited for her to

crawl beneath the covers. Alex rested back against the pillows, hugging her knees and the quilt up to her chest.

Jack sat on the edge of the bed, facing her. "Just talk to me."

Her eyes searched his for several seconds before she tucked her hair behind her ears and tried to shrug off the importance of this discussion with a laugh. "There was an incident when I was sixteen. Tonight's call was like the ones I used to get back then. I'm sure it doesn't have anything to do with Nick's death or your investigation."

"I don't care. I want to hear about it."

The false smile quickly disappeared. With the light from the bedside table illuminating her face, Jack could read all the nuances of emotion that crossed her unadorned features. He didn't like any of what he saw there—except the courage. "My mom died when I was a toddler. I barely remember her. So my dad and my big brother raised me."

"That explains your love for cars and the tomboy getup, not the phone call."

"I'm getting there. When I hit puberty, I was like any other girl. I wanted pretty clothes. I wanted a boy to like me. But I was different in one fairly significant way." She released the quilt long enough to gesture to her breasts. "I sprouted these when I was twelve. By fourteen, I was the talk of the locker room. By sixteen…"

Ah, hell. He caught her fingers on their way back to the quilt and laced them together with his own. He needed to hold on to something, too, because he had a feeling he wasn't going to like what she had to say. "What happened?"

"Well, there was a senior in school. Hank Buell—"

"The jackass from the restaurant?"

Alex looked down. "Hank was a real catch back in high school…"

"Tell me about Hank."

"I had a serious crush on him back then. He was an all-state wrestler. Raven-haired. Cute and funny. He was the first boy who talked to me about cars rather than asking my bra size." Her fingers jerked like a vise around Jack's, but he absorbed the pressure without complaint. "Hank asked me out and I was on cloud nine. We dated three or four times, kissed, petted a little."

A black hole of protective jealousy opened up inside Jack, but he quickly buried the reaction. "I'm guessing the next thing you'll tell me is how he urged you to go further? Maybe said all the girls were doing it, or if you really cared about him…?"

Alex nodded. "It was a beautiful warm spring night. He brought me flowers. Took me on a late-night picnic up in the hills north of town." Jack pulled both of her hands between his, massaging away the sudden chill he felt there. "The first time really wasn't very good. He said, maybe if I stripped for him… You know, touched myself, he could—"

"Alex…" That crackle in his voice warned Jack that he didn't have his emotions as fully in check as he'd like.

"In the middle of pretending I was enjoying myself, I heard applause. And laughter. Lights flashed. Hank had sold tickets, and I was the show. Somebody took my clothes and…ow!"

Jack popped his grip and immediately released her when he realized his anger wasn't in check at all. "I'm sorry." Playing that see-if-you-can-convincingly-seduce-me game with her on a secluded country road had probably been a painful reminder of that horrid night. "Did you report it? Him? Them?"

"Shh. It happened ages ago." Alex reached for his hands again, gently brushing her thumbs across his white knuckles.

Oh yeah, look at who was being the strong one and who wasn't getting his job done now. "Buell is still here in Dahlia. His father and brother, too, must be constant reminders. I suppose they turned it around and blamed you for it."

"It's okay, Jack. There was no real crime committed, just poor judgment on my part. I've learned to deal with it."

He wanted to punch something. "By hiding your gorgeous figure? Looking for dates in another town?"

The trace of a smile on her lips eased some of his anger at the torment she must have endured. "You're the only man I ever succeeded at picking up. And I had to nearly get arrested to do it."

Jack tipped his head to the ceiling, exhaling months of regret over that one. When he was sane enough to look at her again, he tried to think like a cop, listening to the account of a crime. But the man in him, who chomped at the bit to right a serious wrong for an innocent woman, added a sharp edge to his voice. "Did anyone do anything to help you?"

"Nick heard about what was going on. He drove into the middle of it and picked me up. Between him and Drew, they scattered the boys and got my clothes back—except for my bra. I guess somebody kept that as a souvenir. The next day, my dad tracked down Hank and beat the crap out of him."

"Good old Southern justice. I think I'm going to like meeting your father. Buell wasn't crass enough to press assault charges, was he?"

Alex shook her head. "But there's no love lost between our families. If Artie wasn't such a good mechanic, and we weren't so shorthanded come race time, Dad never would have hired him. I think Dad's the better man for moving on, but the Buells…" He followed her gaze to the cell phone beside her bed. "I thought I'd heard the last of it."

"You think it was Hank who called?"

"I couldn't recognize the voice. But it felt the same."

"You felt threatened." He couldn't seem to keep his fingers from the feminine cascade of her hair. He didn't like that his partner had paid the price he had, but he understood the logic. What he didn't understand was how a man—a boy—could take such pleasure in destroying a sweet, sexy woman like Alex. For what purpose? A few quick bucks? To show off his conquest to his buddies? The feeling of power over someone else? "You don't think the call was related to the investigation I dragged you into?"

She reached up to still the stroking of his fingers, and lean her cheek into his palm. "Once you finally allowed me to speak, I volunteered, remember?"

He nodded.

"I don't know who all the boys were, watching that night. But it didn't matter—even if they weren't there, they heard about it. For months afterward, I got phone calls at home and snide remarks at school, calling me a tramp or worse." The catch in her voice cut right to Jack's heart. "Someone must have seen us tonight. And whoever was in front of my house smoking his cigarette was hoping for a repeat performance, I guess. Sounds like I'm back to being Alex, the town slut."

"Shut up." He didn't want to hear her take any of the blame for that incident.

"What?" He could see that his harsh words stunned her.

"Just shut up." Not caring about mud or propriety or her father upstairs, Jack scooped her into his arms, quilts and all, and pulled her into his lap so he could hold her tight. So *he* could hold on to something warm and beautiful before the black hole where his soul belonged consumed him. He buried his lips against her hair and rocked her back and forth. "Don't say that word. Don't believe it."

There was a whole new slew of names he was putting on his shit list in this town. They'd pay for hurting the people he cared about.

Cared about? Hell. He'd only known Alex Morgan for what? Five hours? Five hours and seven torturous months of wishing she was in his bed and at his side during those awful days surrounding Eric's murder and funeral.

It had taken him months of running into Rosie every day in a coffee shop before he'd decided he wanted to ask her out. But he already felt more connected to this sweet, baffling bundle of trouble than he'd felt in a year-long relationship with the woman he'd lived with.

His partner would have loved to analyze that one. Something Freudian, Jack was sure. Something reckless that made no sense beyond the fact he'd wanted that mystery woman from the streets of Nashville so badly. Jack wasn't sure he wanted to take the time to figure it out himself. Mostly because he wasn't entirely comfortable with where he thought this insane relationship with Alexandra Morgan might take him.

He needed her arms looped around his neck, holding him tight, before the haze of vengeance that burned behind his eyes began to recede.

"Jack?" Her lips brushed against his jaw. He'd been quiet for too long. He'd gone to that dark, angry place inside him and had lost track of the time. "Are you okay? You're not having second thoughts about me helping you, are you? I can deal with this. I've dealt with it before."

He didn't have to find all the answers tonight. He just needed to be a cop. He needed to look out for Alex the way he would any partner he worked with.

She'd been scared. She'd been used and hurt in ways he couldn't fathom. But she had more strength and courage in the tip of her nose than the entire male population of Dahlia put together. She'd handle this undercover operation just fine.

"Not a one. Just as long as you remember my rules." He kissed the tip of that brave little nose and stood up with her in his arms. For a moment, he simply enjoyed the perfect weight of her, molding to his body. Something deep inside him lurched with the memory of how their bodies could meld together in other ways that were equally perfect. He longed to test the instincts that told him a relationship with Alex Morgan would hold as much pleasure as it would adventure. But was he really in a place where he could handle that kind of commitment?

More importantly, was Alex?

With every honorable instinct he could muster, Jack set her back on the bed, alone, keeping his feet firmly planted on the floor. He tucked her beneath the covers, robe and all. "If you get another call like that, or you think someone is following you I want to know about it ASAP. For now, leave your phone off and go to sleep. I'll be parked right outside, keeping an eye on things. No one is going to get to you tonight."

"*You* did."

"Only because you hung up on me. I can be a very determined man when I'm trying to find out the truth." She looked so young and vulnerable lying there that Jack felt every one of the fifteen years separating them. She needed someone closer to her own age to sweep her off her feet and rebuild her confidence as a desirable woman and make her world the fairy tale she deserved.

But she was stuck with him. At least until his investigation was complete.

Jack leaned over and kissed her forehead. "I'll lock the door behind me when I leave. You might want to, uh, check for muddy footprints before your dad wakes up in the morning."

Then, ah hell, he kissed her mouth. Kissed her again when she responded, parting her lips for him. He kissed her a third time because a taste of this woman never seemed to be quite enough. When he leaned in to kiss her a fourth time, common sense finally smacked him in the back of the head and he pulled away. He'd better leave before he climbed under those covers with her. His presence would be harder to explain away than the footprints.

"Sleep tight, Trouble. We have work to do in the morning."

"It is morning."

"Then I'm the one who needs some sleep. I'll be out in my truck. Good night."

"Good night, Jack."

THE STREET WAS DEAD. A thorough check of every parked car reassured Jack that he was the only nocturnal animal sitting inside a vehicle in front of Alex's house.

But he had no doubts that someone had been out here. The hilly street was full, nearly bumper-to-bumper, along each curb. Yet when Jack had arrived, there'd been one empty parking space—and a trio of cigarette butts out on the grass where he had pulled in. Putting faith in Alex's claim that someone had been watching her, Jack bagged the butts as evidence and tucked them inside his jacket next to the one he'd recovered from the track. He was miles away from a lab to get any DNA tests run, but he'd find an hour to take them into Nashville tomorrow, to see if they could put a name to the bastard who'd terrorized her. And if they matched the one from the track, then *he'd* be the one doing the terrorizing.

He pushed his seat back, giving his legs a little more room to stretch out beneath the steering wheel, wishing the upholstery didn't still carry enough of her scent to mess with his concentration when he needed to be rethinking his plan of action to include bodyguard duty. Jack reached for the cup of coffee he'd bought at the twenty-four hour truck stop out on the highway. He'd planned to be staking out after-hours activity down at the speedway, not here in town, parked across the street from the Morgans' house. He owed his dead partner and his boss in Nashville a speedy investigation, but somehow, protecting Alex from phone calls and past nightmares seemed a more pressing problem at the moment.

Especially since resurrecting that nightmare was probably his own damn fault.

Jack sipped from the plastic cup. Though the call and his investigation might not be related, he had a sneaking suspicion that there *was* a connection. Alex said she'd gone years without any harassment, and suddenly, now that he'd publicly announced them as a team, some prick wanted to torment her again?

More than likely, it was an attempt to scare her off. But off what? Interest in him? Something at Morgan's Garage? Her amateur investigation into her brother's death? Had his claim on Alex stirred up some vindictive nightmare from her past?

The coffee was too bitter to really enjoy, but Jack took another drink. It was still warm, and loaded with enough caffeine to keep him awake until sunrise. He could manage thirty-six hours without sleep, but he'd have to come up with yet another plan to keep an eye on Alex tonight because he suspected that by the end of the day he'd be ready to crash. In bed with him would be the safest place, if she'd go for it. Maybe he should approach Alex's father, or one of her friends, like Tater Rawls or Drew Fisk, for help in keeping an eye on Miss Trouble.

Then again, maybe he was selfish enough to not want any help. He glanced up the slope of Alex's yard to the curtains hanging at her bedroom window. Doing something positive for Alex would be a lot more beneficial for her than tracking down Hank Buell and finishing the beat-down George Morgan had started. She wanted to be a lady? A fair damsel who was treasured by men, not ridiculed by them? All she needed was a man with a little bit of patience to see the woman hiding behind the tough talk and overalls. Under the guise of maintaining their cover, he could teach her that sex was a beautiful thing, not just a bad memory.

Jack wasn't much for games, but he could play an undercover role with the best of them. He'd mull that one over a little bit— Alex Morgan's knight in shining armor. He had a lot more Terminator than Sir Galahad in him. But knew how to treat a lady like a lady. And he had a whole lot of ideas about how he could show Alex just how sexy and desirable she was. Of course every last one ended up with her in his bed. Or his lap. Or...

A bright pair of headlights bounced off his rearview mirror, interrupting his planning and momentarily blinding him. Jack shaded his eyes and turned to the side mirror.

Seems he wasn't the only one keeping watch in Dahlia tonight.

The white Suburban pulling up behind him didn't need its lights flashing for him to recognize an official vehicle. Jack set his coffee in its holder and straightened, ready to do battle if need be. He made sure his jacket covered the gun tucked into the waistband at his back and waited. The man behind the wheel put on his flat-brimmed hat before climbing out. His good buddy, Henry Buell. Watching the sheriff waddle up beside his truck soured Jack's mood and put him on guard.

Neither man bothered with greetings as Buell braced his hand on the edge of Jack's open window. "My deputy said he'd spotted an unfamiliar vehicle parked outside the Morgans' house." The sheriff casually adjusted his belt and turned to spit into the grass. "I got another call saying someone saw a man breaking into the back of the Morgans' house around two this morning. You wouldn't know anything about that, Mr. Riley, would you?"

Jack waited for those beady dark eyes to face him again. "You wouldn't know anything about who'd be keeping that close an eye on Alex and her back door, would you?"

Buell smiled. "The free parking ordinance is just for night time on the residential streets. Come eight o'clock, when folks are off to work, you'll need to move, son."

Jack wondered if Buell had ever enforced the rules so vigilantly with his own sons. "I'll be finished with my coffee right about then, sheriff. Driving Alex to work. Appreciate you lookin' out for me. I'd hate to get a ticket."

Jack's sarcasm wasn't lost on Buell, and Buell's warning wasn't lost on Jack. Alex Morgan wasn't the only one being closely scrutinized in Dahlia. But was it just the good ol' boys being suspicious of a newcomer? A father making sure his boys didn't find more trouble than he could get them out of? Or was Buell guarding something else, altogether?

With a tip of his hat, the sheriff walked back to his Jeep. As soon as he disappeared around the corner, Jack was on the phone to Daniel Rutledge, his liaison in Nashville.

The phone rang twice, then tumbled off its receiver before anyone spoke. "Yeah? This is Rutledge."

"Sorry about the early hour, but I'm discovering it's hard for a stranger to get much privacy here in Dahlia. Did you get the plate number I texted you?"

"Riley?" The grogginess disappeared from the attorney's voice. Jack imagined him pushing back covers, sitting up, going on alert. "You already stirring up the locals?"

"And then some. Grab a pen. I need you to run a few names for me."

"What have you found?"

"I spotted a couple of guys unloading car parts at the track. No drugs, but the parts were fitted to conceal a shipment if they wanted."

"Get me a description. I'll match it up against the parts we have in evidence here." The kid *was* ready to work. "What are the names?"

"Henry Buell—he's the sheriff here in town—"

"The sheriff?"

"And his sons, Hank and Artie Buell. I want to know if any complaints have been filed against them. Ever. DUIs. Restraining orders. Harassment. Criminal mischief."

"Criminal mischief? Are we talking the same case?"

Jack checked the rearview mirror to make sure Buell hadn't circled around to eavesdrop on his conversation. "The Buells act like they're running the show in this town. That kind of power makes me suspicious. There are too many secrets here. And apparently, there's some bad blood between the Buells and another family—the Morgans."

"As in Nick Morgan?"

"His father and younger sister. You know them?"

He heard the pen go down. A drawer opened and shut. Dan Rutledge was getting an early start to his day. "Nick and I went to law school together. He's the one who brought me evidence of the track's illegal activities in the first place. He died in a car wreck before we could get any names. The papers he had burned with him. My office's investigation stalled out after that, until you and your partner uncovered the operation in Nashville."

"Alex Morgan doesn't believe her brother's death was an accident."

The movement on the other end of the line stopped. "That woman is a thorn in my side. Her relentless curiosity is making it difficult to keep our investigation hush-hush."

Though the insult set Jack's teeth on edge, he kept the emotion out of his voice. "I think she can help us."

"As methodical and discreet as Nick was, everything I hear about Alex is that she's loudmouthed and impulsive. Hardly someone I want to trust with the kind of information we've been collecting."

"I need you to return her call."

"Why?"

"Because I think she's right."

"About Nick's death being murder?"

"She's got an inside track on who the players are in Dahlia and at the speedway. She helped establish my cover and is giving me suspect insights you can't get off any report."

He heard the disdain in Rutledge's tone. "Has she been talking to you? She claims she's got some of her brother's notes and wants to know if they're evidence that can prove someone had the motive to run his car off the road."

Jack sat bolt upright, glancing up at Alex's window again. "You knew she had evidence and didn't ask to see it?"

"If it was something useful, Nick would have had it with him when he crashed into that canyon. At best, she's a biased source—at worst, she's a flake. She's looking for a reason to justify a cruel twist of fate, and I feel for her pain. But I can't make it go away. The sheriff there ruled Nick's death an accident."

"The sheriff here is a pile of horse crap." Jack knew the young attorney was his boss on this particular investigation, but he needed to set the record straight. "He's hiding something. I trust Alex's instincts more than I trust his word."

"So it's 'Alex' already, huh?" A long pause punctuated by a heavy sigh indicated Rutledge was reluctantly conceding. "Fine. I'll run a check on Buell and his sons, I'll get you an owner for that plate number and I'll take a closer look at Nick's accident report. If I find any anomalies, I'll give you a call." The shuffling noises at the other end of the line told Jack that Rutledge had resumed his morning routine. "But I'm not trusting Alex Morgan with information that our task force has been keeping under wraps for months now."

"You should. I've already told her most of what I know."

"Are you crazy, Riley?"

"Talk to her, Daniel. We owe her that much."

9

THE BANDANNA WAS BLUE TODAY.

The overalls and the attitude were the same.

"Those are the papers Mr. Rutledge said to give you—the ones I've been trying to get him to look at. He's finally taking me seriously." Jack obeyed the tug on his arm and circled around Alex's desk to sit. She tested the door to make sure it was closed, then pulled a chair over and propped it beneath the knob before turning to face him.

"Expecting company?" he asked.

"No. But I'm not taking any chances if someone *is* watching us." She waved his attention back to the folder on her desk. "That's why I wanted to come in early, before everyone else reports for work. I don't want Dad to know I have that file. If he finds out I've been snooping around on my own, he'll go into overprotective-marine mode. And if it's nothing more than a pile of papers Nick fished out of the trash, I don't want to get his hopes up. Just read them, okay?"

Her office chair creaked as it took his weight. "Yes, ma'am."

And then the pacing started. Her chin was tilted, the fists were on her hips. Jack had to look hard to find any trace of the vulnerable woman who'd phoned him in the middle of the night, terrified. "I can't believe I've called him twice a day for two weeks with no answer, and you dial him once and snap—he's suddenly interested in what I have to say." She groaned. "He still doesn't believe I know anything, does he? You twisted his arm."

. "I told him he was being foolish to overlook any possible clues." Jack wouldn't be so arrogant. "Let's see what you found."

With a closed door and a good forty-five minutes of privacy before anyone else reported for work, Jack opened the binder marked "March–October '07." It looked like a haphazard collection of business papers—purchase orders, receipts, computer printouts, ledger sheets.

While Jack turned pages, Alex walked circles around the room. "So Nick was working on the same case you are?"

"I didn't know until Rutledge confirmed it this morning. Your brother's instincts were good enough to alert the state attorney general's office. Rutledge made the connection to our end of things in Nashville." He stopped at a receipt stapled to a spreadsheet with two different totals circled in red. Jack was no forensic accountant, but even he could see the discrepancies in income, payouts and profit margins. Somebody was hiding some money somewhere. "Any idea whose papers these are?"

Alex shrugged. "Nick wrote 'Andrew Fisk' on the folder. But that's probably just because Mr. Fisk hired him to go through things. I found several different signatures when I looked at the files. Drew, who is still managing the track until Whip Davis takes over. But that won't be until he and his fiancée, Cardin Worth, return from their honeymoon."

"Here's your buddy, Hank." After Alex's suspicions regarding last night's phone call, even seeing his signature dashed across the bottom of a delivery receipt turned Jack's stomach. "He works at the track? You run into this guy every weekend?"

"It's a small town, Jack. It's hard to escape your past." He hated the way she shrugged off the pain and anger that having Buell around all the time must cause her. "Hank makes a lot of deliveries for the Fisks' aluminum plant. They built the stands at the track, and sometimes fabricate replacement parts for cars that race in Dahlia."

Hank Buell delivered fabricated car parts? Jack filed away that nugget of information. He already knew the rat smoked. That gave him two strikes in Jack's book.

"Even my dad's name is in there," Alex continued. "I don't even know if the papers came from one office. Maybe it's just some work Nick discarded and I'm the only one hoping it's important."

This *was* important, especially if the bulk of Nick Morgan's evidence had been destroyed in his accident. "We're only talking a few hundred dollars," Jack cautioned, "but there's enough funny accounting to indicate a much bigger problem. I definitely want Rutledge and his experts to look at this."

Jack closed the file and smiled at Alex. But it faded quickly. Funny, he'd thought she'd be more excited to find out she'd uncovered a trail of criminal activity with this information. But she was still circling the office, staring into some other place and time. "Someone in that file killed Nick over funny accounting? Couldn't they just pay back the difference if he reported them?"

"Alex, sweetheart…" The grim truth would be more of a comfort to this woman than a useless platitude. "It's a way to hide money. These are small amounts—maybe someone's early efforts to hide the fact they stole from petty cash."

"My brother was not killed over petty cash."

"Neither was my partner."

"Your partner?" The pacing stopped. "You said a cop was killed—"

"Forget about it." Shit. How had that slipped out? What was it about this woman that made him drop his guard and forget his common sense?

She circled around the desk. "Jack… You lost someone you were close to?"

He couldn't stand to see those deep green eyes narrowed with pity. Ignoring the question, he stood suddenly, sending her desk chair rolling back until it hit the shelves behind him. "I'd better check the garage to make sure it's clear before I move this file to my room."

He needed to talk about work, focus on the investigation. He did not need to deal with this woman's curiosity or concern.

But she wouldn't let it rest. "What was your partner's name?"

No. He couldn't do this. Instead of talking about Eric, Jack retrieved her chair and placed it between him and Alex, who was resting her hips against the desk. "Before a perp starts hiding a big influx or payouts from drug money, they practice padding smaller bills and receipts. Small successes give them the cajones to go after the big money."

She crossed her arms in front of her, the tilt of her eyes warning him that she understood exactly what kind of diversionary tactic he was using. But, for the moment, she gave the personal questions a rest. "Why would Nick suspect someone at the track was selling drugs in the first place? We know all the people there. They're our friends."

"Friends change if they get into money trouble, get greedy, develop a habit. Drugs are big bucks. The bastards who traffic them are dangerous. Whether you're taking them or selling them, drugs change people. Period."

"Thanks for the public service announcement, Officer Riley." There was no humor to the bite of her sarcasm. "I still can't believe anyone in Dahlia would hurt someone as good and kind as Nick."

Jack met her eyes. "You can't?"

He almost came around the chair at the shiver that rippled through her body. "That was nine years ago, Jack. They were just boys playing a stupid prank."

"Did that phone call last night feel *stupid* to you?" When she conceded the truth with a shake of her head and the resumption of her pacing, Jack felt only marginally victorious about changing the subject and making his point. "Don't you dare defend what they did to you, or think for one minute that you deserved that. I don't know if that event is related to what's going on now, but trust me, kids who can come up with sick tricks like that grow up into the kind of men I'm looking for."

Way to go, Riley. Those are some real words of comfort.

He shoved his fingers through his hair, trying to shove some compassion into his brain, as well. "Look, Alex, I'm not trying to be a bastard here."

"Yes, you are." She whirled around. Walked right up to him. "You don't want to talk about your partner and you're trying to shut me up."

"Is it working?"

"If you're grieving for a friend, you can't keep it bottled up inside."

"Didn't think so." When she threw up her hands and turned to walk away, something inside Jack leaped to have her back at his side. He grabbed her arm, swung the chair around and pulled her into his lap. Despite the stiffness of her arms braced between them, he felt instantly better with the warmth of her bottom resting atop his thighs. He stroked a loose curl free from the grip of her bandanna. "Eric Mesner was more like a brother than a friend. Doesn't mean I want to talk about him."

"Was he killed in the line of duty?"

Jack simply nodded. "By the same people I'm after now." He spread his fingers with a gently protective grasp around her hips, determined not to inflict any more of his pain on her. "I need you to understand just how serious, how dangerous these people can be. It galls me to think about anybody hurting you. Ever."

Instead of "Thanks, Jack" or even "You're a pig," she mimicked his actions and smoothed the spikes of hair off his forehead. "You look like crap today."

Jack fell back in the chair, laughing. Great. No damage done if she could still dish it out. "That's it. Shred the old fart's ego. That'll shut him up."

"There's nothing old about you, Jack, except maybe that old soul inside you that sees everything in black-and-white or doom and gloom."

As much comfort as he found in touching Alex, there was

something even more soothing about her laying her hands on him without any kind of hesitation. She framed the sides of his face, dragging her thumb across the stubborn line of his bottom lip. "You're not exactly how I imagined you were all these months. You're rougher around the edges. There's a whole lot less sweet talk. But you're a good man, Jack. I'm glad we're in this together."

"You're not exactly what I imagined, either." She pulled her hands away self-consciously. Jack caught them and put them right back. "Touch me, Alex—I want you to. I…need you to."

Her cheeks blossomed with color. "You *need* me?"

"Yeah." Hell of an admission from big Black Jack Riley. But he was tired. His emotions were raw. And this woman brought an amazing light into his dark, isolated world. A little mutual petting might be a good thing for that "old soul" of his. Lifting her bottom, he adjusted Alex more snugly in his lap and invited her to do what she would to him. "Hell, yeah."

Her soft, tentative touches grew bolder the longer he sat there without responding. Outwardly, perhaps. But his eyes weren't missing a thing, and every cell inside him was reviving, volunteering to be the next one graced with Alex's touch.

Guileless in some ways, a sensual delight in others, Alex Morgan was completely irresistible in everything she did. He watched her fascination with his responses to each tender caress, darting his tongue out to catch her thumb when it passed by a second time. Seeing the pleasure she took in exploring his face was an unexpected turn-on. Watching the self-assurance grow in her expression as she saw the pleasure even these simple touches gave him aroused something potent and male deep inside him.

With his upside down schedule, he probably needed a shave. But she seemed to like scraping her palms over the prickly stubble almost as much as she enjoyed toying with his hair. Would her hands be so bold, so thorough, if they were exploring the eager flesh behind his zipper?

"Didn't you get any sleep last night?" she asked, tracing the shadows under his eyes.

He leaned his forehead against hers and groaned his misery, deciding that was a safer move than grabbing her wandering hand and placing it right where he wanted it most. "I'm okay, Trouble."

Misreading his guttural response, Alex cupped his jaw again and pushed him back far enough to search his eyes. "You have enough on your plate without worrying about me, don't you? Praying the bad guys don't find out what you're really up to before you catch them. Pretending you aren't missing your partner—your friend?" Her eyes darkened with the bitter sorrow she must be reading in his face. "I'm right, aren't I?"

His head jerked with a nod.

She pressed a gentle kiss to the corner of his mouth, another to the opposite side. Caught off guard by her insight into Eric's death and the way the pain of losing his friend tore him up inside, something salty and hot burned beneath Jack's eyelids. Her soft, cooling kisses were suddenly there, as well. "You're hurting already, and I only add more stress. I swear I don't mean to. Tell me about your partner."

"Eric Mesner," he stated matter-of-factly. "They shot him up." Those words were harder to squeeze past the tension knotting his throat. Oh man, he did not want to cry. Gettin' busy with Alex, yes. Crying? Hell no.

"I'm so sorry. Shh." Alex pressed her lips against his. "It's okay."

"How is Eric being dead ever going to be okay?" That better not be a tear she was kissing from his cheek. He slipped his hands inside the loose gape of her overalls and hugged his arms tight around her back, crushing her against his chest. He wanted to feel *her,* not the pain. His lips found the velvety arc of her bottom lip, but words tumbled out, getting in the way of sealing the kiss. "Eric was smarter than me. Saner. Patient. Loving. He had a family. He made *me* family. He had everything to lose."

Alex wound her arms around his neck and rubbed her soft

cheek against his coarser one. "You lost, too. When you love someone that much, you lose, too. I know."

He tugged at the double-layered tank tops she wore, needing the contact with the warm, soft skin underneath to distract his shaking hands. "I just need to find the bastards who shot him and let him bleed out in the street. That's all I need."

"Oh my God. How awful." She squirmed, trying to pull back far enough to read his expression, look into his eyes. "You were there when he died? He suffered?"

"Long and slow before I got there."

With a hot, angry breath, Jack buried his face against the juncture of her neck and shoulder and squeezed her until the images of blood and shock and his own angry screams could be pushed aside. He had soft woman against his mouth to muffle the urge to release those screams. And soon he was tonguing, tasting, suckling her delicate skin. "He was barely alive when I got to him. He…" A hot tear, not his own, dripped onto his ear and trailed along his neck. "He…" No. Jack jerked against images of his partner's lifeless body lying heavy in his arms, of an empty street, mocking the brave man who'd fallen there ignored and alone. "Oh, God." His teeth nipped down a little too hard and Alex grunted at the unintended pain. Jack immediately pulled away. But he couldn't release her entirely. He couldn't make himself let go. "I'm sorry, babe. I'm sorry." He couldn't do this. "Let's not talk about it, okay?"

Her fingers cupped the back of his head and neck, pulling him back to her embrace. "Jack, you need to talk."

"I just need you." He dragged the straps of her overalls off her shoulders, kissed the swell of her cleavage, followed her erotic scent down to the cleft between her breasts. He moved his hands to lift the heavy globes, knead them through her clothes, push them up to bury his nose between them. "I don't want to talk."

Her fingertips clawed at his shoulders, stretching the cotton of his T-shirt, trying to hold on to that hug. "You're just like my father. You don't want the world to see any kind of weakness, so the grief festers away inside you and goes on and on—"

"Don't lecture me." He found the hooks cinching her bra together and released all four of them, freeing her bounty to his eyes and lips. He greedily went straight for a pebbly tip and pulled it into his mouth. Her skin was fiery and responsive beneath the pull of his tongue. He ignored her strangled gasp and her fingers digging into his shoulders. He squeezed the pale globe's heavy weight up against his tongue. "Don't tell me what to feel."

"I'm not." Her voice jerked in time with the needy impulses of his hands and mouth. "You're…hurting. I'm only…trying…to help."

"Enough!" Jack shot to his feet, sending the chair spinning as he dropped Alex onto the top of the desk. But the call of her body couldn't be denied. When she tried to jump down, Jack spread her knees open and moved between her legs. He pulled her to the edge, aligning her hottest feminine softness against his own hardening need. "I'm here to work, not sit through some down-home, Dahlia-style psychoanalysis. I don't need that kind of help."

"You need something." She braced her hands against his chest, squeezed her knees around his hips, squirmed right against his arousal. "Jack!"

He pinned her thighs open as he rubbed himself shamelessly against her. "Yes, I miss Eric. It pisses me off that he's gone and I haven't found justice for him yet. But I will deal with whatever I'm feeling later. I have to do my job first. I have to finish the damn job!" He finally paused when he heard the roaring in his own ears, saw the faint pink mark he'd left on her shoulder, saw the mixture of shock and pity on Alex's pale face. He made a valiant effort to rein it all in, to ease his hold on her, to back away. But he was failing miserably. "I am not going to break. Believe me. I'm as tough as I look."

Damn, if she didn't look as though she saw right through that lie.

"You have to grieve." Her fingers crept up to frame his jaw again, to feather against his hair, to draw his mouth down for a gentling, healing kiss. But the instant he hardened his mouth over hers, she pulled away, sprinkling kisses along his jaw and neck, whispering wise words for her limited years and tormenting him with what he couldn't have. "I know what it's like to be the one left behind. The guilt you feel. Nick had so much more to offer the world than I ever will."

He plucked a metal button loose at her waist. "That's not true. Don't say that."

She skimmed her hands down over his arms, making every muscle quake beneath her touch. "Some days, the only way to get through the grief is to promise myself that I'm going to do more with my life—care deeper, be stronger than I thought I could be. I want to make a difference in the world. I may never measure up—"

"Don't say that." He tipped her chin up to kiss away her doubt. *He* was the one who'd never measure up. He'd never have half of what Eric had lost. "Don't ever say that."

"But I have to try. I have to honor Nick's memory and try." Another button went by the wayside. Now she was kissing the center of his chest, moving over a muscle, touching his heart. "I want him to look down from heaven and be proud of me. Just like I know your partner is so proud of you."

"No." He tried to set her away, but wound up pulling her overalls taut at her crotch, thinning the barrier that separated the helpless push of his hips from the heat and temptation of her feminine center.

Alex gasped at the contact. Her fingertips clutched his chest. She pressed her face against his neck, moaning as his thumb followed the seam of her pants down between her legs.

"Jack." The more she tried to squeeze her legs together to relieve the torment, the more Jack rubbed. And still she tried to reason with him. "You have to…let it go." Every gasping breath was a hot, moist caress against his skin. "You...have to let yourself...feel."

"I don't want to feel." The denim was damp now, fragrant with her alluring scent. "Don't make me feel anything but this."

A profound need to bend Alex over that desk and take back the emotions she'd stolen from him, to lose his pain buried deep inside her blossoming heat spasmed through Jack. No, no, no! Damn it. He wasn't going to hurt. He wasn't going to feel. He had to keep his wits about him, stay in control and get the job done. Alex was his cover, his source for information—a freaking tempting lay—but not his salvation.

She was clinging to his shoulders now, panting, reaching for something he couldn't quite give her. She pressed a kiss to his neck. Another to his chest. In between gasps, she found his nipple through his shirt and tongued it until it stood as erect as his aching dick. But he didn't need gentleness. He didn't need patience or understanding. His body was screaming for release. Raw. Mindless. Fast. Hard. He wouldn't cry. He couldn't grieve. He needed...

"Let go, Jack," she whispered against him. "You don't have to be patient or teach me anything this time. Let me help."

"Damn it, Trouble—Alex." He kissed her mouth. Kissed her cheek. Kissed that damn bandanna. "I need... Do you know what I'm asking?" He thrust his thumb deliberately against her swollen heat and she whimpered. "I need you. Everything." Last night in his truck had been good, but he'd needed this, wanted this, forever, it seemed. "Please let me..." Jack pulled away, barely able to stand. He held his shaking hands up, surrendering himself to her will. "Or say no. There's a crappy cold shower in a room not twenty yards from here."

He held every screaming cell inside his body in check until she answered.

"Yes, Jack." With those deep green eyes holding his gaze, she reached down to her waist and pulled her tank tops up and off over her head. The bra tumbled down her arms and quickly followed. She knocked aside items on top of the desk before setting the wad of tops behind her. Then, like the helpless man he was, he watched her lie down on top of the clothes and vee her legs open, offering her body, herself—her healing mercy—to him. "Yes."

With a hell of a lot more urgency than finesse, Jack untied his boots, unhooked his belt. He retrieved a condom from his wallet before shoes and pants disappeared. Alex slithered out of her plain white panties while he sheathed himself.

When she sat up to reach for him, Jack pushed her back down onto the desk. "Don't I need to help?" she asked.

"No." Her pale skin stretched taut across her weepy mound, and Jack breathed deeply the heady fragrance that was this woman's alone. She lay there before him, a naked, willing sacrifice spread-eagled on an altar, just for him. Ready to be taken. Ready to be his. Ready to give him what he'd needed for so long. "Just be there for me. Let me look. Let me touch. Let me take."

With his left palm holding her writhing hips flat on the desk top, he slipped two fingers inside her, testing her readiness. Her body jerked against his palm. Clenched around his fingers. Her fist pounded the desk and she moaned. She was slick and tight and gasping for a deep breath as desperately as he was. Her breasts bounced up and down in erotic display, beckoning him as she twisted helplessly against his probing hand. Her eyes locked on to his, telling him in yet another way how primed and ready she was for this.

He pulled his fingers out of her and slicked her own moisture around her clit and thighs, trailed it around the rosy areola of each proud, perfect breast, making her whimper and pulse with every stroke. "You're a beautiful woman, Alex. Never doubt that." For a moment, he considered stooping down and taking her with his mouth, making her come again and again. But he hadn't even taken the time to remove his shirt. His dick was hard and swollen and butting against her thigh, telling her exactly what he needed. "Never doubt how much I want you."

Alex propped herself up on one elbow and touched herself, wetting her fingers before reaching for his straining cock. When she wrapped her hand around it and squeezed, Jack cried out, lurching against her grip. The innocent little vixen smiled. "I want you, too, Jack." Her breathless command was a pure carnal invitation. "Don't make me wait any longer."

Jack removed her hand and pushed her back onto the desk. She was as golden and perfect down below as she was on top, but Jack spared little time to admire the view. Unwilling to wait a second longer, he pushed open her thighs, pulled her right to the edge of the desk and buried himself inside her. Buried himself to the hilt. Pushed down into her and ground himself against her, gritting his teeth against the promise of release, even as she cried out and arched her back. She was tight, damn tight, and little ripples of muscles were grabbing him like tiny hands inside her.

He meant to go in slowly, pull out, enter her again—ease her into growing accustomed to the size and shape of him. But he needed her. Damn, how he needed her.

"Are you all right?" He moved one hand to brace himself against the solid oak of the desk. He could barely breathe, barely see around the haze of need swirling behind his eyes. "Damn it, Alex, are you all right?"

Her back relaxed against the desktop, yet she was breathing so hard he could scarcely hear her. "I didn't know…you could come in just…one…time."

"Oh, hell, baby." He would have laughed if he had the strength in him. But Jack Riley was a driven man. He was already moving inside her. "Let's go, baby. Let's do it."

She snatched at his wrist, moved his hand back down to the thatch of hair where he was pumping into her again and again. "Take me, Jack. Take me. Take me."

Even with the fever building inside him, he understood her

request. While he rammed himself deep into her welcoming heat, he sought out the responsive nub between her nether lips and pressed his thumb against it. Alex bucked on the table. Papers flew. He pulled his other hand from the desk and ran it along her abdomen and stomach, easing her back into position. He retreated a fraction of an inch and plunged in as deeply as he could again.

Thoughts of lonely nights and solo showers and mindless grief tried to sneak into the mix of rocket fuel charging through his system, filling his groin with a powerful surge not unlike an engine running at smooth top speed. He moved his hand to a straining breast and anchored himself to the decadent pleasure this woman gave him.

"Jack…it's okay." He closed his ears against the tender voice and focused on the hard nipple and swollen nub beneath his hands.

"Jack…"

He rocked against the desk, thrust into her body. Squeezed. Rubbed. The need in his body shifted to a higher gear, erupted through his pores, demanded satisfaction.

The desk moved across the floor with a grinding screech and he felt the finish line slipping away from him. "Stay with me." He pulled her body partway off the desk to sheathe himself again. She wrapped her legs around him, hooked her heels behind his thighs, opened wide and gave him everything he wanted. Unable to make sense of her urgent words, he felt the traces of her second orgasm begin to squeeze him, urging him on. But he wasn't there yet. He wanted something more.

"I need…" No. A powerful emotion latched on to the desire screaming through his veins. He felt strongly about this woman, about this joining. But he didn't want to feel…"Oh, God, sweetheart, I need…"

Jack looped his arms beneath Alex and scooped her up against his chest. As though he was behind the wheel of a speeding car that threatened to spin out of control, Jack felt things inside him buffeting him from every direction. Three long strides carried them across the room. And then he had her up against the wall, her arms and legs wrapped tightly around his body, her breasts crushed against his chest, his mouth covering hers in a fierce kiss as he drove himself home.

Jack roared as his release overtook him. The explosion deep inside her was the most powerful, most humbling, most freeing moment of his entire forty years. He was dizzy with the force of it. Drained.

"Oh, Jack…Jack…Jack." Alex's gasps of weary satisfaction matched his own. She continued to pulse around him as their ragged breathing pushed their sweaty chests and sticky stomachs against each other. She had her fingers in his hair, whispering sweet little somethings into his ear as Jack buried his face against her breast.

Dots of hot moisture hit his cheek and trailed rivulets down through his beard. "Sweetheart, don't. Don't."

Jack pulled her away from the wall, snugged her in his arms and held her close as Alex wept the tears he couldn't shed.

"ARE YOU GOING TO TALK TO ME?" A leather office chair wasn't the most comfortable place for a man to sit when he was naked. But bare skin on warm leather wasn't the discomfort that concerned him. He felt even more exposed inside—all because of the woman in his lap.

Alex sat with her knees curled up, her head tucked beneath his chin, while one hand rested almost protectively over his heart. He wasn't the only one exhausted by that out-of-control desktop session. As their bodies cooled, Jack trailed his fingers in a long line up and down her bare back, lifting her hair to cup her nape, sliding down to the flare of her hip. "I'm not used to you being this quiet for this long. I'm not sure what to think when you're not arguing with me."

"I'm just…tired."

Understandable. He was physically and emotionally spent.

But he was also the one with the experience. She was the one who'd been used and terrorized by a lover before. They both needed a gut check.

"Come on, Trouble," Jack coaxed. How terrifying must it be to have a man of his size and life experience come unglued like that? "Are you hurt? Did I scare you? Unless you have a camera hidden somewhere inside your office, you don't have to worry about anyone seeing us."

"It's none of that. I pushed you too hard to let your real feelings out. I thought I could help, but it's like opening a wound. I only made things worse for you, didn't I?" She stirred restlessly, pulling her arms down to hug them around her knees. She was being self-conscious now? After what they'd just done? After all he'd revealed? "I warned you I wasn't very good at this relationship stuff."

Jack's eyes were gritty with the emotions he'd buried for far too long. The grief and rage that had been trapped inside him had found an outlet that no police psychiatrist, no clergyman, no well-meaning friend had been able to tap into until this tough-talking tomboy-goddess had simply held him, welcomed him, dared him to open up and give himself—all of himself—to her. "You're far better at it than I am. You've got a big heart. I hope I didn't take advantage of that."

"You didn't." She inched a little more space between them, but Jack's hand on her hip asked her to stay with him a while longer. "I'm still having a hard time resolving Fantasy Jack with what it's really like with you."

"Fantasy Jack?"

She sat straight up now, dropping her feet to the floor. The heat he felt warming his cheeks was nothing compared to the deep blush on hers. "I shouldn't have said that out loud. Since we met last October, you kind of, um…" she gestured meaningless circles in the air, "when I imagine…"

"I think I can fill in the blanks." He hoped Fantasy Jack had done a better job of seeing to her needs than he had. He grimaced at how this morning's encounter must compare to her knight in shining armor dreams. "You know, it's hard for a man to live up to the heroes in fairy tales and fantasies."

"I know." Was that disappointment? But then she turned and looked at him with a wry smile. "It has been different, but I like the real thing better than…oh." She pressed her fingers to her lips to hide her embarrassment.

"Than what?"

"My washcloth."

"Ah, hell." Jack wrapped his arms around her and pulled her back to his chest. As much as she knew about the darker side of human nature, she was still so damn young and naive about the craziest things in this world. "It can be better for you, babe. It *should* be better. Next time I'll make sure of it."

"Next time? We could do this again?"

Jack nodded at her curious, hopeful expression. He didn't deserve the rush she was giving his ego. "I'm not a cop 24/7, Alex. I won't be on this case forever. If you let there be a next time for us, I promise it won't be the quickie like last night in my truck, or the catharsis that this was. There's a way a man's supposed to treat a lady. Slow, gentle—"

"But exciting, right? I…" Her eyes dropped for a moment before looking back up into his, exacting a promise he intended to deliver. "I'm learning a lot from you, Jack. I'm learning that sex can be a wonderful thing. That it's more than hormones and hot spots. It's kind of…empowering, isn't it? I love how it makes me feel…with the right man."

Exciting? Empowering? Exactly. "I'll make sure it happens that way for you."

"Next time," she murmured, snuggling back against his chest. "You know, I've never done it in a bed. I know that's the usual place, but…"

Laughter rumbled deep in his chest as Alex chattered on about some interesting possibilities for more sex. This woman had the resiliency of…Alexandra Morgan. There was no one else like her in the world—at least not his world. She'd endured cruelty and grief and still came out swinging. She had self-doubts, but an instinct about people far wiser than his own at times.

Something deeper than the sex, more profound than the physical release, had bonded them in a way that left Jack feeling closer to this woman than he'd felt to anyone in his entire life. Closer than Rosie. Closer than Eric, even. He'd let Alex Morgan into a place where she alone knew his deepest, darkest secrets. He felt raw. Beholden. Like she already owned half his heart.

He wasn't exactly comfortable with that kind of closeness. It was as if she'd gotten inside his most personal undercover role and could expose him if she was so inclined. How was he supposed to trust someone else with that kind of power over him?

The solace he'd found in Alex's willing body made him feel at once lighter, calmer, and yet, somehow more burdened than he'd been an hour ago. She'd unleashed a dam of emotions inside him. And, until he sorted them all out, he needed to be careful or he'd wind up giving his whole heart to another woman who didn't want it.

10

THE SOUND OF MALE VOICES in the hallway startled Jack from his drowsy speculation. By the time a key scraped into a lock across the hall, he was wide awake. Alex jumped off his lap, dove beneath her desk and crawled across the floor to retrieve their clothes.

Apparently, the time for cuddling and reflection was over.

She jerked her panties up over her hips and tossed Jack his jeans. "Come on. Dad will come looking for me any minute. We always start our work day with a cup of coffee and discuss our schedules and plans."

Carefully peeling himself off the chair, Jack picked up a sock and began to dress. "Alex…" She hooked, buttoned, gathered papers, straightened a picture frame—moving too fast to get a touch or word in. "This doesn't change anything."

"I know." She pulled on her yellow tank top, and then the blue one.

Jack slid into his shorts and jeans. "We still have to work at the track today, still have to get those papers to Rutledge."

"I know."

"And I still think you're the classiest lady I've ever known."

"Lady?" She paused in the middle of tying a boot. "I don't think so."

When she straightened, Jack grabbed the strap of her overalls and fastened the last hook for her. "*These* don't keep you from being a lady." He leaned in and kissed her pale mouth, bringing back its warm, rosy color. Everything was still a mess inside him, and he didn't know where to begin or where he needed to end up. He just knew… "Thank you."

"Jack, I…" A rap at the door silenced whatever she'd meant to say.

"Alexandra? You in? I didn't see your car out front."

Her father? Great. How teenagery was this scenario?

Alex squeezed his forearm, trying to reassure *him*. Hell.

"We can't talk about this right now." She turned and shouted toward the door. "Good morning, Dad. I'm just finishing up some paperwork. I'll be right out."

"What paperwork? Honey, you're not spending my money to sponsor another driver, are you?"

Alex hurried over to the door to push the chair aside, but stopped and popped up mid-slide. Uh, oh. What was she thinking now?

"Trouble?" Jack scooted the desk back into place, waiting for an answer.

"Alexandra?" Her father knocked again. "Is someone in there with you?" The knob rattled and turned. "Alexandra?"

With one quick shove of the chair and a pat to make sure her bandanna was on straight, she opened the door. "Morning, Daddy." Alex stretched up on tiptoe to kiss her father's cheek and trade a hug. But *Daddy* was looking over her shoulder, straight at Jack. Uh, oh. Jack was too old for the lecture he saw brewing. Could Daddy tell Jack had just had sex with his daughter?

"Dad, this is Jack Riley, the driver who's renting our back room. Jack, my father, George Morgan."

The two men shook hands. "Mr. Morgan."

"Jack. Word's already out about you down at the coffee shop." George's suspicious green eyes traveled from Jack back down to his daughter. "This isn't the back room."

"We were having a meeting." Alex jumped back into the conversation. "I have a plan, a way to boost promotion for the garage and bring in new business."

Was that the brainstorm that had struck moments ago?

George splayed his hands at his hips. "Funny how my daughter's never mentioned you before."

"Dad—"

"Long-distance relationships are hard to maintain. We've kept ours very low-key, in case it didn't work out." Jack dared to drape a possessive arm over Alex's shoulders and pull her to his side. If they were playing the roles, they needed to play them for her father, too. "She's told me about how the gossip works in this town."

The stern suspicion turned to surprise. "She told you?"

"Yes, sir. I'm very aware of protecting Alex's reputation."

Surprise became a glimmer of acceptance, if not necessarily approval. "Not to be rude, but how old are you?"

"We're both legal age, Dad."

"Yeah, but he looks a little more legal than you are."

"Dad." Alex nudged Jack aside. "I want to tell you about my idea."

She'd played along with everything he'd asked of her thus far. A business meeting, eh? Jack could play along, as well. "Yeah, I'm anxious to hear you explain the plan, too."

"This one's always getting ideas in her head," George groused with a mixture of love and trepidation in his voice.

Alex rolled her eyes at them both. "Come on in and have a seat, Dad." She took one look at the desk, then turned and pushed her father back into the hallway. "Better yet, let's talk in your office." They were all settled with chairs and coffee before Alex continued. "My promo idea is a good one, and it won't cost you a thing."

"Sounds too good to be true. How do you figure that?"

As Alex and Jack sat side by side on her father's couch, she reached over to squeeze Jack's knee. "We're going to sponsor Black Jack at this weekend's races."

"I told you not to be buying anything but car parts."

"I won't, Dad." Jack imagined that smile could convince Daddy to agree to just about anything. He knew *he* found it hard to resist. She set down her coffee and crossed to her father's desk.

"I've decided to donate my time and expertise to prep Jack's car for the race."

"*You're* going to soup up his car?"

"I'll be a one-woman pit crew. We'll put a *Morgan & Son's* logo on Jack's racing suit and decal it on his car. All I need from you is the space to work. And a couple of days off to get it all done."

George took Alex's hands in his. "You're serious about getting into this business, aren't you."

"Yes. Sorry, Dad, but you're never going to make a Southern belle out of me."

He gently tweaked his daughter's chin and smiled. With a sage nod of acceptance, George leaned around her to address Jack. "And you're okay with this arrangement? We wouldn't be paying you anything." He glanced up at Alex. "We're not paying him *anything,* right?"

Jack unfolded himself from the couch and joined them. "I've been out of racing for a while, sir. Believe me, I'm glad to have the help to…" A startling realization put the charade on hold for a fraction of a second, and turned Jack's entire plan to get into Dahlia, get the truth and get back out, sideways. "She's helping me get back to where I want to be. Your daughter seems to have a real gift for fixing things."

And he wasn't talking about cars.

THIS WASN'T RIGHT. The wires weren't original and the engine block looked a couple of micrometers short of being properly aligned inside the chassis. And what was that extra seam of solder inside the wheel well for?

Alex's heart skipped a beat, then pumped a little faster.

Someone had tampered with this car.

She guessed that shouting for Jack to come and look at her discovery while the garage was busy with mechanics and customers wouldn't fit his rules for undercover work. So she took a deep breath and pretended her heart wasn't racing with excitement as she scooted off the fender of Drew Fisk's Corvette and pulled the shop rag out of her back pocket to wipe her hands. "I'd definitely say it's your alternator, Drew. It just doesn't seem to want to hold a charge."

Her friend muttered a much more civilized curse than the gasket she would have blown at learning his sixty-grand investment was a piece of recycled junk inside. Drew closed the hood. "I just spent a fortune on these two cars. I can't afford to add repair bills on top of that."

Alex tried to offer a bright side to having a new sports car die after three days. "Well, the 'Vette is this year's model, so it has to be under warranty. Why don't you just take it back to the dealer?"

Drew skimmed a hand over the top of his trim blond hair. His face had gone pale beneath his tan. "I didn't go through a dealership. The guy I bought the Mustang from threw in the Corvette to make it a real sweet deal."

"Too good to be true, hmm?" Alex squinched up her face in sympathy. When Drew had come into the garage this morning, asking for a favor, she'd been willing enough to help. But this was one she couldn't fix. It was, however, something she really needed to show Jack. Wasn't that how he'd said the drugs were being smuggled into Nashville? Through modified cars and parts? Hello! She'd just seen the evidence that one of her friends had possibly been duped by the very men Jack was looking for. Maybe they could find out where the car had come from. "Will you be sending this back to Nashville for repairs, then?"

"That's a hell of an expensive mistake to make." Drew turned nearly 360 degrees, perhaps checking to make certain no one was eavesdropping on his misfortune—or maybe just looking for an empty place where he could throw something without hitting anyone. "Are you sure it can't be fixed here? Grandfather will freeze my trust fund again if he finds out I've been taken on a stupid deal like that. First, he sells the track out from under me, and now he'll start checking every business deal I make."

"We'd have to order in the parts, but I suppose we could do it." Wait a minute. "What do you mean, sell the track out from under you?" She pulled a boxed set of socket wrenches from her tool chest and dropped them into her portable tool box for the trip she and Jack were taking to the track this afternoon. She used the task of packing the rest of her tools to scan the garage for a sign of where Jack might have gone. She spotted him having a conversation with her father near the office exit—hopefully about cars, and not her. Or Jack's investigation. "I thought the Fisks selling the speedway to Whip Davis was a group decision, that you had some big job lined up somewhere else in the family business."

"Are you kidding? I have no desire to end up like my father— tied to his work twelve months a year, living every day trapped in his corner office or on an airplane." Drew circled around his car to take Alex's arm and turn her full attention back to him. "You understand what it's like. I love the excitement of the track, getting my hands dirty down in the pits, the thrill of finding that next great car and driver who are going to make the Fisk name famous. I want to create my own fortune so that I don't have to follow Grandfather's boring old code of Fisk family behavior and expectations."

Startled by his touch, but not afraid, Alex patted his hand and smiled. She could understand the drive to be his own man. After all, she was desperately trying to be her own woman, and make her father as proud of her as he'd been of Nick. But Drew Fisk getting his manicured nails dirty down in the racing pits? She doubted she'd ever see that day. "I never knew you had goals like that, Drew. I thought you were all about Fisk family traditions. Trophy wife. Plantation life. Running empires."

"Very funny. I'm serious. That track was my baby."

She smiled at the rare glimpse of real passion etched beside his eyes. "So you want to discover that next great car and driver?"

"Did I hear someone mention my name?" The shift in Drew's gaze warned her a split-second before Jack walked up behind her.

Drew released her and retreated a step as Jack rested his hands at either side of her waist. She felt a kiss at the crown of her hair before he stepped around her to shake Drew's hand. "Fisk. Good to see you again."

"Jack."

Jack nodded toward the Corvette. "Problem with your ride?"

"She died on me this morning. I thought maybe it was all that rain we had the past few days getting up under the engine, but Alex says it's the alternator." Whatever warmth and camaraderie had been in Drew's voice a moment ago had cooled now that the conversation included Jack. No doubt, like her father, he was reserving judgment on the stranger who'd allegedly laid claim to her heart—or at least her bed.

Either Jack didn't sense the change, or he didn't care. He flattened his palm at the small of Alex's back. "Are you sure your dad doesn't mind you taking the day off to put my car through its paces?"

Drew's frown filled his voice. "Aren't you going to order the parts for my Corvette? I want to get it fixed as soon as possible."

"Sorry, she's spoken for." Jack pinched the back of her overalls and tugged her toward the next garage bay. "Come on. I want to hit the track while the sun's still shining and the asphalt's dry."

"I'm coming. Here, make yourself useful." She picked up her tools and pushed the heavy box into his hands. Turning back, she gave Drew an encouraging smile. "Don't worry. Ask Artie to call in the order. He maintains your drag racers. I imagine he can take care of your street car, too."

"Artie?" Drew grimaced.

Alex laughed. "Go talk to him. He's downstairs in the lube pit."

Leaving Drew behind to dig through the Corvette's glove compartment and whine to himself about his own foolishness, Alex looped her arm through Jack's and whispered. "You and I need to talk. But not here."

Jack was pulling her along as much as she was pushing him. "No. You and I need to talk."

"About what? Oh, wait." Alex snapped her fingers and pulled away. She'd nearly forgotten. "Hey, Drew?"

Apparently not finding what he'd been looking for, he slammed the car door shut and straightened his jacket. "Decided to take pity on me, after all?"

"I tell you what, if Artie gets the parts, I'll make the repairs on your car first thing next week. After the races."

"Promise?"

"Only if you do me a favor."

The frustration lining his face eased. "Anything for you, Shrimp."

"Could we borrow your keys to the track so we can open it up and do a couple of test runs on Jack's car?"

"So that's whose engine you'll be tuning this weekend."

If there was anything suggestive in Drew's comment, Alex overlooked it. She knew people were talking about her and Jack. She supposed that was the point, really, to get people used to him as a fixture around the track and town so that he wouldn't attract so much attention. They'd gossip about that new driver in Dahlia and what he was up to with Alex Morgan. Hopefully that would distract them from the fact that he was asking lots of questions and poking his nose around in track business. "Thanks, Drew. I appreciate it."

"Just make sure you lock the gate when you're through. There'll be a couple of deliveries from Jim DiMarco in concessions and a replacement awning from Dad's plant later this afternoon. Other than that, you should have the track to yourselves."

On impulse, she stretched up on tiptoe and kissed his cheek. "You're the best. We'll try not to beat your car too badly come Saturday."

He dropped the ring of keys into her hand. "You care to make a small wager on that?"

Large hands closed around Alex's shoulders and steered her

back toward the Camaro in the next bay. "I'm the man to make a bet with if you're talking cars," Jack challenged. "You think your Ford can beat my Chevy?"

"A hundred dollars says yes."

Alex realized a hundred bucks was a drop in the bucket to a Fisk, but what happened to Drew just blowing sixty grand on a lemon of a car and getting called on the carpet by his grandfather for throwing his money away?

"Make it five hundred and you've got a deal."

"Jack!"

Drew nodded and extended his hand. "You're on."

With the two big men done trading testosterone, Jack turned to catch up as Alex stalked away.

"What was that about?" she asked. "We haven't even towed your car out of the garage yet and you're betting you'll win?"

"Testing a theory. Is Fisk always that anxious to make a wager?"

"I suppose. I mean, the man comes from money. If he wants to play…" Alex stopped, sending Jack colliding into her backside. She was already turning before he could ask if she was all right. "I get it. The numbers in that file of Nick's. If Drew is losing money gambling…"

Jack dipped his face close to hers, keeping his voice at a whisper and urging her to do the same. "There were plenty of padded numbers in those papers to cover a few five-hundred dollar bets. And your father just told me the last person your brother talked to before he left for Nashville that night was Andrew Fisk. They'd set up a meeting for when he got back to town. That'd throw up a red flag to anybody who didn't want your brother talking about his suspicions."

Alex thumbed over her shoulder. "Drew's grandfather, Andrew Fisk?" A shocked *O* rounded her mouth. "The man is pushing eighty. You don't think a sweet old gentleman like Mr. Fisk is running dope through his own racetrack, do you?"

Jack pressed a finger to his lips, reminding her to keep her voice down. "What I'm thinking is that a lawyer spending that much time at the track offices is likely to run across more than doctored books. Whatever he planned to tell Fisk's grandfather probably set off the chain of events that led to his…accident."

"Wait a minute. You talked to my father about your investigation? I don't want you to upset him."

"I just asked him about Nick. Offered my condolences. He's the one who started talking about your brother's work. Let's get out of here before someone overhears us."

He stepped around her to the four-wheeler they'd already tethered to Jack's Camaro and set her tool box in the rear basket. Rather than waste a drop of the expensive fuel used to run the drag racers, or risk any kind of damage to the delicate motor inside, it was customary to tow the car onto the track instead of driving it across the parking lot.

Once he'd strapped her tools in safely, Jack straddled the ATV and patted the seat behind him. "Let's move it, Trouble."

Alex was slower to climb on. She wondered how a man could be overwhelmed by deep emotions in the throes of passion, and then turn it all off and become this calculating investigator again, trusting no one and sharing none of the need or even concern he'd shown for her in the privacy of her office that morning. She hugged him tight with her knees and arms, missing the private Jack more than she cared to admit.

The mild warmth of the midday sun was a welcome comfort to the lonesome chill working its way through Alex's body. As they rode the four-wheeler across the lot to the track's brick arch entrance, Alex tried to take a lesson from the master. Turn down her emotions. Think like a cop.

She leaned into his back, hoping that he could hear her above the vibrations of the four-wheeler's motor. "Do you really think of Drew as a suspect? He was a friend of my brother's from as far back as I can remember."

Jack slowed as they approached the Dahlia Speedway's white

metal entrance gate before looking over his shoulder to answer her. "Every crime needs three things, Trouble. Motive, means and opportunity. I've got nothing to prove your pal Fisk is covering debts by moving drugs through his business." He stopped and idled the four-wheeler, putting out a hand for her to hold on to so she could climb off and unlock the gate. He held on, waiting for her to face him before finishing his answer. "If Fisk has problems with money, that's motive. He comes from a family of business entrepreneurs, so I'm guessing he has the means to travel and meet these people. And if he's running the place, he's got all the opportunity in the world to manage the cars and cash and goods that come in and out of this speedway."

"Drew would never be a part of killing Nick or your partner. His financial problems don't make him a criminal."

Those steel-gray eyes didn't flinch. "No. But they make him a suspect. You watch out for him. Even if he's not a part of this, he's not above taking advantage of you."

"I watch out for every man in this town." Alex pulled her hand away. The dart of her eyes let Jack know he was currently included on that list.

"How much did you plan to charge him for working on his car?"

"Just for parts."

"And which one of you is the millionaire who can afford to pay for the work?"

"Doing a favor for a friend isn't the same as letting someone take advantage of me." She fished Drew's keys out of her pocket, reminding Jack that Drew was doing them this favor. "In fact, I believe someone might be taking advantage of his gambling and investment problems. If the clues all point to him, as you suggest, he'd make a perfect fall guy for someone working behind the scenes, right?"

"I suppose." Jack followed behind her, pushing open the gate once she'd unlocked the chain. "What's your theory, Detective?"

"Very funny. Remember, back at the garage, I said I needed to tell you something?"

"Yeah?" He towed the Camaro through the gate, then waited for her to climb on before heading over to the staging area.

"Drew's Corvette—the one he bought in Nashville a few days ago." They drove onto the 1/8 mile strip of asphalt and lined the Camaro up in the staging lane beside the starting tower. "I didn't have time to get a really thorough look at it, but someone had modified it under the hood."

"Modified the motor?"

"No." Alex got off and unhooked the tether from Jack's car. "To me, it looked as though someone had removed the engine so they could reshape the interior wheel well."

Jack rode the four-wheeler over to the nearest pit and jogged back to pull his fireproof racing suit from the driver's seat of the Camaro. "You think there was a hidden compartment built into the car?"

"Things are tight inside a Corvette. Whoever did the work didn't put it back together very well. I think that's why it stopped running. Drew said he bought both the Corvette and his racing car from the same guy in Nashville. Maybe both cars have been modified to transport drugs." She unstrapped Jack's helmet while he pulled his black racing pants on over his jeans. "Tonight, after the garage is closed, I can get back in there for a better look."

"*We* will go back in for a closer look. You're not doing anything on your own in this town. There are too many people I don't trust."

"I can tell my dad that you and I have a date."

Jack shrugged into the matching fireproof jacket. "Your dad suspects that you and I have done a little more than date."

Alex busied her hands with zipping up Jack's jacket, ignoring the familiar sting of disappointment in herself. "He was so hoping to have Suzy Homemaker for a daughter. Instead he got stuck with Alex the tomboy who sleeps with mystery men before he even gets a chance to meet them. No wonder the slut rumors have started again."

"Don't say that. From everything I've seen, George is very

proud of you." The flinty hardness of his eyes softened, giving Alex a glimpse of the man who could show he cared. "What he got stuck with was a loyal, talented daughter whose heart is big enough to carry both of you through these tough times. He loves you, Alex. He's a lucky dad. And for the record, you've slept with one *man*." His voice deepened. "Anyone who tries to say you're anything but a lovely, loving woman will answer to me," he growled.

Alex tilted her chin to read the powerful flux of emotions that darkened Jack's features. A smile blossomed across her mouth and deep inside her heart. "Who needs a knight in shining armor when I have a fierce warrior like you on my side?"

Jack laughed. Sort of. "You know, the sage old warriors usually don't make it to the end of the movie. We teach what we know to the young bucks, and then they wind up with the girl."

With his helmet hugged between them, Jack was too far away. His joking doubts about a lasting relationship with her put even more distance between them. But Alex was a woman with an idea on how to fix problems like that. She grabbed the collar of his black jacket. "I have a feeling that you're one old warrior who's going to make it all the way to the end of the flick."

Alex tugged on his collar and pulled him down for a kiss. She held on tight and kissed him hard, kissed him deep.

In a matter of seconds, the helmet was gone, and so was the cop. The Jack that wrapped his arms around her and lifted her onto the hood of the Camaro was the lover who held her tight and took his own sweet time kissing her.

Alex was breathless and dazed and a little less afraid of giving her heart to this man when he tore his mouth from hers with a groan and rested his forehead against hers.

Smiling, he pressed a kiss to the tip of her nose. "Does this mean I get the girl?"

"You'll get her tonight," Alex promised. "Our date at the garage, remember?"

"That's work. I'm interested in play."

"Wasn't that one of your rules, Jack? Pretend that we're lovers?"

"Screw pretend. I want to screw you."

It was no *milady,* but in that deeply pitched husky voice, the honest request was more of a turn-on than anything her imagination could devise.

Alex gave him a quick kiss and then pushed him away. She jumped to the ground and retrieved his helmet, planting it in his gut and earning an "oof" and a smile. "We'll talk about that later. But first, let's see if this car has as much fire in it as the man who's driving it."

11

"YOU LET ME DOWN, BABY."

Jack pulled off his helmet, tossing it out the window before attacking the harness that strapped him into the Camaro's safety cage. The vibrations from the Outlaw class engine were still shaking through his body. He didn't need to see Alex's honey-blond head shaking back and forth over on the sidelines to know that hadn't been a good run.

His line hadn't been straight and he'd hesitated a fraction of a second too long before shifting the car from third to fourth, missing out on the maximum power boost it should have given him. If there had been a car in the opposing lane, Black Jack Riley would have been left in his competition's fumes and dust. A few things had changed since his glory days of drag racing back in high school. Namely, the driver. He was rusty.

Seeing Alex grab her toolbox from the four-wheeler and jog toward him, with those delectable bouncing Bettys leading the way, Jack grabbed on to the roof and hauled himself out of the car. He'd better stand up for what was coming. His disappointing run was bound to earn a pointed debate with the sexy ace mechanic.

He unzipped his jacket and flung it onto the Chevy's roof, feeling the cool spring breeze on his hot skin like a steadying breath. Instead of moaning about what hadn't worked, he'd better look for the positives. But the list was short as he circled the car. He grunted a laugh. At least the chute had deployed to let the air resistance help drag him to a safe stop. Alex reached the hood of his car and set down her tool box. Jack met her halfway as she pulled her earplugs out and let them dangle around her neck. "All right, Trouble, let's hear it."

He gave her points for pausing a moment to at least pretend she was thinking through her response. "People are going to laugh you off the track." She pulled her stopwatch from her pocket and showed him the time. "Yes, you shaved a half second off your first run. But at 8.1 seconds, you won't even clear the prelims to make it to the weekend races when the big crowds are here. This bad boy comeback you're trying to intimidate people with won't be very impressive if you're sitting in the stands."

Jack propped his hands at his hips and tipped his head up toward the clear blue sky. "You know, I'm all for honesty in a relationship, but if you want to shred my ego why don't you just say I'm too old to play at this game anymore."

Four fingers latched on to the waist of his pants and pulled his attention and body to the front of the car. "You'll be too old the day I'm too girly. Quit feeling sorry for yourself, Stud Man, and help me get the hood off."

"Stud Man?" Jack arched an eyebrow. "What—"

But she'd already run to the other side of the car to unscrew the hood clamps. "I'll see what I can do. If I can get the parts, I can make this thing go." Jack unfastened his side and lifted off the hood, leaning it against the car while Alex pulled out a flashlight and shimmied up onto the fender. The motor itself was probably still too hot to touch, but she was already checking wires, shining the light down into the bowels of the engine. "Yeah. I can get some more horsepower out of this baby. I'd have to add another coolant tank, but it looks like there's room to rig that up under the seat. I'll add an air spacer, too, to keep the carburetor cooler and increase the torque. Don't worry. I'll get you down under six seconds, maybe even five. If you stay on the track and drive a straight line, we could win. Or at least keep you around till Sunday."

Jack wasn't sure how long he stood there, mostly enjoying the view of her ass as she started adjusting things in the engine. Even without the fireproof jacket, he was making himself sweat imagining all the things he could do with Alex bent over a car like that. Then his eighteen years of investigative experience finally kicked in. The reminder hit him like a slap in the face. This week wasn't really about him and Alex, or even about racing. He had a prime opportunity here with no one on site except for the two of them. What was he doing just standing there? Justice for his partner—and now Alex's brother—was waiting.

"Hey, Trouble." He announced himself before he palmed her butt to warn her of his intentions, and stuck his hand inside her right pocket to pull out the ring of keys she'd used to open the gate. "Hearing you talk cars gets me about as excited as hearing you talk dirty."

"Do you want me to talk dirty to you?"

He leaned over her and kissed the blush warming her cheek. "Desperately. But I have some work I need to do first. Will you be okay here for a few minutes? I want to take a look through the supply room. Follow up on something I found earlier this week."

Alex glanced over her shoulder. "It'll be locked up."

He jangled Drew's keys. "Not for long."

She slid back to the ground, tucking a loose curl beneath her bandanna and leaving a cute little smudge next to the worried frown on her forehead. "What if someone finds you snooping around? Do you need me to be your lookout?"

"I need you to stay right here with the car and provide anyone who shows up a plausible reason for me being here. See if you can get this baby into racing shape again. I'd like to run another eighth-mile before we take her back to the garage." He pressed a quick kiss to the smudge and turned toward the viewing stands. "I'll be back in fifteen minutes."

ALEX WAVED TO JIM DIMARCO as the bald man drove his un-marked truck through the track gate—waved as though he was a long lost friend she hadn't seen in years. She waved and gestured, desperately hoping he'd drive over and talk to her. She wanted his attention right here at the drag strip with her instead of at the guest services area where Jack was still looking for evidence.

When Jim pulled up and shifted into neutral, Alex wiped her hands and strolled over for a chat. "Hey, Jimbo. Hey, Crank."

As usual, Jim's partner in the food delivery business was sitting beside him, waiting to provide the muscle to unload the supplies from the back of the truck. He glanced her way. "Miss Alex."

Jimbo, on the other hand, made up for his short stature with a friendly, good-ol'-boy charm that always made her smile. He hitched up the sleeve of his Fisk Aluminum racing team jacket and leaned out the window, nodding toward the Camaro. "So what's goin' on here, little darlin'? Did you get yourself a new toy?"

She tilted her head up to the truck cab. "It's my boyfriend's car." Though there was nothing boyish about Jack, it sounded like a reasonable response. "Pretty sweet, isn't it? I'm fixing it up for him."

"Would that be Black Jack Riley?" Jimbo seemed inclined to chat. Good. Hopefully, Jack would have heard the truck and would be locking up by now.

"You've heard of him?"

"Down at Pammy's over morning coffee with the guys. Word is he's been paying you surprise visits." Jimbo scanned the empty stands and track buildings. "Is he here?"

Keep your attention right here, buddy.

Alex walked up to Jimbo's door. Making up stuff outside her bathtub fantasies wasn't as easy as she'd hoped. She avoided his question and jumped on the first thing that came to mind. "Have you heard good things about him? I mean, what are people saying?"

Jimbo chuckled as he faced her again. "It depends on who's talking," Jimbo answered. "Pammy and the ladies were throwing out words like 'tall, rugged mystery man.'" Crank snorted.

Alex winced. Folks in Dahlia really were talking about her again. "But the men are more interested in what he's driving and what his stats are." He nodded over her head toward the car. "What's she running?"

8.1 seconds wouldn't impress anybody around here. Counting on her expertise and Jack's determination, Alex lied. "About 5.2. I'm hoping to get it down a few more tenths of a second."

Jimbo nodded. "Nice. That should give him a shot at the money. How'd you two meet?"

"Yeah." Crank was joining the conversation? The bearded man leaned forward. "Seems he showed up out of nowhere."

The question caught her off guard, changed the topic and rattled her composure. "How did we meet?"

Jimbo shrugged his shoulders. "Don't take this the wrong way, but we kind of thought you didn't like guys."

"Really?"

"The word I heard was that you didn't want to have anything to do with men, you know, in that way. I knew Hank Buell always had a thing for you, so I figured that's why you two only hooked up that one time."

Hank was still talking about that night? Figures he'd turn it around and make that humiliating virgin sacrifice for the boys her fault. "I guess I'm a one-man kind of a woman. And Hank wasn't it."

Jimbo ran his fingertips over his smooth, shaved head. "That's good to know. I mean, when Drew Fisk steered me away from asking you out, I just always figured it was because you didn't like men."

Like there was no other reason to turn away from a bastard like Hank or the disturbing innuendoes of how the men in town were still talking about her sex life. A fuse of anger lit and simmered through her veins, giving Alex the courage to move her hands to her hips and tilt her chin higher. "You can lay those rumors to rest, Jimbo. I think Jack Riley is hot. Hank Buell doesn't know the first thing about making a woman feel like a woman. But Jack does. As soon as I met him in Nashville, I knew he was the man I wanted."

Jimbo raised his hand in surrender to her vehement defense of her relationship with Jack. "Down, darlin'. I believe you. Of course, with a car that runs the eighth in five seconds, even I'd be interested. Hell, if I'd have known that a fast car was all it took to get you hot and bothered, I'd have—"

"Jimbo." Crank's stern warning put the kibosh on the conversation. "We've got a schedule to keep."

"No." Where was Jack? Alex grabbed the door of the truck as Jimbo shifted it into gear. "Can't you stay and chat?"

"Sorry, darlin'. But we're on the clock. I'm guessing you are, too." He winked. "Have fun with that Chevy."

Alex stepped aside and Jimbo drove the delivery truck over to the concrete-block buildings behind the stands. She wondered at the double entendre of his last comment, suspecting that was how a lot of the locker-room talk about her in town was going.

But gossip she could survive. She was an old pro at that. Worrying that she hadn't bought the tall, fierce warrior she was falling in love with enough time to get himself someplace safe, however, was a whole new experience.

NICE WORK, SWEETHEART.

Jack had long suspected that Alex Morgan's mouth could be a potent weapon. He was just glad she was using it for the forces of good.

He'd heard the delivery truck driving through the gate, but she'd distracted its occupants and given him plenty of time to lock the door and hide out inside the darkened men's room while the two men unloaded enough boxes of cotton candy and funnel cake mix to give a small army a sugar high. He'd have to find an appropriate way to thank Alex for giving him ten uninterrupted minutes to conduct his search. A half dozen long, leisurely ways to advance the sexual education she craved sprang to mind.

Jack waited until the truck was heading toward the main entrance before he risked leaving his hiding place. After trading a reassuring wave with Alex, he pulled out Drew Fisk's key ring. Having the keys instead of his lock-pick tools made getting in and out of the track buildings easy. Searching through all the boxes Crank and Jimbo had unloaded would be a more time-consuming task. But if even one box held the drugs he'd been looking for, then Jack had himself a case.

The grinding rumble of a diesel engine stopped Jack with his pocketknife poised over the box in his hand. What was this? Grand Central Station?

Instinctively changing his grip on the knife to a defensive position, he crept out of the storage unit and peeked through the bleachers. Instant recognition charged his pulse and sharpened his senses.

A black pickup truck and toter trailer were pulling into the speedway arena. Jack ducked behind a support post. The truck was the same make and model as the one he'd seen the other night. In the light of a clear spring day, he could read the Fisk Aluminum logo on the side of the truck. A second delivery, like Drew had said. Would this one be just as suspicious?

Today, the truck and trailer were heading straight over to the edge of the infield grass near the drag strip where Alex was draped over the fender of his Camaro again. Unless there was a car inside that trailer, the driver had no business being there. As muddy as it was, a truck that size could easily damage the grass around the asphalt staging area.

But it wasn't concern for Dahlia's newly remodeled strip that kept Jack from retreating inside to search for drugs.

It was the black-haired man who climbed out of the truck.

The hairs on the back of Jack's neck stood up in warning as the man approached Alex. He must have startled her, judging by the way she scrambled off the car. Even then, Jack knew Alex's mouth could keep a man at bay for the few minutes it would take him to find out whether there were any drugs hidden inside those boxes. For one moment, the cop in him who wanted justice for a murdered partner turned to the potential evidence just beyond his reach. A split-second later, cursing his own conscience, he pulled the door shut and locked it behind him.

There were different types of threats a man had to answer to in the world.

And right now, the one that made Alex Morgan turn pale and shrink against his car was the only one that mattered.

JACK SLOWED TO A STROLL and fixed a casual smile on his mouth as he came up behind Hank Buell. The slow-rolling drawl unmistakable.

"I have a right to be here, sugar."

"Fine. Be here. Just quit spreading lies about me and go do your job. And leave me to do mine." Alex's tone was tough enough, but there was a pinched look about her mouth that told him she was getting through this encounter on sheer guts.

Hank pulled the stub of a cigarette from between his lips and flicked it to the ground. "What job's that, sugar? Waitin' on your man?"

"I hope so." Jack announced himself, circling around the black-haired man. Oh, yeah. This ought to be fun. "Hank."

Jack draped an arm around Alex. She tensed for a moment, then leaned into him, clenching a fistful of cotton shirt at his back.

"Riley." Hank Buell's shoulders straightened and his stance widened a fraction. He was on guard. Must have felt some kind of threat from Jack.

Good.

"Is this him?" Jack didn't have to specify "the bastard who sold tickets." Alex knew what he was asking.

"Yes."

Keeping one eye on Buell, Jack tucked a couple of fingers beneath Alex's chin and tilted her mouth so he could kiss her hard, publicly claiming her in no uncertain terms. When he felt the tremor of her response softening her lips beneath his, Jack pulled back an inch, stole one more kiss, then tucked her possessively to his side.

She looked calm, but Jack could feel her hand trembling at his back. Knowing this man could make her afraid pissed Jack off.

But he knew how to hide what he was feeling, too. "Have you learned any better manners about how to treat a lady?"

"Look at you buttin' into my business again." Buell tucked his thumbs in the back pockets of his khaki work pants and laughed. "Seems you have a knack for causing trouble wherever you go, Riley. We were having a polite conversation, weren't we Al?"

His dark eyes sought out Alex's for confirmation.

"He didn't hurt me or anything." To her credit, Alex didn't shy away from Buell's gaze. "But I did ask him to leave."

"'Nuf said." Jack pointed to the cab of Hank's truck. "Goodbye."

Buell's skin flushed beneath his tan. "I am not watching my step just to please you, pal. We live in the same town, work around the same track. Alex and I are bound to run into each other. I've moved on from our past relationship."

"What you did to her had nothing to do with relationships."

"You still on about that?" Hank shifted his glare from Alex up to Jack. "We were kids then. Stupid kids. It's time she got over it and grew up."

Jack pulled his arm from Alex's shoulders and stepped forward. The need to protect her, to right the awful wrong this town had done to her, thundered in his ears so loudly that the crunch of gravel at the front entrance barely registered. "You're telling her to grow up?"

"Jack…"

He shoved Hank up against the truck. "You apologize to this lady right now, you jackass."

"Apologize?" Buell shoved Jack's arm away. He was just as mean sober as he'd been drunk. "I'm the one who got blackballed by her brother and daddy. You think I could get a job in this town when I graduated from high school? I had to call in a favor from Drew Fisk just to get the crap factory job I started with."

"Pity you didn't take the hint and move on."

"This is my town, Riley. Not yours."

"Jack, let it go." He felt a tug at his back.

He ignored it. "This woman is under my protection. You stay away from her, understand?"

Maybe if Buell hadn't grinned, maybe if he'd just kept his mouth shut, Jack would have let him walk away.

"Don't know what you see in her. I never did like used cars, myself."

With that crack, Jack grabbed Buell by the shoulder and spun him around to meet his fist. The satisfying crunch against Buell's cheek laid him flat on the ground.

"Jack, stop!"

But he was already advancing as Buell scrambled to his feet.

"Not now!" Alex latched on to his right arm with both hands, pulling him far enough off balance to give Hank the chance to land a punch to the left side of his ribcage.

Jack swore as pain bloomed in his side. He dodged a second blow and jerked free of Alex's grip. He bent low and charged forward, catching Buell in the gut with his shoulder and driving him to the ground. The two men rolled across the grass and dirt. Buell kicked. Jack punched.

The blip of a siren finally registered. Then there were hands pulling Jack off Buell. Another pair of arms helped Hank to his feet. When his opponent lunged forward, Jack squared off to meet him.

"Jack, please."

The small hand at the center of his chest calmed Jack's need to mete out punishment more quickly than the arms that bound his shoulders or the tan uniform that blocked his path to Hank. Jack nodded at the worried look on Alex's pale face, indicating he was in full control of his fists and temper now. He nodded again at Drew Fisk, the man who'd tied his shoulder up in a wrestling hold.

"I'm done," he assured them both. "I'm good."

He even retreated a step when Fisk decided it was okay to release him. Jack saw the black-and-white with the spinning lights on top now. He saw the dark gray clouds gathering in the sky to match his mood. He saw Sheriff Buell chuff his son on the shoulder and hustle him back to his truck. "You get on over there now," he ordered.

"Ow!" Hank protested. "What are ya gettin' on me for? He took the first swing."

Short on breath after dealing with the tussle, Sheriff Buell panted when he turned and advanced on Jack. "That right, Mr. Riley? You started this? I knew you were gonna be trouble."

"Back off, you tin-plated—"

"Shut up, Jack." Alex pushed him away another step, wedging herself between Jack and sheriff. She backed her shoulders into his chest, blocking him, protecting him. "Hank insulted me. Jack was defending my honor."

Hank snickered from the truck. "Honor?"

"You son of a…" Jack pulled Alex aside and surged forward.

"Stop right there, Riley."

"Look out!"

Her shove against his bruised ribs didn't stop him. Henry Buell's gun, pointed right at her head when she jumped between them again, did.

Shit. Jack picked her up and moved her aside, putting his shoulder between her and the barrel of that gun. "This is getting out of hand, Sheriff."

Drew positioned himself in front of Alex, too. "Buell. Put that damn thing away. You know your son. I'm sure Hank was out of line."

"Listen, Fisk, your granddaddy may own half the county, but he doesn't own me." Buell sucked in his gut to holster the gun, but his beady black eyes made it clear he didn't appreciate the interference. "And a young pup like you never will."

"Maybe not, but the Fisks do influence votes." Drew's tone was devoid of his usual cultured Southern charm. "And if you still want your job come November…"

"Are you threatening me? Fine. Get out of here, Hank. Go on about your business." He tipped his hat to Drew with mock deference. "Mr. Fisk here insists."

"But Dad, I have a delivery to—"

"Git! Do your job." The sheriff waited while Hank groused all the way into the cab of the truck and started the engine. Then Sheriff Buell walked up to Jack, pointing a pudgy finger a little too close to Jack's chin. "I'm issuing you a warning, Riley. You keep your hands off my boys." The point of the finger shifted over to Drew. "Or not even Fisk here will stop me from throwing your butt in jail."

It was a good thing Alex had such an tight grip on Jack's hand, or he'd be tempted to add assaulting what passed for a fellow officer in this town to his list of infractions for the day.

As it was, he shifted to lace his fingers with hers and hold on to the calming strength and emotional stability he seemed to have lost since coming to Dahlia. "I'm okay, Trouble." After the sheriff turned off his lights and sped away through the track's front gate, Jack raised Alex's hand to his lips and pressed a grateful kiss to her knuckles, ignoring the bruises and scrapes that now dotted his own. "I'm sorry I lost it, but I'm okay."

Drew straightened the sleeves and lapels of his jacket as he turned to apologize. "He's pretty sensitive where his sons are concerned. Probably because they've given him so much grief over the years."

Jack didn't want to hear excuses. "There's something he can do about that. It's called parenting."

Drew shrugged. "Too late for that, don't you think? At any rate, I wouldn't have brought him over here if I'd known what was going down between you and Hank. The sheriff was at the garage to meet up with Artie, and when he left, I hitched a ride." He held out his hand. "I need my keys. Grandfather summoned me out to the house for a family meeting. That's never a good thing. Especially with my new car in the shop. I'm sure I'll have to explain that one." Jack pulled the keys out of his pocket and dropped them into Drew's open palm, clasping his hand over them to shake the other man's hand and thank him for his help. Drew nodded, then winked at Alex. "Y'all take your time and finish up. I'll be back later to lock everything up."

Alex released Jack to wrap a hug around her friend's neck. "Thanks, Drew. For everything."

"No problem, Shrimp." He squeezed her right back, holding on until Alex pulled away. Then he walked to the door of Hank's truck and knocked to get his attention over the grind of the engine. "I'll help you unload whatever's in the back if you'll give me a ride out to Grandfather's."

As Drew walked around to climb into the passenger seat, Hank leaned out the window. His cheek was already red and puffy from Jack's fist. "I'll be beatin' your ass on the track this weekend."

Jack hugged Alex to his side. As long as Hank kept his distance from her, he was welcome to try.

ALEX TWIRLED AROUND IN the dressing room of Beverly's Closet, admiring the deep blue-green silk and ivory lace of the robe and nightgown she wore. Who knew such a pretty thing existed in her size?

Beverly Stillwell, the boutique's owner, was a successful businesswoman for a reason. Alex had ventured into the alien territory of ladies' shops off the courthouse square of downtown Dahlia in order to find a tailor who could sew a couple of *Morgan*

& Son's Garage logos onto Jack's insulated racing jacket. But the stylish older woman with the platinum hair and bejeweled wrists and fingers had seen the way Alex was drawn to the rainbow of colors in her lingerie display. Pale blues and sunny yellows. Rich reds and a sleek steel-gray that reminded her of how Jack's eyes darkened when a need or emotion that was too powerful to control got hold of him.

Despite Alex's protests that none of the beautiful skimpy things would fit her short and busty dimensions, Mrs. Stillwell had tutted her into silence, taken a few quick measurements, and brought her a tray full of beautiful things to try on. And there wasn't one plain white cotton and elastic over-the-shoulder-boulder-holder in the bunch.

Sure, this particular gown had a wider strap than the one displayed on the mannequin out front, and an underwire helped support and contain the twin curses. But it was a damn sight more feminine than her father's plaid robe.

Alex smoothed her hands along the silk at her hips, wondering if Jack would even recognize her in something this feminine. She almost looked like the princess of her fantasies. The deep color flattered her pale skin. The lace tickled her nipples, making her feel unexpectedly sexy. All she needed was a tall man in black—her warrior knight—standing behind her in the mirror for the fantasy to be complete.

"Come on out here and let me see you," Mrs. Stillwell urged.

After one more twirl, Alex obliged. The shop owner's approving nod triggered an unexpectedly confident smile. "It looks good, doesn't it, Mrs. Stillwell?"

"Sugar, you call me Miz Beverly, like everyone else does. 'Mrs. Stillwell' reminds me of my mother-in-law." She winked. "Bless her heart, I never did like her and she couldn't stand me."

Alex snorted a laugh through her nose. She quickly covered her mouth, finding nothing feminine or princesslike about the horrible noise she made when something amused her. "Sorry."

She imagined the embarrassment that bubbled up had stained her cheeks as rosy a pink as the silk blouse Miz Beverly wore.

But Beverly Stillwell was the class of Dahlia's grande dames, and her smile never wavered. "I knew that color would be wonderful on you. You don't need this, though." She pulled the bandanna from Alex's hair and encouraged her to shake out the strands that were curling with the rain and humidity. "Lovely. Looks as though it might need a bit of a hem—unless you have some heels to wear with it."

"I don't have any high heels." Not since the silver mistakes she'd trashed in Nashville.

"Hemming it is, then. I can send it to Mrs. Spooner along with the jacket if you like."

Alex was tempted, but asked, "Where would I wear something like this?"

Miz Beverly laughed. "Well, now, that part's up to you. But a man almost always likes to see something pretty on his girl." She dropped her voice to a whisper, and Alex leaned in, absorbing every word of advice. "Though, to tell you the truth, they generally prefer to see you naked. But I think he'll appreciate a woman who makes an effort to wear something like this for him. And he'd certainly be proud to see just how beautiful the woman he loves can be."

Alex pulled back, her smile fading. The woman he loves? Lusty impulses aside, there was no way the big-city cop with the emotional baggage was ever going to love a country tomboy car geek like her. Especially when Jack seemed so hung up on the age difference between them. His maturity was a part of what attracted her to him, but it was by no means the only thing.

Broad shoulders, strong arms and gorgeous eyes didn't hurt. And those kisses—in every way she could imagine, he'd taken her mouth in a kiss. Savagely. Gently. In laughter. In tears. He'd kissed her to keep her quiet and because he just couldn't resist. And, she imagined there were even more ways he could seduce her mouth.

How could all of those kisses possibly be an act?

The turmoil inside must have reflected on her face because she felt the older woman's hand gently squeezing her shoulder. "Alexandra?"

The bell over the shop's front door jingled, saving Alex from having to analyze or explain what she was feeling.

"Miz Beverly?" A familiar man's voice hit her like a punch to the stomach, robbing Alex of the confidence and hope that her time with Beverly Stillwell had given her. Sheriff Buell. Alex snatched back her bandanna and turned toward the dressing room.

But he moved surprisingly fast, despite his rotund belly. He suddenly appeared in the doorway to the dressing rooms. "Ma'am." Though he tipped his plastic-wrapped hat to Beverly, his gaze had settled on Alex. More specifically, on Alex's breasts. "My God, Alex Morgan in a nightdress. What are you doin' in here, girl?"

She instinctively hugged her arms in front of her, feeling his damning scrutiny as much as she had back at the track. "I had business. I needed a tailor."

His gaze finally wandered back up to her eyes. "Riley's a lucky man."

"Now, Henry," Beverly pushed against the sheriff's chest and turned him around, "you're going to scare off my best customer of the day. Everyone else must be staying home because of the rain." She scooted him out to the main floor. "You come and tell me your business at the counter."

Appreciating the escape, Alex ducked into the dressing room and threw on her clothes. With one last regretful stroke across the silk, she left the nightgown on the tray with the bras and panties. She grabbed her jacket and hurried on out, barely slowing as she interrupted what sounded like a man and a woman changing plans. "Thank you for everything, Miz Beverly." *From making me feel welcome and feminine right down to your advice about men.* "I have to get back to work. Dad needs me at the garage today and I've already taken too long a break."

Beverly came around the counter, her expression baffled as she tried and failed to catch her. "Is there anything—?"

"Will Mrs. Spooner be able to finish the jacket by the qualifying prelims tomorrow night?" Alex paused after opening the door, hoping the kind, intuitive woman could read the apology in her eyes. "Please tell her I'll pay extra for a rush job like this."

Beverly nodded. "I'll call you when it's ready."

"Thank you, ma'am."

If Alex had spared a glance for the sheriff, she might have seen him excusing himself and catching the door before it closed behind her.

"Hold it right there." His meaty fingers closed around her arm, stopping her. Alex swung around, but the badge on his chest kept her fist at her side. The forecaster's prediction of another evening of rain had been accurate. The cold drops hit her face as she tilted her chin to meet the warning in Buell's dark eyes. "You tell your man Riley that if he comes after either of my boys again, not even Drew Fisk is going to be able to talk me out of pressing charges against him."

Alex twisted her arm from his grasp. "My *man* doesn't start the fights he's gotten into with your boys. He just finishes them."

The sheriff dipped his head, spilling water off the brim of his hat onto Alex's shoulder. She twisted away as if the cool water had singed her. "Don't you get sassy with me, girl. I'm the law in this town."

"Henry Buell." Beverly Stillwell had come out beneath her awning, her tone as protective a rebuke as Alex imagined any mother might give. "You let that girl go. She has a job to get back to."

He touched the brim of his hat, his expression a friendly good-ol'-boy smile now. "Don't rush off on my account. But if you are headin' back to your daddy's, you tell Artie I need to speak to him, all right? He must have turned off his phone."

So why didn't he just call the garage? They'd still be open for another half hour. But she wanted this conversation to be done. "I'll tell him."

Leaving Buell and his warnings and her hopeless dreams behind, Alex booked it back to her car. She'd unlocked the door and tossed her bandanna across the seat before she saw the brown envelope tucked beneath her windshield wiper.

Alex reached between the car's frame and door and pulled the soggy paper free. The rain soaked through her hair and trickled down her scalp as she looked all around the square for some sign of who had placed it there. Though only a few cars were still parked along the sidewalks, it seemed that she was alone on the street. And yet…

Feeling more spooked than she cared to admit, Alex climbed inside her car and locked the doors. She wiped the rain from her face and tucked her hair behind her ears before opening the envelope.

She pulled out the contents. "Oh, God."

The rain had made spots on the old instant photograph's finish. But the image was clear. It was from that night. She looked so young and helpless, her arms uselessly trying to hide her naked body, her eyes red and swollen with tears. Hank Buell, belting up his pants, and another boy, little more than a blur of blond hair, were fuzzy images laughing in the background.

Anger surged through her, blotting out shame and fear. She was about to crush the image in her fist when she saw the message, typed on a sticker and glued to the back of the photo.

It'll be worse than this if you don't send your boyfriend back where he came from.

"You son of a bitch." Tossing aside the crude picture, she pulled out her phone and dialed Jack's number.

"Riley," he answered on the second ring.

"Jack?" Damn. She hated when her breath caught like that. It revealed far more than she ever intended.

"Trouble? What's wrong?" She heard a stern man's voice in the background, warning Jack back to some meeting. Jack ignored him. "Is it Buell again?"

"Which one?" But sarcasm didn't help. The anger seeped out of her, leaving her helpless. "I got another message. On my car. With a picture this time."

"Shit. I'm still in Nashville at Rutledge's office, arranging for backup at the track this weekend."

"Oh." That explained the voices in the background. Jack had said he was taking in some evidence he'd found and reporting to his task force team leader. "Okay." She nodded, discarding the belief that she just might be more important than the job he had to do. "I'll deal with it."

"Don't you dare hang up on me. What did it say?"

She didn't need to see the photo again to recall the threat. "It says I should get rid of you. Or…" *Just say it.* "Or they'll hurt me worse than they did that night in high school."

Alex had heard Jack cuss up a blue streak and talk his way in and out of whatever lie he needed to maintain his cover. She'd been soothed and seduced by the deep timbre of his voice and had heard him cry out his physical satisfaction against her naked skin. But she'd never heard him this quiet. Not for this long.

The silence worried her. She finally understood the "talk to me" rule. "Jack?"

And then she heard a rush of sound. The screech of a chair, voices protesting his hasty departure, a door opening. "We'll finish this later," he said to the men in the room with him. "You get anything on the DNA or car parts I brought in, you call me." Then he was back on the phone with her. "Trouble? You still there?"

"I'm here."

"Are you anywhere near a fax machine?"

"Dad has one at work."

"Is he still there?"

"Yeah."

"Good. I want you to send me a copy of that note and anything else that came with it." She wrote down the number he gave her. "You go to the garage and stay with George until I can get there."

"But I don't want my dad in any danger—"

"*He* won't want you in any danger, either." A door slammed. "Fax me the note. As soon as I get it into forensics, I'm leaving. You don't have to tell George anything. Just stay with him until I get there. Okay?"

Alex nodded. "I'll see you at the garage."

12

ALEX GRITTED HER TEETH and pushed with all her strength against a stubborn nut that wouldn't turn. Jack's rebuilt motor had been going together nicely with her design modifications and a few purchases from the local parts store. Until now.

Because of shipping delays, she'd been forced to cannibalize a couple of key components from an old GM motor of her dad's. But even with some reshaping on the sander, the spacing was off, and the bolt refused to tighten. With the motor secured on a chain and steel sawhorses, she should have been able to get the leverage she needed. But the stubborn thing just…wouldn't… turn.

The wrench bit cracked, slipped.

"Ow!" Her knuckles scraped across the iron block and the tension of the day blew up in her face. "Stupid, stupid, stupid!"

She slung the broken wrench into her tool box, thinking the crumpled up photo and vile message made a better target for her wrath. Where the hell was Jack? He'd promised he was on his way an hour ago. She'd locked up the garage and had kept her hands busy out in the shop while her father finished up some paperwork in his office. She hadn't told him about Jack or the message yet. And she was hoping she wouldn't have to say anything to worry him until she had the proof in her hands to show him who was responsible for Nick's death.

She'd wanted Jack to tell her the threat meant nothing, that she should throw the photo away and pretend the jerk-ass Buells couldn't harm her or make her feel afraid the way she'd pretended for nine long years. But she *was* afraid. Afraid of Jack's long, cold silence. Afraid that calling him back to Dahlia would put him in danger. Afraid that locked doors, her father and the marine-issue pistol he kept in his office weren't enough to stop the dangerous men who'd already killed her brother and Jack's partner in order to keep their secrets.

Being afraid was getting mighty damn old.

Alex picked up the wrench and pulled off the broken socket head. She didn't know if she was pining away for a man who was only hers for the duration of their undercover charade, or if the fear she felt for Jack's safety meant their relationship had never been a charade for her at all.

She hurled the broken socket across the concrete floor. "Stupid, stupid, stupid!"

Her heart nearly stopped as a familiar friend materialized from the shadows where she'd cast the offending part. "I'll hold it down for you if you want to kick it a couple of times." Tater raked his fingers through his shaggy blond hair, grinning from ear to ear.

Once she could breathe again, Alex answered. "Go on, let it out."

By the time Tater had had his laugh and retrieved the broken piece for her, Alex was smiling, too. "What are you doing, all spiffed up in clean jeans and a dress shirt? Got a hot date?"

"I might."

"With Sandy Larabie?"

Tater winked. "I might."

Good. Alex was pleased to see a guy she liked as well as Tater find someone special. "You two have a good time."

"No Jack yet, eh?" he teased, misinterpreting the cause for her mood. He thumbed over his shoulder to the empty bays in the garage behind him. "Looks like your dad has another couple hours of payroll work ahead of him. You want me to wait until Artie or someone else gets back to keep you company? He's over at the track setting up the Fisk team's trailer and tent for the races tomorrow."

Artie keep her company? No thanks. Alone was definitely preferable to one-on-one time with him. "Nah. Like you said, Dad's here. You go on. Don't keep Sandy waiting."

"You're sure there's nothin' else I can do to help?"

Alex held up her broken wrench. "Not unless you've got a rachet bit I can borrow."

"Help yourself to my tool chest. And if you can't find what you need in there, check Artie's locker downstairs. He's been braggin' about that European alloy set he bought with his winnings from the Moonshine Run. To hear him tell it, if he doesn't have the tool you need, then it doesn't exist."

"I'll keep that in mind. Thanks, Tater." She locked the main door behind him and sent him on his way with a wave.

Short of pestering Jack with another phone call or raising her dad's suspicions by hanging out with him in his office, Alex had nothing to do but continue her work. Besides, if she wanted to get Jack's Camaro in shape for the races tomorrow, she didn't have time to sit around and worry about Jack's safety—or her own.

A quick scan of Tater's tool chest revealed it was as neat and tidy as his hair was a rumpled mess. So it was easy to see that he didn't have the odd-sized part she was looking for.

With a sigh of resignation, Alex walked to the lube pit and turned on all the lights. She peered over the steel railing, working up her nerve to climb down the ladder attached to the wall. As much as she loved working on motors, she hated going down into the concrete vault where Artie drained the oil and worked beneath cars. Sounds always seemed muffled down there, and the lights, especially after dark like now, never seemed bright enough to illuminate the deepest corners. The mice and spiders she knew scurried around down there didn't help. And years ago, before she'd been old enough to work at the garage, a man had fallen into the pit and died. Maybe it was a little girl's imagination about ghosts that made the pit such an uncomfortable place, or maybe it was the very real scents of stale cigarettes and Artie Buell that made the pit so loathsome.

However, the lure of Artie's state-of-the-art ratchet set meant she was climbing down that ladder. The Moonshine Run trophy displayed for all to see easily identified Artie's locker. Since he was the only one to work down here, nothing was terribly neat. Though she felt a little awkward about getting into Artie's things, she rationalized opening his locker by remembering that she and the other mechanics often shared and traded tools as needed. Besides, Tater had given her permission.

By the time she'd jimmied the handle open and pushed aside an illicit whiskey bottle to reach the metal box that housed his swanky European ratchet set, Alex wondered if sorting through the mess inside was worth the trouble. When she pulled the box forward on the eye-level shelf, two cigarette cartons came with it. She caught the cartons in her arms, along with the Fisk Racing cap that had hooked on the box and was dragging the contents of the entire shelf out with it.

"Good grief," she fussed, juggling everything to keep it from hitting the floor. Sneaking booze into the workplace against her father's rules was bad enough—she'd have to report him for that. But Alex's distaste for the man and his habits grew with the discovery of something much more sinister. A dozen tiny plastic bags spilled out with the rest of the junk. "What's this?"

After stuffing everything back onto the shelf as haphazardly as she'd found it, Alex carried the bags to Artie's work table and turned on a work light to study the tiny crystals sealed inside. She had no firsthand experience, but she'd taken enough health education classes through school to suspect that she was looking at crack or crystallized heroin, bagged and ready for sale on the streets. Stretching up on tiptoe, she counted the loose bags on the shelf. A search through the rest of his things uncovered three larger bundles, wrapped in enough plastic to mask the contents inside—or protect them from bursting open within the hidden compartment of a modified race car.

She didn't know whether to feel victorious or scared spitless.

Was this what Jack's fast-paced life was always like? Walking that fine line between acceptable risk and certain danger? It was like being behind the wheel of a powerful engine, gunning it at the starting line. Sometimes, you won the big prize. Sometimes, you crashed and burned. What a rush. What a scary, satisfying, she'd-better-call-someone-who-knew-what-he-was-doing rush.

Alex pulled out her phone again and called him. "Jack?" Damn. Voice mail. He was either on the road or back in his meeting. Alex left a brief message. "I found them. I found the drugs. In Artie Buell's locker. Call me when you can so I know what to do. I…I really wish you were here."

How did a himbo like Artie come up with the brains to organize a drug smuggling operation? Of course, hiding the goods in an unlocked locker wasn't the smartest move a criminal could make. That kind of arrogance and stupidity sounded more like the Artie she knew. But he'd certainly have the means and opportunity Jack had mentioned to alter the race cars and stash the drugs inside. As long as someone told him what to do, he'd be a good worker bee. And Alex had a short list of suspects to share with Jack as to who might be giving the orders.

Tucking the bags deep into her pockets, Alex closed the locker door so quietly that even the mice couldn't hear it. Just in time. The jangle of keys from the garage above her warned to run for the ladder before the footsteps she heard reached her. Too late.

"Well, isn't this a surprise?" Alex looked up beyond the rungs of the ladder to see Artie standing at the top. Grinning. Leering. Had he seen anything? He pocketed the keys that had gotten him inside the locked garage. "What are you doing down there, sugar?"

Don't panic. He hasn't caught you at anything. Yet. Act the part you're supposed to play. She had to clear her throat before the words would come. "I needed to borrow one of your tools. Tater said you had a new socket set."

"'Zat so." She backed away as he turned and gripped the sides of the ladder with his hands and feet, sliding straight down, blocking her escape. She jammed her hands into her pockets to mask the bulk of the drugs she'd confiscated, but Artie didn't seem to notice, his eyes lingering on her chest as he strolled toward her. "You ever want something from me, all you have to do is ask."

About the time the stench of his coveralls reached her, Alex's brain and her bravado finally kicked in. "What are you doing here? I thought you were at the track, setting up Drew's pit area for tomorrow."

"I was." Alex retreated when he kept advancing, kept smiling, as though finding her in his work space was the sweetest surprise of his night. "But I finished. It's still muddy at the track, so me and the boys thought we'd come back here and do a little partying."

Me and the boys?

Alex jerked her chin to find they had an audience. The overhead lights reflected off Jimbo DiMarco's shiny shaved head. He grinned. "Evening, Alex."

"Hey, Jimbo." He was wearing his Fisk Racing jacket. So was the bearded hulk standing at the railing beside him. As usual, Crank had little to say. He didn't even respond to her acknowledging nod. Drew Fisk's crew for the races, they had every logical—legal—reason to be here. But they were one man short. Alex prayed the fourth member of their team wasn't with them.

"Hey, sugar."

So much for praying. She turned toward the voice. "Hank."

The elder Buell brother braced his hands against the railing and looked down at her. Looked inside her. Licked his bruised and swollen lip and smiled. A remembered dread spread like ants crawling across her skin. She was surrounded. Just like that night. The setting was different. She wore clothes four layers deep. But the feeling was the same. All eyes were on her. She felt exposed, outnumbered, afraid.

Alex's breath caught in her chest, grew shallow. Every muscle in her tensed with the urge to bolt. But backed against Artie's work table, with her path to the ladder blocked and three men waiting like vultures at the railing above her, where did she think she could run?

"Well?" Artie prompted, sliding a toothpick from one side of his mouth to the other. If the smell of his breath was any indication, the party had already started. "Tell me what you need."

Why hadn't she heard them sooner? Had she been too focused on breaking a lead on Jack's case? Were they sneaking in so her father wouldn't know they were here after hours with alcohol on the premises? Were they here for the drugs?

What was she doing, just standing here, trembling as though the past was repeating itself? She was a smart, college-educated woman who'd returned to Dahlia because her father needed her. She wasn't the girl Hank had terrorized nine years ago. She wasn't even the same inexperienced woman who'd left seven months earlier to find a man who could see her as more than a mechanic or pair of boobs. This was no role she was playing. She was Jack Riley's woman. Down in her heart, she was beginning to understand that loving a man—loving the right man—made her strong. These jackasses better start realizing that she wasn't an easy victim anymore.

"I'm here to work, Artie. Not play." She shoved him back a step and pulled out the broken socket piece. She studiously kept her gaze from lighting anywhere near Artie's locker and asked, "Do you have one of these? It's an odd size I need for a custom job."

"You're in luck, sweet thing." Artie grabbed the bit along with her hand and pulled her with him to his locker.

She held her breath as he pounded the lock with his fist and swung open the door. What if he saw something out of place? What if he suspected she'd already sorted through the contents inside?

"Artie." Hank chided his younger brother from above. "Leave it." Did Hank know what was in that locker, as well? Now there was a man she could believe had the will and know-how to organize an operation like this. He shifted his dark eyes to Alex. "You get on up here, girl."

"I don't answer to you, Hank."

"Pretty bold words for a little lady all by herself. Where's that badass boyfriend of yours?"

Jimbo circled the railing to thump Hank on the arm. "What are you doin', Hank? I thought we were here to get the car."

"I'm having a conversation with the lady, so you back off." His eyes hadn't gotten any friendlier when they returned to her. "Come on up here and talk to me, Al. I'm not gonna hurt you."

Right. And all this rain wasn't going to make the track slick. Her heart didn't know whether to race or stop cold.

Artie nudged her toward the ladder. "You better git."

Resisting the urge to adjust the extra lumps in her clothes, Alex grabbed the first metal rung and climbed upward. She got the crazy notion in her head that if she delayed long enough, Jack would come storming to her rescue. Not that she wanted to think she was in any real danger from Hank with the other men around, but then, she hadn't suspected she was in any danger that night in the tenth grade, either.

But she didn't even get the chance to dream. Artie's palm was on her bottom, pushing her to climb faster. "Move it."

"Keep your paws to yourself." She smacked his hand away and hurried up, stepping between Jimbo and Hank on the garage deck, finding herself boxed into a triangle when Artie scrambled out behind her. With no place to go and no chance to shove all three men out of her way, Alex turned to the one weapon she had left in her arsenal. She tilted her chin to the most dangerous of the three. "Get out of my way, Hank. I have work to do."

"Now, now, sugar." His once-handsome smile, now bruised by Jack's fist and tarnished by her own memories, was as menacing as the hand that cupped the side of her neck and pulled her closer. "All work and no play for all these years?" She twisted out of his grasp, but that only made him reach for her with both hands, holding her face still as he moved closer. "Here I thought you'd sworn off sex. If I'd known you were lookin' to get some more experience, I'd have helped you out." His eyes hooded in some drowsy representation of passion. "You didn't have to go all the way to Nashville to find a man."

Alex seethed beneath his touch. "I don't see one here."

Hank's fingers tightened like vises against her jaw and scalp. He brushed his lips across hers in a mockery of a kiss. "You aren't woman enough to know what a real man is."

"You bastard." Alex squirmed. His grip tightened painfully and she clawed at his hands to free herself. "Damn it, Hank."

Jimbo closed in behind her and she jerked, knowing a moment of terror. "Hey, pal, I didn't sign on for this."

"Nobody's askin' you to stay." Hank released her face to wrap his arms around her. "You owe me an apology for what your boy-friend did to me."

Alex shoved at Hank's chest before he got too close. Why didn't anyone do something to help? "Jack will be here. We have a date." She punched his mouth with her fist, aiming straight for the imprint Jack had left behind. "Let go!"

"You bitch." Hank grabbed her arm and twisted it behind her. She cursed the sharp pain that shot through her shoulder and Hank laughed, rubbing his body shamelessly against hers. The blood from the cracked lip she'd reopened dripped onto her shirt. "Jimbo, didn't you tell me you saw Riley headin' down the highway out of town?"

"A couple hours ago."

These men were watching Jack? Taking note of when and where he went? Alex tried to get her footing, tried to kick. She had to find him, had to warn him. Had to get Hank off her before he discovered the bags she'd stolen.

"He's coming back," she insisted.

Hank leaned in. His hot breath whispered against her ear. "He's gonna be late."

She raised her knee, fighting in earnest. "What did you do? Get your hands off me." With every kick, every protest, Hank's grip tightened. His black eyes turned cold and mean.

Artie was laughing now. He had his phone out. Oh, God. Was he taking a picture? Texting the image to someone? "She's a handful, big brother. Need some help?"

But Hank lifted her off the floor and reached into the pocket of his jeans. "Get out of here." He tossed a ring of keys to Artie even as he shoved her up against Tyler's tool chest and knocked a couple of drawers open. She was in trouble. "Take Drew's car. Open her up and get her ready for tomorrow."

Crank uttered a foul word and pulled Jimbo and Artie away. "Let's get out of here."

"No!" Hank squeezed her breast and Alex screamed. "Don't leave me with him!"

"Hey, man. Shouldn't we—?"

"Get out of here," Hank ordered. "And you?" He slid his tongue against her neck and groped her again. "You need to stop fightin' me. How many layers of clothes you wearin', girl?"

The packages inside her pockets shifted, squeezed upward. Oh, no. No, no. He couldn't find the drugs on her. "Get off me!"

A gunshot rang out through the garage, pinging off metal and thunking off concrete and plunging the entire building into a taut, dangerous silence.

Hank released her and Alex's feet sank to the floor as her father reached around him and pulled her to his side. "What the hell is going on out here?" George Morgan looked more elite force than motor pool as he leveled his service pistol at Hank. Alex held on tight to the back of his shirt, trying hard to breathe, trying harder not to curse or cry. "Keep your hands off my daughter," he barked, "and get the hell out of my garage."

Holding his hands up in surrender, Hank tried to reason with a father guarding his daughter's life. "Now, George—"

"Now, nothing. Get out." George used the barrel of the gun

to back Hank up beside his brother. "And you. Pack your stuff and go with him. You're fired."

Artie's mouth dropped open. "What? Why?"

"Because you're a son of a bitch, Buell, and I'm tired of making nice while you refuse to grow up or even say you're sorry for what your family did to my girl."

"You don't think I've been payin' for that night—"

"Did I hear a gunshot?" The outside door opened and Drew Fisk came charging in. Alex finally took a normal breath as the odds against her and her father changed. Drew slowed to a stop beside Hank and Artie, eyeing each one with first concern and then disdain. "What the hell is going on?"

George hugged Alex to his side. But the gun never wavered. "There's been a change of plan, son. If you're going to have the Buells working for you, then you're going to have to store your car somewhere else."

Drew's wide, stunned eyes swept over Alex. Her arm and jaw ached. She probably had marks on her. "Hank, did you—"

"Shut up. We can take him."

"He has a gun, you idiot." There was more ruthless business mogul than playboy best friend in the look Drew gave Hank. "George Morgan is a reputable businessman in Dahlia, a man to respect. Until you outgrow your vindictive need to own this town and the people in it, you'll never know what that feels like."

For a moment, Hank glared right back, exchanging a silent message that Alex couldn't understand. When Hank dropped his gaze, then turned to look straight at her, she pressed her hand to her chest, hiding both the drug package and the fear he burned into her heart. "I guess you'll never know the real truth about the good men of this town, either."

"What?" Alex frowned. What kind of spiteful remark was that?

It didn't matter. Drew was already herding Hank and his buddies toward the unlocked door where they'd come in. He pushed a button to open the garage door in front of his Mustang.

"I'll grab what's mine out of my locker," said Artie in a voice that was far too agreeable to be trusted.

Wait! How did she stop Artie from moving the rest of the drugs without endangering herself or Drew or her father? How did she get Jack or anyone else here in time to arrest him? It was pretty obvious that calling the sheriff wouldn't be an option.

Perhaps sensing her need to end this nightmare, George pointed his gun at Artie and shooed him toward the others. "Just get out. You can come back in the morning for your tools."

"Okay, old man." Artie held his hands up in surrender. "Just don't shoot that thing."

Alex watched from behind her father's strong, protective shoulder as Artie, Jimbo and Crank loaded the car onto Hank's toter trailer to drive it over to the track. She hugged her arms around herself and shivered. She felt dirty and helpless and frustrated that these men were going to get away with hurting her and her family all over again.

She wanted Jack. Needed him desperately. And not because he was a cop.

"He'll be late."

Had Hank done something to Jack? Had the four of them ganged up on him? Had they tampered with Jack's truck or run him off the road?

Maybe her father understood her a little better than she gave him credit for. Maybe he could even read her spinning thoughts. Letting Drew take over watching the Buells and their buddies leave the garage, George Morgan hugged her close and pressed a kiss to her temple. "Call him, honey. Tell Jack I'm taking you home."

ALEX WAS NECK DEEP IN A hot sudsy bath, soaking the aches of her body and washing the feel of Hank Buell off her skin, when she heard the door knob turn.

She recognized Jack by scent alone. "You're late."

The dampness of the night outside clung to his jacket as he

shrugged out of it and set both his holster and badge on the vanity across from the tub. "I like not having to break in to come see you. Your father had his chat with me and went upstairs." Jack untied his boots and tossed them in a corner. Then he was kneeling down beside the tub—like the knight of her fantasies, only stronger, tougher, sexier. Real. His fingers trembled as he touched each bruise dotting her jaw and neck. A tight muscle beside his mouth flinched. He brushed a wet curl off her cheek and leaned over to press the gentlest of kisses there. "He said if I wanted to stay the night it was my choice. I say it's yours."

Alex laid her soapy fingers over his stubbled cheek and soothed the tension stamped there. "Stay, Jack. Please? I'll be through here in just a minute."

When she fished her washcloth from the water to resume her bath, he plucked the soft terry from her fingers and took over the duties for her. "George said you just got in here."

"You'll get your clothes wet."

"Yeah?" He squeezed out the excess water and tenderly wiped it over the line of bruises left by another man's hand. Alex closed her eyes beneath his gentle ministrations, feeling every stroke along her shoulders and arms, down her legs and between her toes. Once he started, he never broke contact with her body, not once. His touch was soothing but sure. He eased away the hurts and left something much more pleasurable in his wake. "Sit up."

He broke the seductive spell only long enough to catch Alex around the waist to give her something to lean against as he reached behind her to wash her back all the way down to her bottom. "I told George everything," he confessed in a soft rumble against her hair. His hand moved the cloth over her hips now, seeking out places much more private to bathe. "That I'm a cop. What I'm investigating. How I got you involved. Facing a father with a gun in his lap isn't the easiest thing. I hope I never have daughters."

Alex hugged the strong arm that crossed between her breasts and blinked her eyes open. "Did you tell him about Nick?"

"That I suspect he was murdered?" Alex hugged him tighter. She was beginning to see that there was much more to being treated like a lady than simply holding coats and opening doors. A gentleman protected a lady. Listened to her. Made her feel like she was worth the effort of being with her. Jack had done all those things and more. "Is he mad at me for not telling him?"

"No, sweetheart. He's proud of you. He's in this fight with us. Something about not losing another child to the secrets of this town." Stroke. Caress. Alex's eyes drifted shut again. "I did get the paternal lecture about not keeping my eye on you 24/7, though. He said that's always been a challenge for him, too."

Alex smiled against the wet sleeve of his shirt. "Are you saying I'm a handful?"

"Oh, yeah. But I like a challenge." He eased her back against the pillow and paused to peel off his soggy T-shirt and toss it after his boots. Then his hand and the cloth were back beneath the water, sliding along the inside of her leg. Alex gasped at the deliberate boldness of his touch, coming so close to her most intimate self, then pulling away, leaving a tightening knot of need hungry for the pressure of his hand at the juncture of her thighs. "Easy, Trouble." He must have felt her flinch. "Just try to relax."

Alex closed her eyes again and tried to do just that. Only Jack's hands sliding over her legs and belly and up beneath her breasts, creating a soft friction even warmer than the bath water, made it difficult to do much more than remember to breathe.

"You were right, Detective Trouble." She tried to concentrate on his soothing voice, though the seductive tones were sinking deep inside her, waking other things beyond her sensitized skin. "I don't condone you taking the risk you did, but the crystallized heroin you took from Artie's locker matches the product Eric was buying from the distributor in Nashville, right down to the make of the plastic bags. I took a detour up by the track to make sure the Buells and their buds were all accounted for, and then I went back through the garage. As I suspected, Artie's locker had been cleaned out and there was no trace of any drugs." His hand was moving gently over the swell of her breasts now. "I'd love to have a drug dog go over Fisk's car that Artie was working on to see if he can hit on where the drugs were moved to. I asked Rutledge to secure a warrant for that."

Alex could barely speak when he swirled the washcloth around the tip of her breast. "You did…all that in the two hours you were gone?"

He moved on to the other breast. "I also got the preliminary report on the cigarette butts I found. The DNA doesn't match up to either of the Buell boys."

Her eyes snapped open. Despite the temperature of the water and the heat generated by Jack's hands, Alex felt chilled. "You mean someone else is watching me? Leaving those messages?"

Jack's eyes were dark and bleak. "You told me Artie wasn't smart enough to run an operation like this. And in my book, Hank's too hotheaded to be in charge. Can you remember anyone else who was there that night? Maybe the blond bastard in the background of that photo?"

There'd been plenty of boys, with every hair color, that night. Alex drew her knees up to her chest and tried to hug the delicious warmth back into her body. "I didn't see Drew until he came later with Nick. Tater's blond. But I don't remember seeing him there. Of course, they didn't have to be there to see the pictures or hear the gossip."

He reached around her to wrap her folded-up body into a hug, lifting her partway up out of the water. "It's okay, sweetheart. We don't have to figure it all out right—" He swore under his breath and pulled back. His splayed fingers hovered above the five bruises on her left breast, bruises that perfectly matched the span of a man's rough hand, bruises left by Hank's vile touch.

For a moment, shame twisted in Alex's stomach. Jack touched

his fingers so lightly to the deep purple and red marks that goose bumps popped up across her skin. Alex looked up and the shame went away. Something strong, needy, more compassionate, flowed into her veins as Jack's eyes narrowed. *Now* he was going to cry? "Jack…"

"I'm sorry I couldn't get to you sooner." He stroked each wound with shaky fingers.

"Shh." She reached over to cup the clenched line of his jaw.

"How can I make it up to you?"

"I'm just glad you're here with me now."

"Don't argue with me on this one. What can I do to make things right?"

She didn't have to think for long. She was transforming into a woman who understood what they both needed. "Be my knight in shining armor. Help me forget what it feels like to be used. It's always good with you, Jack. I'm never afraid when I'm with you."

"Then I'm not going anywhere."

In a feat of strength and determination that made her feel as feminine and cherished as any fairy-tale princess, Jack scooped her up out of the water and carried her down the hallway to her bed. After putting his gun and a condom on the bedside table, he stripped down naked and crawled beneath the covers to gather her up in his arms.

He took his time, kissing her deeply, thoroughly, completely. On her mouth, her breasts, the aching mound between her legs. His hands wandered where they would, gentle one moment, more urgent the next—retracing every inch of her that he'd washed earlier, replacing the memory of any other man's touch with the brand of his own. By the time her skin had cooled from the bath, the delicious weight of his body was covering hers, sliding inside her, setting her on fire from the inside out.

Stretching her body taut, he guided her hands up to hold on to one of the wrought-iron curlicues of her headboard. He withdrew, then entered her again, teasing her a little more deeply with each slow, delicious foray and retreat. Anything softer than iron would have bent in her hands, she wanted him so badly. He pulled out one last time, tormenting her when she was so ready for all of him. "Jack," she whispered, writhing beneath him, wanting.

And then they found a rhythm that taught her there was still more pleasure to be had. Everything inside her was building, reaching, needing, loving.

"Now," was all he said.

He slid his thumb down between them, pressing the switch that made her come unglued as he emptied himself inside her.

Jack swallowed up her blissful cry with a kiss.

13

"WHERE THE HELL IS ALEX?" Jack shouted the question above the roaring engines of the two cars gunning their motors at the starting line. The telltale beeps and flash of red, yellow and green lights indicated a heat was about to start. "She should have been back by now. The stores don't stay open past five on a Friday night here in Dahlia."

Daniel Rutledge stopped snapping pictures of the suspects they were surveilling and pulled off his ball cap with the press card ID pinned to it. He combed his fingers through his short blond hair, using the offhand movement to glance around at the other teams prepping cars and lining up in the staging lanes. "I told my man to stay with her. You want me to give him a call?"

"Yes!" Jack pulled out his own phone, checking to see if he'd missed a call from her, explaining why her trip into town was taking more than an hour. He wasn't worried about the Camaro's motor or where he placed in the rankings or the surprise gift Alex had been so excited to go pick up from a shop called Beverly's Closet. He was worried that neither her father nor the undercover agent Rutledge had assigned to her could stay ahead of the trouble that woman seemed to get herself into.

No message. "Anything?" he asked Rutledge.

Daniel pocketed his phone. "My man's still parked in front of the shop. Says she hasn't come out yet."

"Send him in to look."

Jack would have gone with Alex himself if Rutledge and the

ten other task force operatives blending into the crowd at the track hadn't decided that tonight was the night they were going to shut down the Dahlia drug smuggling operation once and for all. Against Jack's knee-jerk reaction to want to punish the man who'd assaulted Alex in her father's garage, Rutledge had decided to let Hank Buell and his entourage work the speedway the way they'd planned. Artie was the only one they could conclusively link to the drugs. Crank and Jimbo had delivered the modified car parts, but that didn't make them killers. Hank had the balls to run a man off the road, but even Jack couldn't yet book him for anything more than assault. They might have the players in their sights, but a lack of brainpower and a bunch of cigarette butts with a stranger's DNA told Jack they hadn't found the man in charge of this operation yet.

Along with the evidence he and Alex had already gathered and turned in, the idea was to catch the men, the modified vehicles and the drugs all in one location, giving them a dead-bang case to take to court. According to Rutledge's legal machinations, such a certain conviction should convince the Buells and their buddies to turn on whoever was running the show. So Jack had agreed to follow the plan.

Jack owed Eric Mesner, he owed Nick Morgan—he owed Alex—the permanent shutdown of the drug pipeline. Eric deserved the justice Jack had promised. Nick's family and this town deserved to know that he had died a hero. And Alex deserved to be safe.

She'd been coping with the constant reminders of the cruel prank that had forced her to rev up her tomboy attitude and shut down her natural feminine instincts and desires for too long. She'd found a way to survive in Dahlia. But it was no way for a woman of her spirit and talents to live. Even when Jack's work here was done, he wasn't going to let her face any more past or current demons on her own. He might even decide that watching over her was a full-time job that demanded his attention here instead of in Nashville.

But that was a decision for later. Right now, he had to get the damn job done. Putting these bastards away—all of them—was the best way he knew to keep her safe.

So what the hell was taking her so long? He was due at the starting line in less than thirty minutes. And while he had no doubts that his car was ready to run, he wanted his crew chief with him. He wanted Alex on the sidelines to fix anything that went wrong. He wanted her close by to make him feel like he was a young man in his prime with just a word or a kiss or a smile.

A sense of foreboding crept up the back of his neck. Jack scanned the ebb and flow of fans and locals, in and beneath the stands. They sported bright team colors and carried armloads of snacks and souvenirs as they found their seats. He spotted Henry Buell moseying through the front gate, chatting folks up more like a welcoming host rather than working any kind of security that Jack could see. Maybe the sheriff was studying the crowd himself, serving as a lookout until his boys could get clear of the track with their car and drugs.

But there was no yellow bandanna anywhere to be seen. No honey-blond curls he recognized. No denim overalls stuffed with courage and curves and heart.

A loud horn and the clamor of the fans blended into the explosive roar of the two cars speeding down the strip. Jack tuned out the din and vibrations and focused his gaze on the drivers and their teams in the speedway's infield. He paid particular attention to the purple-and-silver awning that marked the Fisk Racing team's trailer and pit area.

His blood boiled beneath his skin as he caught sight of Hank Buell and his buddies, Crank and Jimbo, who'd stood by and done nothing to help Alex when Hank had turned abusive. Hank stood at the hood of Fisk's Mustang and shouted orders to his brother, Artie, who was leaning over his cell phone, texting a message. He smacked his brother in the back of the head, demanding his attention. But Artie made some kind of protest, pointing to the leader board and list of names for the upcoming time trial match-ups posted on the viewing tower. Then Hank was reading the phone, scanning the crowd, looking straight at Jack.

Suddenly, Hank and his crew were moving around their car as if they'd just been called to the starting gate. Nothing suspicious about that. Hell.

"I think we've been made."

"What?" Rutledge shouted over the cheers and boos of the crowd as the eighth-mile times were posted.

Enough of this. Something was wrong. Jack tossed his helmet inside the Camaro and pulled out his phone. He jogged toward the front gate and Morgan's Garage, where he'd find his truck and enough quiet to make a phone call. "Round up Buell and his crew," he told Rutledge. He nodded toward the Fisk tent. "They know something's going down. Seize the car and the trailer now. Have the sheriff help you so we don't lose track of him, either. And get ahold of Artie Buell's phone and find out who the hell just gave him the heads-up."

"Wait a minute," Rutledge snapped. "I give the orders here. We have a plan."

Screw the plan. "Has your man found Alex yet?"

"No."

"Then I will."

"Pick up, sweetheart." Jack tucked his gun into the back of his jeans and pocketed his badge as he bypassed the line of cars waiting for a parking space and jumped the curb. He spun onto the highway and raced his truck toward downtown Dahlia. He pressed on the accelerator and jammed on the horn to warn oncoming traffic that he was flying in their direction. "Come on, Trouble, answer your damn phone!"

Fourth ring. Fifth ring. *Do not go to voice mail!*

"Hello?"

Thank God. "Trouble? The Buells just got an alert that we're on to them. They're scrambling, but Rutledge and his men will round them up. I need you to stay with—"

"Yes, this is Alexandra."

What the hell? Jack ratcheted down his relief at hearing Alex's voice and tried to think like a cop. Tried to think like a record-holding driver who was hitting curves on the road about fifty miles above the posted speed limits. "Are you still at Mrs. Stillwell's store? Is your dad with you? Did Rutledge's man find you?"

"Miz Beverly's just fine."

She was freaking him out. Something was way wrong with the dulcet tones and screwy answers to his questions. "Are you still at the shop?"

"I'm fine, too. Why don't I meet up with you after your run?"

Answer the damn question, woman! "Are you at the shop?"

"Good luck racing tonight. I know you'll win that bet."

Bet? What bet? The only wager he'd made was that theory he'd tested with... "Are you with Drew?"

"I have to go. I'll catch up with you later."

"Are you in his car? Where's he taking you? Whatever you do, leave your phone on. I can track you. Talk to me, Alex. What's going—?"

She disconnected the call without answering any of his questions.

She hung up on him.

Jack lost his focus for a split-second and nearly blew off the road. Now he knew she was in trouble. Finding the truck's balance again, he decelerated onto the brick streets of downtown Dahlia.

He stopped long enough to find an agent nursing a concussion behind the counter at Beverly's Closet. He found Beverly Still-well and George Morgan tied up and gagged in one of the dressing rooms. He called Daniel Rutledge and told him to track down the signal on Alex's cell and put an APB out on Andrew Fisk III.

Then he followed a vague hunch about deep hidden gullies and roads to Nashville.

"Come on, baby," he urged, climbing into the hills outside Dahlia, coaxing a few extra mph out of his truck.

Losing Eric had gutted him. But he was healing. With Alex's help, he was finally healing.

If he lost the woman who'd jumpstarted his heart he'd never recover.

"WHERE ARE THE DRUGS?"

Running into Drew at Miz Beverly's shop had been a pleasant surprise. It had seemed odd, though, that he wasn't at the races to watch his new car run. It had been odder still to note the sheen of sweat beading his upper lip. The oddest part had been her father disappearing when he and Drew had gone into the back room to find out why Beverly was taking so long to retrieve Jack's jacket. She'd suspected the truth when Drew came back out by himself. Showing her the gun hidden beneath his suit coat, and inviting her to join him for another ride in his Corvette, confirmed it.

Alex looked straight into the wavering barrel of Drew's gun as they veered off the main road and headed up into the hills along the same road where her brother had died. She bit her tongue and refused to answer.

"The people I work for don't take kindly to someone stealing their merchandise. They'll want money or some kind of payment that isn't pleasant. And it's not coming out of my hide."

The hand on the wheel clutched the last, flaking embers of the cigarette he'd pulled from the glove compartment. That explained the expensive cologne. He was covering up an old habit that he couldn't quite shake.

Apparently Drew had been covering up a lot of things.

"Is that where you're taking me? To your so-called friends? I thought *I* was your friend, Drew."

"It's business, Alex. I have a delivery to make or I don't get paid."

Alex gripped the armrest and dashboard and rode every bump

and curve as night descended around them on the remote county highway. She prayed Drew wouldn't remember her phone was on after hanging up. If he did, she hoped that she'd wedged it far enough between the seat and door so that Jack and anybody but the Buells would arrive before Drew could get around her to dig it out. Even as she mourned the loss of a friendship that she'd known almost from the day she'd moved to Dahlia as a child, Alex was trying to get her head around the facts. "You ran my brother off the road, murdered him—murdered your best friend—to cover up your drug smuggling operation?"

"Ten thousand dollars or the drugs, Alex. Or you'll have to find some other way to pay," he warned. "Artie said you were in his locker. I don't know how you got so many bags out, but you were the only one who could have taken them."

"What if Artie took the drugs?" she challenged. "After all these years, you're saying you trust him more than you do me?"

Muttering a curse, he cracked open his window and flicked the cigarette butt outside. For one crazy moment, Alex considered grabbing the gun or the steering wheel and fighting her way free. But she wasn't that crazy. Shooting the driver or losing control of the Corvette at these speeds would probably ensure her own death, as well.

"Artie may not be the brightest bulb on the tree, but he knows how to fix cars the way I want them. And he knows where his paycheck comes from. He's not so stupid that he'd cross me."

"Oh, but I am?"

He slid her a patronizing glance. "You're not exactly in a position to be mouthing off to me, Shrimp."

"Don't call me that." Her stomach turned from more than the hills and valleys of the road. "That's what my brother called me."

Drew shook his head. "Nick went all good guy on me. He was going to my grandfather with printouts that showed where I'd laundered the money from our Nashville sales. I would have paid him off if he'd given me the chance."

"Nick would have expected better from you."

"Don't get all righteous with me. You're nothing in this town. But folks would listen to Nick. I'd be disinherited and out of a job."

"Not to mention in prison." The crest of the hill where Alex had seen two sets of skid marks was just beyond the next ridge. She dug her fingers in tighter. *Where are you, Jack? Find me.* She hoped he'd understood the message she'd been trying to give him.

"When he wouldn't listen to reason, Hank and I followed him to Nashville. We had to stop him."

Drew Fisk had stood there at her brother's funeral, holding her hand. All these months since, he'd hugged her and advised her and tried to fill the shoes of the very man he'd taken from her life. "You're a third generation millionaire, Drew. You've got a degree from Princeton and opportunities the rest of the world doesn't usually have. Why drugs?"

"I needed the money. I may be the heir to millions, but Grand-father's such a penny pincher that he rations out the money with an eye dropper. That's why he's selling the track. He says I'm squandering his fortune, tarnishing the family name with my lack of success. I got in too deep with my gambling debts, and the mob offered me a way out. Get their drugs to Nashville—get their money back out. Hank owed me for landing him a job and covering his ass in this town. And Artie does whatever Hank tells him. He was a natural at refitting the cars to hide the drugs, and Hank…"

"He's the muscle? Your thug? Your connection to all things evil?" Tears of anger burned behind her eyes. "You killed Nick!"

"I didn't want to."

"Do you expect sympathy from me?"

"I tried to scare you away from this business. All your poking around into Nick's things. The phone calls. The questions I couldn't answer. Hell, I even hoped you'd turn to me for protec-tion. Then I could explain everything away nice and neatly. But no, you had to go find that old man to warm your bed."

"Scare me away?" The cigarette fit. The watching was possible.

Wait a minute. Her grip went slack as her body chilled. "You're the blond boy in the background of that picture from that night. You didn't rescue me—you were a part of it."

Drew laughed, but there was no humor in it. "You honestly think Hank is smart enough to see an opportunity and turn a profit? He isn't now and he wasn't then. He just wanted to get laid and have Artie take a few pictures to prove he'd had you."

"*You* sold the tickets to all those boys."

The smug bastard actually seemed proud of the fact as he shifted into a lower gear to climb the next hill. "And my grandfather says I'm not a motivated businessman."

Alex wanted to reach across the seat and slap the grin off his face. "Is Hank and Artie's father part of this, too?"

"Not at first. But Henry knew his boys were up to something. At first he just looked the other way. Pretty soon, for a cut of the money, he was running interference for us."

"Saying Nick's death was an accident so there'd be no investigation."

"Who knew you were so smart about anything except cars?" Were they actually slowing down? Did he think stopping at the scene of Nick's death would make her break down and tell him what he wanted to know? "I already sent a message to the others and told them to meet us here. Look familiar? Will you listen to reason any better than Nick? Tell me where my drugs are, Alex, and I might let you live."

As the engine gradually powered down, Alex became aware of another sound. Low and growling. Powerful and smooth. There was another finely tuned engine out on the road tonight. Her pulse beat with anticipation. Her heart hoped.

And then she saw the headlights, piercing the darkness through her side-view mirror. Her knight in shining armor drove a big black truck instead of riding a white horse. She wouldn't have it any other way.

"Did you kill that cop in Nashville, too? Eric Mesner?"

"How did you know…?" Gravel crunched beneath Drew's tires as he pulled onto the shoulder of the road. "My associates in Nashville took care of him once we found out he was a cop. Let me guess, Jack Riley is more than a fast driver."

"He's a very fast driver. And he's right on your ass." The car had slowed enough that Alex figured she wouldn't break her neck. She opened the door and tumbled out.

"Get back here, you crazy bitch!"

The next few seconds were a blur of noise and fear and adrenaline. Alex rolled over rocks and grass and slammed into the trunk of a tree. Brakes squealed. Drew cursed as he leaped from the car. A zillion pinpricks of pain burned across her scalp as he grabbed a handful of hair and jerked her to her feet.

"No!" Alex screamed.

Drew's gun dug into her temple. "Get up!"

Lights flashed. Drew spun around. Alex twisted away from him, her bandanna ripping from the top of her head as she fell to her scraped knees. He snatched at the strap of her overalls.

And then she heard the most beautiful voice in the world. Jack's.

"Try it, Fisk. Give me a reason to blow your sorry hide away."

Drew dropped his gun and raised his hands in surrender. "You're Nashville PD?"

Jack's gun never moved from the target between Drew's eyes. "That's right. And you're under arrest. We'll start with kidnapping and assault and work our way up to murder. You okay, Trouble?"

Alex scrambled to her feet. "I am now."

"Then get over here." He held out his arm and tucked her to his side. "And you?" With his gun, he motioned Drew to the ground. "Get down in the dirt where you belong."

14

Three weeks later

"THANK YOU, DAD. It means a lot to me." Alex didn't try to hold her tears in check as the painters on the scaffolding over the first garage door pulled away the tarp to reveal their handiwork.

Morgan Family Garage

The bold red letters said much more than the fact that her father had made her an equal partner in the family business. It honored her brother's name, yet made her feel included, as well. He believed in her abilities in the office and under the hood of a car, even though she wore overalls to work instead of a business suit. He trusted her instincts about money and people, even though she'd have to hire a new mechanic now that Artie was in jail awaiting trial with his brother, Hank, Jim DiMarco, Oswald "Crank" Peterson and Drew Fisk.

He accepted her as she was. Not a poor replacement for Nick, nor a pale shadow of her mother, but a unique woman who calibrated engine blocks better than she cooked a casserole. He finally saw that she was a woman of skill, determination and strength. Her ideas might be a little outside his traditional box, but her heart was always in the right place. She could help take down the bad guys and share the truth about her brother's murder.

He loved her. Unconditionally. And he was making sure the world—or at least Dahlia, Tennessee—knew it.

A girl could get used to that. She might start thinking she

deserved the same kind of respect and acceptance from all the men in her life.

"Now, now." George Morgan pulled a handkerchief from his pocket and dabbed at her eyes. But Alex brushed aside the tender gesture and wrapped her arms around his waist, loving when he folded her in a hug. She let the tears flow until she felt his skin warming her cheek through his damp shirt. "Good grief, honey, you're going on the way your mother used to whenever I brought her flowers or something."

Reluctantly, Alex pulled away. But the unexpected comparison made her smile. "So you think I have a little bit of Mom in me, after all?"

He chucked her gently on the tip of her chin and grinned. "I see more of her in you every day. She'd be proud of the young woman you've grown into. I know I am." Her eyes stung and filled up again. "Now stop that. I can't have my director of resources and development tearing up every time someone pays her a compliment."

"Right." Alex sniffed. Loudly. "Oops." The noisy pronouncement warmed her cheeks and earned a smile from her father.

He winked. "Good to know some things never change." He pointed across the crowded parking lot to the speedway and the sound of the loudspeaker announcing the Outlaw Modified Street Car Division time trials that were about to start. "You'd better get going. Last I saw, Jack was still on the phone in your office. If I'm paying money to sponsor him, I want him at the track racing."

Alex swiped the last of the tears from her eyes and grinned. "Yes, sir. I'll get our driver up to the track ASAP. Tater's still with the Camaro, right?"

"As far as I know. I'll head on over to help him get the car to the staging lanes. Just make sure you lock up before you come over, okay?"

Alex stretched up on tiptoe and kissed his cheek before dashing inside to her office.

"That's right, Daniel. Yeah, I'll tell my captain." Alex quietly closed the door, smiling at the sound of Jack's voice, and how even disguised in those clipped, professional tones, it danced across her ears and made her heart beat a little faster. "I just wanted to let you know that I'll be around to supply whatever assistance you need on the case." After tapping her watch to point out the time, she unfolded the racing jacket with the new red-and-white logo from the box from Beverly's Closet. Updated racing gear wasn't the only thing she'd picked up from Miz Beverly this morning. But Alex was saving that surprise for later. She lifted Jack's helmet from the corner of the desk and waited for him to finish his conversation. "I will. Thanks, Daniel."

"Well?"

Jack shut off his phone and dropped it into his weekend bag along with his badge and gun. "It's official." As he changed his clothes from city cop to weekend drag racer in the middle of a very successful comeback, Jack explained the phone call to Daniel Rutledge. "I applied for the job. With Sheriff Buell's hasty retirement, Dahlia will be needing a new sheriff. It'll take me a couple of months to get everything off my desk in Nashville, but…" He paused, tucking his black T-shirt into his racing pants and circled around the desk to take the helmet and jacket from her hands. He set them down on top of the desk and reached for her. "If you think there's enough reason for me to move to Dahlia…?"

Alex smiled, tilting her chin to lock on to those steel-gray eyes as she aligned her hips against his. She reached up to brush a silvering spike of hair off his forehead. "Let's see. You cleaned up the drug smuggling ring in town. You made friends with my dad and Tater and Sandy Larabie. You're making more than respectable progress in your runs at the track—"

He pressed a finger against her lips and shushed her. "I was hoping for a more personal answer to my question. I don't like this weekend relationship of ours. Don't get me wrong, I love our weekends, but Monday through Thursday gets mighty lonely without you. Would it freak you out if I was around all the time?"

Losing two people they loved had brought Jack and Alex together. Finding love in each other would keep them together.

"Remember that night when Hank…" She dropped her gaze to where her plain, strong hands rested against Jack's chest. "That night when I found the drugs, I asked you to stay."

"And I did. I'd have been camped out on your doorstep even if you hadn't invited me into your bed that night." He tipped her chin back up, asking her to have the confidence to look him in the eye and speak her heart. "Talk to me, Trouble. What are you saying?"

"Stay, Jack. I want you to stay."

A slow smile spread across his face. "So the sage old warrior *does* get the girl in the end, hmm?"

Alex nodded. She rose up on tiptoe, wound her arms around his neck and welcomed his kiss. Welcomed him into her life and into her heart.

He traced the seam of her lips with his tongue and Alex willingly opened for him. He claimed her mouth, driving his tongue inside to slide along hers. Alex suckled the strong line of his bottom lip, scraping her palms against the masculine prickle of his evening stubble. He shucked off her bandanna and tunneled his fingers into her hair, turning her head to give him access to the soft skin beneath her ear and the sensitive column of her neck. Jack nibbled his way down to her collarbone, sending warm ribbons of desire curling into the tips of her breasts and down low into her feminine center.

When he suddenly stopped and lifted his head, Alex blinked, momentarily disoriented by the haze of pleasure still swirling through her head. "Jack?"

He hooked a finger beneath the collar of her T-shirt and pulled it across her shoulder to expose the emerald-green strap of satiny material that held up her bra. "What's this?"

Alex brushed his hand away, remembering the plans she'd

made for tonight after the races were done. "It's for the fashion show later."

"Fashion show?"

"We have work to do first. Then we can try my little project." She turned to grab his jacket and helmet off the desk.

He moved in right behind her, setting his racing gear back down and trapping her against the solid oak with his body. "I seem to recall your *projects* getting me into a whole lot of trouble."

"I think you like having a little trouble in your life, Jack Riley." He wrapped his arms around her waist and Alex shivered at the chest to bulge-behind-his-zipper contact. "Miz Beverly found me a whole bunch of pretty things in my size. And I intend to model them for you and let you take every last one of them off me."

"Who knew I could be such a slave to fashion?" He dipped his head and pressed a hot, wet kiss to that sensitive bundle of nerves at her nape. Her knees turned to jelly. "Do you still have that little black hooker dress? I'd love to take that off you, too."

Alex turned in his arms. One of them had to be strong here. "Later, Jack. Right now you've got a time trial to run at the speedway. I want to see if my Alex Morgan–special engine can take the competition."

"I'll take the Alex Morgan special anytime. Day or night." Jack picked her up and set her on the edge of the desk. He pulled her knees apart and moved between her legs. He reached for the strap on her shoulder and Alex surrendered to what they both wanted. "Now let's see what girly thing you have on under these overalls."

They finished just in time to make the starting line for the race.

* * * * *

Celebrate 60 years of pure
reading pleasure with Harlequin®!

Step back in time and enjoy a sneak preview
of an exciting anthology from
Harlequin® Historical with
THE DIAMONDS OF WELBOURNE MANOR

This compelling anthology features three stories about the outrageous Fitzmanning sisters. Meet Annalise, who is never at a loss for words… But that can change with an unexpected encounter in the forest.

Available May 2009
from Harlequin® Historical.

"I'm the illegitimate daughter of notoriously scandalous parents, Mr. Milford. Candidates for my hand are unlikely to be lining up at the gates."

"Don't be so quick to discount your charms, my dear. Or the charm of your substantial dowry. Or even your brothers' influence. There are as many reasons to marry as there are marriages."

Annalise snorted. "Oh, yes. Perhaps I shall marry for dynastic reasons, or perhaps for property or influence. After all, a loveless, practical marriage worked out so well for my mother."

"Well, you've routed me on that one. I can think of no suitable rejoinder." Ned rose to his feet and extended his hand. "And since that is the case, let me be the first to wish you a long and happy spinsterhood."

Her mouth gaped open. And then she laughed.

And he froze.

This was the first time, Ned realized. The first time he'd seen her eyes light up and her mouth curl. The first time he'd witnessed her features melded together in glorious accord to produce exquisite beauty.

Unbelievable what a change came over her face. Unheard of what effect her throaty, rasping laughter had on his body. It pounded a beat upon his ear, quickly taken up by his pulse. It echoed through him, finally residing in his stirring nether regions.

So easily she did it, awakened these sensations within him—without any apparent effort at all. And she had called him potentially dangerous? Clearly the intelligent thing for him to do would be to steer clear, to leave her to the tender ministrations of Lord Peter Blackthorne.

"You were right." She smiled up at him as she took his hand and climbed to her feet. "I do feel better."

Ah, well. When had he ever chosen the intelligent path?

He did not relinquish her hand. He used it to pull her in, close enough that he could feel the warmth of her. "At the risk of repeating Lord Peter's mistake and anticipating too much—may I ask if you'll be my partner in battledore tomorrow?"

Her smile dimmed. Her breath came a little faster. His own had gone shallow, as if he'd just run a race—and lost. He ran his gaze over the appealing lift of her brow and the curious angle of her chin. His index finger twitched.

"I should like that," she said.

His finger trembled again and he lifted it, traced the pink and tender shell of her ear, the unique sweep of her jaw. Her pulse leaped beneath her skin, triggering his own. Slowly he tilted her chin up, waiting for her to object, to step back, to slap his hand away.

She did none of those eminently sensible things. Which left him free to do the entirely impractical thing.

Baby soft, the skin of her lips. Her whole body trembled when he touched her there.

He leaned in. Her eyes closed, even as she stood straight against him, strung as tight as a bow. He pressed his mouth to hers. It was a soft kiss, sweet and chaste. And yet he was hot and hard and as ready as he'd ever been in his life.

She drew back a little. Sighed. Their breath mingled a moment before she slowly backed away.

"Oh," she breathed. Her dark eyes were full of wonder and

something that looked like fear. He took a step toward her, but she only shook her head. His outstretched hand fell to his side as she turned to disappear into the wood. This was the first time, Ned realized. The first time, since he'd come to the house party at Welbourne Manor, that he'd seen her eyes light up.

* * * * *

Follow Ned and Annalise's story
in May 2009 in
THE DIAMONDS OF WELBOURNE MANOR
available May 2009
from Harlequin® Historical.

Available in the series romance section,
or in the historical romance section,
wherever books are sold.

We'll be spotlighting a different series
every month throughout 2009
to celebrate our 60th anniversary.

Look for Harlequin® Historical in May!

**60 years of Harlequin,
600 years of romance
in Harlequin Historical!**

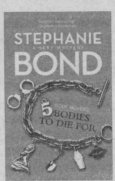
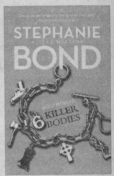

REQUEST YOUR FREE BOOKS!

2 FREE NOVELS
PLUS 2
FREE GIFTS!

HARLEQUIN®

Blaze

Red-hot reads!

YES! Please send me 2 FREE Harlequin® Blaze™ novels and my 2 FREE gifts (gifts are worth about $10). After receiving them, if I don't wish to receive any more books, I can return the shipping statement marked "cancel". If I don't cancel, I will receive 6 brand-new novels every month and be billed just $4.24 per book in the U.S. or $4.71 per book in Canada. Shipping and handling is just 25¢ per book. That's a savings of 15% or more off the cover price! I understand that accepting the 2 free books and gifts places me under no obligation to buy anything. I can always return a shipment and cancel at any time. Even if I never buy another book, the two free books and gifts are mine to keep forever.

151 HDN ERVA   351 HDN ERUX

Name	(PLEASE PRINT)
Address	Apt. #
City	State/Prov.	Zip/Postal Code

Signature (if under 18, a parent or guardian must sign)

Mail to the **Harlequin Reader Service:**
IN U.S.A.: P.O. Box 1867, Buffalo, NY 14240-1867
IN CANADA: P.O. Box 609, Fort Erie, Ontario L2A 5X3

Not valid to current subscribers of Harlequin Blaze books.

Want to try two free books from another line?
Call 1-800-873-8635 or visit www.morefreebooks.com.

* Terms and prices subject to change without notice. Prices do not include applicable taxes. N.Y. residents add applicable sales tax. Canadian residents will be charged applicable provincial taxes and GST. Offer not valid in Quebec. This offer is limited to one order per household. All orders subject to approval. Credit or debit balances in a customer's account(s) may be offset by any other outstanding balance owed by or to the customer. Please allow 4 to 6 weeks for delivery. Offer available while quantities last.

Your Privacy: Harlequin Books is committed to protecting your privacy. Our Privacy Policy is available online at www.eHarlequin.com or upon request from the Reader Service. From time to time we make our lists of customers available to reputable third parties who may have a product or service of interest to you. If you would prefer we not share your name and address, please check here. ☐

HB09R

HARLEQUIN *Blaze*™

COMING NEXT MONTH
Available April 28, 2009

#465 HOT-WIRED Jennifer LaBrecque
From 0–60
Drag racer/construction company owner Beau Stillwell has his hands full trying to mess up his sister's upcoming wedding. The guy just isn't good enough for her. But when Beau meets Natalie Bridges, the very determined wedding planner, he realizes he needs to change gears and do something drastic. Like drive sexy, uptight Natalie absolutely wild...

#466 LET IT RIDE Jillian Burns
What better place for grounded flyboy Cole Jackson to blow off some sexual steam than Vegas, baby! Will his campaign to seduce casino beauty Jordan Brenner crash and burn, once she discovers what he really wants to bet?

#467 ONCE A REBEL Debbi Rawlins
Stolen from Time, Bk. 3
Maggie Dawson is stunned when the handsomest male *ever* appears from the future, insisting on her help! Cord Braddock's out of step in the 1870s Wild West, although courting sweet, sexy Maggie comes as naturally to him as the sun rising over the Dakota hills....

#468 GOING DOWN HARD Tawny Weber
When Sierra Donovan starts receiving indecent pictures of herself—with threats attached—she knows she's going to need help. But the last person she needs it from is sexy security expert Reece Carter. Although, if Sierra's back has to be against the wall, she can't think of anyone she'd rather put her there....

#469 AFTERBURN Kira Sinclair
Uniformly Hot!
Air force captain Chase Carden knows life will be different now that he's back from Iraq—he's already been told he'll be leading the Thunderbird Squadron. Little does he guess that his biggest change will come in the person of Rina McAllister, his last one-night stand...who's now claiming to be his wife!

#470 MY SEXY GREEK SUMMER Marie Donovan
A wicked vacation is what Cara Sokol has promised herself, although she has to keep her identity a secret! Hottie Yannis Petridis is exactly what she's looking for *and* he's good with secrets—he's got one of his own!

www.eHarlequin.com